"A BEAUTIFUL, HEARTFELT, AND HONEST STORY THAT SENDS LOVE UP FROM EVERY PAGE."

—JOHN COREY WHALEY,
PRINTZ AWARD–WINNING AUTHOR OF *WHERE THINGS COME BACK*

PRAISE FOR *ASK THE PASSENGERS*

A 2012 Los Angeles Times Book Prize Winner

A 2012 *Publishers Weekly* Best YA Book

A 2012 *School Library Journal* Best Book

A 2012 *Kirkus Reviews* Best YA Book

A 2012 *Library Journal* Best YA Literature for Adults Book

A 2012 *BookPage* Best Children's Book

A 2012 Los Angeles Public Library Best Teen Book

A 2012 Lambda Literary Award Finalist

A 2013 YALSA Best Fiction for Young Adults Book

A 2013 Rainbow List Top Ten Book

A 2013 Capitol Choices Noteworthy Titles for
Children and Teens Book

A 2013 Children's Cooperative Book Center Choices Book

A Junior Library Guild Selection

★ "Funny, provocative, and intelligent, King's story celebrates love in all its messy, modern complexity." —*Publishers Weekly*, starred review

★ "Another thoughtful, and often breathtaking, achievement for King, whose star is ascending as quickly as one of Astrid's planes." —*Booklist*, starred review

★ "King's thoughtful, sad, funny, and frank book…will appeal to any mature teen resisting the pressure to conform or rebel [and to] anyone who wants to define herself on her own terms." —*SLJ*, starred review

★ "A furiously smart and funny coming-out-and-of-age novel."
—*The Horn Book*, starred review

★ "For kids still struggling with their own truths, it can be hard to believe how much light there is once you come out of the cave. This is a book that knows and understands that, and it's one that readers will believe." —*The Bulletin*, starred review

"Hits it out of the park.... It shouldn't be a shock to anyone by now that A.S. King has written another masterpiece with *Ask the Passengers*.... [A] book worthy of any shelf." —*San Francisco Book Review*

★ "Quite possibly the best teen novel featuring a girl questioning her sexuality written in years." —*Kirkus Reviews*, starred review

"Astrid is a model of strength and compassion.... Good reading for everyone." —*VOYA*

"King has penned a work of realism that is magical in the telling."
—Cooperative Children's Book Center

"So special and perfect and true and right. This book is made of stardust and guts; I'll hold it in my heart forever." —LAUREN MYRACLE, *New York Times* bestselling author of *Shine*

"I'm sending love to Astrid Jones, for being one of the most reachable, realistic characters that I have ever dared to adore. And I'm sending love to A.S. King, whose positively brilliant writing style never ceases to amaze me. *Ask the Passengers* made me smile, cringe, laugh, and believe in the absolute power of the human spirit. Amazing. Simply amazing." —HEATHER BREWER, *New York Times* bestselling author of the Chronicles of Vladimir Tod series

"In *Ask the Passengers*, A.S. King exquisitely creates a tender, multilayered portrayal of the takeoffs, nose-dives, and loop-the-loops of sexuality, friendship, family, and love." —ALEX SANCHEZ, author of *Rainbow Boys* and *Boyfriends with Girlfriends*

"In Astrid Jones, A.S. King has created a memorable, thoughtful, funny, questioning protagonist whose search for answers reminds us how important it is to ask the questions in the first place." —SARA RYAN, author of *Empress of the World*

"A warm, thoughtful, and thought-provoking novel about the paradoxes of love, sexual identity, and the magic of connectedness." —MALINDA LO, author of *Adaptation* and *Huntress*

"A.S. King is one of the most engaging and innovative writers in the field. *Ask the Passengers* is a wonderful novel about tolerance and the limitations of definition; it should be required reading in all high schools." —MATT DE LA PEÑA, author of *Mexican WhiteBoy* and *Ball Don't Lie*

"This book really should be read by everyone....It's just that awesome. More power to you, A.S. King!" —the-soul-sisters.blogspot.com

"*Ask the Passengers* was my first A.S. King novel, and I can now see why this author is so wildly popular." —fictionfolio.com

"[A.S. King] is one of the most powerful voices in YA literature today." —nextbestbook.blogspot.com

"Such an important book for all to read...The story teaches invaluable lessons on identity, kindness, and love. The world needs more of that." —thebookishbabes.blogspot.com

ASK THE

PASSE

NGERS

A NOVEL BY
A.S. KING

LITTLE, BROWN AND COMPANY
NEW YORK • BOSTON

Little, Brown and Company

Hachette Book Group
237 Park Avenue, New York, NY 10017
Visit our website at www.lb-teens.com

Little, Brown and Company is a division of Hachette Book Group, Inc.
The Little, Brown name and logo are trademarks of Hachette Book Group, Inc.

The publisher is not responsible for websites (or their content) that are not owned by the publisher.

First Paperback Edition: September 2013
First published in hardcover in October 2012 by Little, Brown and Company

Library of Congress Cataloging-in-Publication Data

King, A. S. (Amy Sarig), 1970–
Ask the passengers : a novel / by A.S. King. — 1st ed.
        p. cm.
Summary: "Astrid Jones copes with her small town's gossip and narrow-mindedness by staring at the sky and imagining that she's sending love to the passengers in the airplanes flying high over her backyard. Maybe they'll know what to do with it. Maybe it'll make them happy. Maybe they'll need it. Her mother doesn't want it, her father's always stoned, her perfect sister's too busy trying to fit in, and the people in her small town would never allow her to love the person she really wants to: another girl, named Dee. There's no one Astrid feels she can talk to about this deep secret or the profound questions that she's trying to answer. But little does she know just how much sending her love— and asking the right questions—will affect the passengers' lives, and her own, for the better"— Provided by publisher.
ISBN 978-0-316-19468-6 (hardback) / ISBN 978-0-316-19467-9 (paperback)
[1. Love—Fiction. 2. Lesbians—Fiction. 3. Family problems—Fiction. 4. Prejudices—Fiction.
5. Gossip—Fiction. 6. High schools—Fiction. 7. Schools—Fiction.] I. Title.
        PZ7.K5693Ask 2012   [Fic]—dc23   2011053207

10 9 8 7 6 5 4 3 2 1

RRD-C

Printed in the United States of America

FOR MY SISTERS,
WHO SAVE ME FROM
THE FLYING MONKEYS.

Question everything.

—EURIPIDES

*The only true wisdom is
in knowing you know nothing.*

—SOCRATES

Know thyself.

—ANCIENT GREEK APHORISM

ASTRID JONES
SENDS HER LOVE.

EVERY AIRPLANE, no matter how far it is up there, I send love to it. I picture the people in their seats with their plastic cups of soda or orange juice or Scotch, and I love them. I really love them. I send a steady, visible stream of it—love—from me to them. From my chest to their chests. From my brain to their brains. It's a game I play.

It's a good game because I can't lose.

I do it everywhere now. When I buy Rolaids at the drug-store, I love the lady who runs the place. I love the old man who's stocking shelves. I even love the cashier with the insanely large hands who treats me like shit every other day. I don't care if they don't love me back.

This isn't reciprocal.

It's an outpouring.

Because if I give it all away, then no one can control it.

Because if I give it all away, I'll be free.

1

YOU'D HATE IT HERE.

MOTION IS IMPOSSIBLE. That's what Zeno of Elea said. And though I've disagreed with the idea every day this week in humanities class, sometimes I think I know what he meant.

It's Wednesday, which is lit mag day. Justin and Kristina are ten minutes late. They are always ten minutes late. This doesn't bug me. I've learned to expect it. And if I run out of submissions, I can always work on layout or advertising or just sit here and read a book. Justin and Kristina have all kinds of stuff to do after school. I just have lit mag.

When the two of them finally arrive, they walk through the door holding hands and giggling. Justin has his SLR digital camera around his neck like always, and Kristina is in a pair of yoga pants and an oversize Yale sweatshirt. Her hair is pulled back into a ponytail.

"Sorry we're late," she says.

Justin apologizes, too. "I had to take some candid shots of the usual suspects: Football practice. Cheerleading. Hockey team running their laps. Yearbook crap."

"I went with him to help," Kristina says. "Could Aimee Hall be any more obvious?"

Justin laughs. "She actually posed for me hugging her tennis racquet."

"It was gross," Kristina says, adjusting her ponytail by grabbing two sides and yanking on them to center it on her perfect head.

When the townies talk about her, they say: *You know that's her natural color?*

They say: *I bet her and that Justin Lampley will have some damn pretty kids.*

They say: *I can't figure out why she hangs out with that weird neighbor girl.*

That's me.

▶ ▶ ▶

"We're going up to Sparky's before they close for the season. You in?" Kristina knows the answer to this, but she asks it anyway. And she knows that I'd kill for a Sparky's root beer float, too.

"Can't. School night. You know the deal." Jones family

small-town rules: no going out on school nights unless for clubs, sports or other school-related activities.

"Maybe Friday, then? It's their last night. It'll be packed, but worth it," she says.

"Uh, Kris, we have a double date on Friday night," Justin says.

"Oh, shit. My bad. Can't do Friday. Double date."

It's so cute, isn't it? It's so 1950s. When I hear them talk like this, I close my eyes and picture Kristina in a blue chiffon dress that poufs out right below her knees, pearls and satin heels. I picture Justin in tightly tailored pegged pants. They are at a sock hop, jitterbugging.

People say: *Did you hear those two double-date every Friday night? Isn't that the way it's supposed to be?*

Justin looks at his watch. "Are you done or what?"

I show him the empty submission box, and he pulls out his phone and starts to wander toward the door.

"You need a ride home?" I ask Kristina. She looks at Justin, who is already texting Chad. We know it's Chad, because Justin gets this look on his face when he texts Chad.

"Sure," she says.

Justin is laughing at whatever clever text he just received and doesn't even hear us. By the time I turn off the lights in Ms. Steck's room, we've managed to nudge him into the hall and lock up. When we say good-bye, he grunts, thumbs typing furiously on his little iPhone keypad. Kristina says she has to grab something from her locker before we go and she'll meet me in the parking lot, so I stop at the bathroom and my locker, too.

By the time I get outside, I see Justin and Kristina standing by Justin's car in the parking lot, talking to a gaggle of their sporty and popular friends. Everyone is nice to Justin because if he likes you, there's a better chance you'll end up in the yearbook. If he doesn't like you? Let's just say Justin can make you look really good or really bad in a picture.

Justin and Kristina have been doing this dating thing since mid-sophomore year, so the people-being-overly-nice-to-Justin thing extends to her. Sometimes, it even extends to me, too, if I show up at times like this when they are mobbed in the parking lot, but today I don't feel like it. They're all probably saying, "Hope you win Homecoming king and queen! You've got my vote!" and stuff like that. I decide to get in my car and wait for the activity buses to leave. I reach into the glove compartment for a bottle of Rolaids and shake out three to chew on.

We say good-bye to Justin once the buses clear, and drive down Main Street of Kristina's historic town. I don't call it *my* town because I don't think of it as my town. I still remember living in New York City, and loving the smell of the sweaty steam coming through the subway vents, and the vendor carts full of boiling hot dogs. That's my town. Not Unity Valley.

Unity Valley is Kristina's town.

Unity Valley is now my sister Ellis's town, even though she was nine when we moved and totally remembers life in New York.

Mom says: *You two have a chance to really fit in here. Your father and I will always stick out because—well, you know—because of our education and our way of thinking. But you two can really be small-town girls.*

6

Ellis bought this. She's living it. As far as I can tell, it's working for her.

Mom says: *We have so much more space here! The supermarket is so big! The roads are safe! The air is clean! The schools are better! No crime! And the people here stop and say hello!*

Sure, Mom.

They stop and say hello, and then once you pass, they talk the back off you like you were nothing. They assess your outfit, your hairstyle, and they garble what you say so it comes out ugly. If I don't hear it firsthand, I hear it secondhand.

About black kids: *I hear that Kyle kid got himself a scholarship. Had to be black to get it. I can't see how that's fair.* Jimmy Kyle got that scholarship to Villanova because he's a straight-A student and wants to go to law school.

About the two Latino freshman girls: *The parents don't even speak English. This is America, isn't it?* Franny Lopez is third-generation American, and her parents don't even speak Spanish. Michelle Marquez's mother has it bad enough without having to learn a second language. Mind your own business.

About my family: *Did you see they have birdhouses all over their yard? I don't know about you, but that's inviting bird shit, and who wants bird shit?*

They say: *It's just not natural that he makes his girl use a hammer.*

Maybe this sort of thing happens in your town, too.

▶ ▶ ▶

"Wish you could come to Sparky's with us tonight," Kristina says.

"I'll live without a root beer float until next summer," I say.

We're a block from our houses, in the prettiest part of town. I used to think the two-hundred-year-old redbrick buildings were so cute, you know? I used to think the cobblestone town center was quaint. It was different and new. And kinda forced on me, but it was cool, too, once I got over the initial shock.

"I can totally bring you a root beer float, you know. Not sure why that's only occurring to me now," she says. "What's better than Sparky's except Sparky's room service?"

"That would rock so much, I'd owe you something big. Like maybe an ear or a toe or something," I say.

She laughs. "You don't have to give me your toe, dude."

"Oh. Good," I say, pretending I'm relieved. "I was planning on using mine for stuff later today, like walking. And standing upright."

Kristina laughs again and even snorts a little. But then she gets that worried look on her face as we approach her house. "Do you think people know?" she asks. She's so random.

"No."

"Are you sure?"

"I'm sure," I say.

"I wish I could be as sure."

"Don't worry. No one knows."

"You're not bullshitting?" she asks.

"No bullshit. Promise. I am the ears of this town. No one knows."

2

AUBERGINES, FOYERS, AND THE HORSE WHO LIVES UPSTAIRS.

WHEN I GET HOME and put my backpack on the desk in the quiet room, I hear Mom's rolling office chair carving tracks into the wood floor upstairs. She rolls to the east side of the office and then rolls back. Each push makes a series of loud clopping sounds, as if there's a dancing horse upstairs.

My mother wears expensive high heels all day while she works, even though she works at home. She wears full business attire, too, and makeup and earrings and has her hair perfectly styled, even though nobody ever sees her. When she breaks for lunch, she clip-clops downstairs to the kitchen and then clip-clops back upstairs—back straight, eyes focused just above the horizon, as if she's still in New York City, walking down Park Avenue, being a big, important art director. When I hear her clip-clopping, I am immediately annoyed. At everything. At Unity Valley. At her. At this house and how I can hear her upstairs because the house is a million years old and there's no insulation between ceilings and floors, unless you count centuries-old mouse nests.

We wouldn't be here if it weren't for my grandmother dying. Mom's mom. She used to tell Ellis and me stories about growing up where there were cornfields and hills to roll down. On our last visit to her Upper West Side apartment, Gram mentioned to Mom and Dad that the house Gram grew up in—one of the oldest on Main Street in Unity Valley—was up for sale.

Even though Gram lived her whole adult life in New York City, she was buried back in Unity Valley, next to her mother, my great-grandmother. We drove by the house fifty times the week of her funeral, and one time we stopped the car and Mom got out and talked to a person walking down the sidewalk. The lady said, "They'll never get what they're asking. The place is too small, and the market is too slow."

That's all it took for Mom to call the real estate agent.

"It's rightfully mine," she'd said. "I remember visiting my grandmother in it when I was little, and always wishing I lived there," she'd said. "We won't move permanently, but we should buy it. It's like an heirloom. I finally have a chance to buy it back into our family."

So she did. A year later, when I was ten and Ellis was nine, we moved. Now we're small-town girls. Except that we aren't. And Mom is a hometown girl. Except that she isn't.

Clip-clop, clip-clop, clip-clop. She descends the steps, and I start to unpack my books onto the quiet-room desk to get ready for the trig homework I've been avoiding all day.

"How was your day?" she asks Ellis, who's been sitting in the kitchen this whole time but hasn't said hello.

"I'm starting against Wilson tomorrow," she says.

"I suppose that's good, is it?" Mom never played sports. So, Ellis's field hockey is her introduction to words like *starting*, *varsity* and *shin splints*.

"It's great," Ellis answers.

"How great? Will we see you on the front page of the sports section soon?"

Ellis rolls her eyes. "It's great for me. And the team. And maybe it means Coach Jane will start me more often."

"I can't understand why she doesn't make you the star of the team. This whole fairness-to-seniors idea is so silly. If they backed talent no matter what age, it would get them further."

I'm still in the quiet room playing invisible, but I want to explain to Mom that you can't make a player *star of the team* by better advertising or better shelf placement, the way she does with her clients' products.

"I think it's fair to let the seniors start," Ellis says.

"Well, it won't help you get your name in the paper, so you'll have to forgive me if I disagree," Mom says. "Help me make dinner?"

Ellis deflates and claims homework time in her bedroom. Mom goes into the kitchen to make dinner without asking me how my day was, even though she knows I'm here.

The quiet room is technically the foyer. In our house, you pronounce that correctly. Foy-*yay*, not foy-*er*. We call it the quiet room because as long as the horse isn't dancing upstairs and the door is closed, it is the quietest room in the house. It's where my mother hopes to read classic novels again one day when she isn't working nine days a week, and it's where I do my homework because Ellis plays loud music when she works in her bedroom and I can't concentrate. And I need to concentrate because trig is killing me.

When I signed up for trig, I certainly thought it would be more exciting than the deep study of triangles. Seriously. Triangles. That's all it's about. When I realized this upon reading the basic definition in the front of the textbook on the first day of school, every cell in my body told me to go to Guidance and change my schedule. I don't need trig to graduate. I've taken plenty of math, and I got good grades. I even got picked for AP humanities—the only class in Unity Valley High School that requires teacher references.

I'm not sure if learning about ancient Greece and classical philosophy is going to get me anywhere, but it's not like trig is going to get me anywhere, either. At least philosophy isn't making me want to jump off the nearest bridge. Okay, well at the moment it kinda is, but that's Zeno of Elea's fault. And anyway, if what he said is true, that motion is impossible, then I wouldn't *really* be able to jump off a bridge, would I?

▶ ▶ ▶

At five thirty, Dad parallel parks in the space in front of our house and goes into the backseat for his briefcase. When he gets to our front walk, he hits the lock button on the car, and it sounds a little honk. He stops to make sure our two front bird-feeders are filled. He checks the water level in the birdbath. Then he walks in the front door to find me pretending to poke my eye out with a protractor.

"Trig?" he asks.

I put my head down in response. I stick my tongue out and roll my eyes back like I'm dying.

"Good luck with that," he says as he heads upstairs.

I can smell the pot on his breath.

▶ ▶ ▶

Mom brings the steaming casserole dish to the table and places it on a hot pad. "Aubergine casserole!" she announces. Yes, aubergine. That's eggplant to us nonspecial, undereducated, small-town people.

She serves it with a cold salad and sprinkles walnuts on top of everything.

Halfway through dinner, Ellis tells Dad about starting against Wilson tomorrow. As she tells him the details, he nods and chews. When he finally swallows, he says, "What time does it start?"

"Four."

"I bet I can swing that," he says. "Even if I'm a little late."

"That would be awesome," she says.

Mom says, "I can't make it." Even though she works upstairs. And she can. Totally. Make it. "But if you want, we can go shopping this weekend."

We all go back to eating aubergine casserole. For the record: The last time Mom took me shopping on a whim was never. And it's not like Ellis has grown out of her clothes. The saddest part is that Ellis still pretends they have the perfect relationship Mom wants them to have. Because Ellis is her last chance, and they both know it.

"It would be nice to see you in the paper," Mom says. "They're always concentrating on boys' sports or the kids who get scholarships."

"I'm a midfielder," Ellis says, which she knows Mom won't understand, so I don't know why she says it.

"But you're talented," she says. "I'm going to get in touch with Mike at the paper and see what he can do. We do each other favors. He could get you in there," she says, pointing with her fork.

"I don't really want to be in the paper," Ellis says.

"Everyone wants to be in the paper!" Mom says. "And it's not like it's the *Times*. No need to be modest."

I can't figure out if that's an insult or a compliment.

When it's my turn to talk about my day, I share lit mag news.

"We got a few poems today that were half decent," I say. "And there's a kid in freshman AP English who writes these great fantasy short stories, and he submitted a few of them. I picked one of those, too."

"Fantasy?" Mom says. "Seriously, Astrid. You're the editor. You should set the bar."

Instead of replying with my usual open-your-mind speech, I send love to my mother. *Mom, I love you even though you are a critical, unforgiving horror show. This casserole sucks, but I like the way you roasted the walnuts.*

"We're starting the first unit of the Socrates Project in humanities next week, and I'm kinda excited," I say. Mom nods, even though she has no idea what the Socrates Project is...because I haven't told her. "I think I'll just be happy to stop talking about Zeno and his dumb motion theories." I haven't told her about Zeno, either.

"And how's Kristina?" she asks. She's using the Kristina tone—a weird mix of jealousy and I-know-something-you-don't-know because she and Kristina text each other a lot and she thinks I don't know this.

"Fine."

"Any word on Homecoming?"

"We vote Friday."

"I know Kristina's really excited about it."

"Yeah."

"I think she has a real chance to win. She has all the right qualities," she says.

I am annoyed that she thinks she knows more than I do about Kristina. Believe me, if she knew half of what I know, she'd probably choke on this awful aubergine casserole and die right here in her four-hundred-dollar shoes.

"What qualities are those?" I ask.

She takes a sip of her wine. "You know. She's just such a great representation of what this town is all about."

"True," I say. Because it's true. Kristina is exactly the opposite of what she seems, and that's a perfect representation of Unity Valley.

Then Dad tells us about how boring it is to work in his new office cubicle all day, talking to people on the phone about microprocessors and systems analytics while looking over his shoulder for the outsourcing memo. (His last job lasted eight months before the company moved to Asia. The job before that lasted eleven.)

"To top it all off, while I was at lunch, someone borrowed my stapler and broke it."

"Aw, poor Gerry," Mom says.

"Hey, that was my favorite stapler. It was ergonomic," he says.

Without a moment's sympathy, Mom launches into her day (hellish clients, dumb photographers, bitchy magazine editors) between gulps of wine and mouthfuls of eggplant. She could go for an hour, I bet.

We all eat as fast as we can to get out of here.

Then, after the dishes are done and the kitchen is cleaned, Ellis goes for her nightly jog on well-lit Main Street with two of her small-town teammates, Dad sits down in the quiet room to read a book, Mom goes back to her office, and I go out into the backyard to talk to the passengers.

3

ASTRID JONES SENDS HER LOVE.
FROM A PICNIC TABLE.

I MADE THIS PICNIC TABLE with Dad the summer before junior year. I was sick of making birdhouses. Seriously. How many birdhouses can two people make before they run out of things to say? Before they run out of space to put them? Our backyard was an ode to nesting and flight—part bird zoo and part art exhibit.

They'd say: *It's very unique.*

Dad had the whole summer off on account of his temporary unemployment, and Mom was staying with friends back in New York City to do some well-paid consulting for a month. Ellis was at summer sports camp for a week, and it was just Dad and me. Dad hadn't discovered pot yet. He was a late bloomer, I guess.

So we built the table and moved it to the back patio, and even though Mom hates eating outside, she lets us do it about twice a summer just to be normal small-town people, the way she wants us to be.

The rest of the time, the table just sits here with nothing to do. So I lie on it and I look at the sky. I see shapes in the clouds by day and shooting stars by night. And I send love to the passengers inside the airplanes. It makes me happy. Anyone looking on might think I was smoking Dad's pot, I bet. Lying here, grinning.

But it feels good to love a thing and not expect anything back. It feels good to not get an argument or any pushiness or any rumors or any bullshit. It's love without strings. It's ideal.

Tonight I spot a small jet and I concentrate on it and I stare at it and smile. Its very existence proves Zeno of Elea wrong. If motion was impossible, there would be no such things as airplanes. Or departure times. Or arrival times. I send my love up in a stream of steady light and in my head I think: *I love you. I love you. I love you. I love you.*

PASSENGER #4657
HEIDI KLEIN, SEAT 17A
FLIGHT #879
NASHVILLE TO PHILADELPHIA

I stare at him because I can't believe he just said that.

"What?" he asks.

"Did you really just say that?" It's rhetorical, that question. I know what he said.

"What?" he says again, this time smiling that smile at me because he knows I can't resist it. This is how he convinced me to let him move into our apartment. He said he'd rather sleep on the couch and pitch in rent than stay in that shitty dorm room with his dorky roommate. Then he smiled just like this.

"I'm fighting with you over how you can't cook anything and how I have to come home from chem lab to a stinky apartment and no dinner and you tell me this now?"

"Yep."

"You love me?"

"Uh-huh."

I can't help but smile back at him. "We only met two months ago."

"So?"

"So you can't love me," I say.

"Why not?"

"Because you don't know the real me, right?"

"We've lived together for two months, Heidi. You make great coffee. You're always late for work. You use moisturizer in your hair as mousse. I've washed your underwear."

"Still doesn't get you out of making dinner once in a while," I say.

"But I still love you."

I still can't believe he's saying this. "Why'd you choose to tell me this now?"

"I don't know. I guess it just came out."

"After two months," I say.

"After two months," he says.

I want to say so many things. I might even want to say...it. But instead, my head fills with signature Heidi Klein snark-and-logic combo. *You can't love me. I don't have a soul, so I don't believe in soul mates. We're nineteen. Next thing you'll be asking me to marry you. Seriously, did you forget to take some meds this morning?*

He looks misty. The way my mother was when I left to go to college in September. I hated all that misty crap. Maybe I'm codependent and I've replaced my mother with Ron. Oh, God. Maybe I need all that misty crap. Shit.

"Can we save this for later?"

He smiles again. His dimples pop. "Let me out," he says. "I need to take a leak."

I get up and let him out and plop down in the window seat for a while. Clear skies—I can nearly make out the landscape below, but it's still blurry. And then something crazy hits me and I say, "I love you, too," without any reason to. It's like I'm not in control of my mouth or something.

And on the one hand, I'm glad Ron wasn't here to hear it, but on the other hand, I hope he gets back soon. I miss him already.

CLAIRE NEVER QUITS.

HUMANITIES CLASS IS a little like a shield I can put on every morning that will protect me from people like Aimee Hall and her pack of gossiping, tennis racquet–hugging compulsive hair-straighteners.

The room is filled with kids who either own Albert Camus T-shirts or read Kafka for fun on weekends. Okay— there are a few people here who just do it because it looks good on their college applications. But no matter what group you fit into, in humanities class you can speak your mind and Ms. Steck will listen. At the moment, we're debating how I can't accept that Zeno got away with questioning motion.

Every time we've talked about his "motion is impossible"

theory, I do the same thing. I stand up. I swing my arms around. I say, "Motion is possible. Check it out!" Today is no different.

"Back it up with an argument," Ms. Steck says.

I swing my arms more wildly and pretend to tap-dance in place. "Motion is totally possible! Hello!"

"That's not an argument," she says.

"I think it is. Imagine the argument was *Astrid has two arms*, but I had only one, and my right arm was a stump, and I could show it to you right here in your face. Wouldn't that be proof enough to move on to the next argument? Wouldn't the stump be argument enough to prove that Astrid had only one arm?" I ask. "So me standing here moving is proof that Zeno was wrong and silly and just wasting our time. Motion is possible, and everyone in this room knows it."

Ms. Steck just looks at me.

I add, "Maybe saying *motion is impossible* was his way of getting out of doing chores. Maybe it got him laid or something. But it's totally ridiculous. Look!" I swing my arms even more wildly.

Two kids—Zeno lovers—in the back row keep trying to explain to me. "That's the point!" one says. The other nods. "To argue things out to the most absurd!"

Ms. Steck reminds me of the arrow—one of Zeno's arguments. The idea is that an arrow shot at a target has to move through time, but since time is made of tiny moments, the arrow, in each tiny moment, is at rest and not moving.

"That's like saying that if I take a picture of Clay"—I

point to Clay, who is wearing his Kurt Vonnegut asterisk T-shirt today—"while he's running hurdles and I freeze that moment in time...that he never really moved during the race."

Ms. Steck says, "Yes. That's a little like what Zeno was trying to say."

"Which brings me back to: This is a waste of time! We all know Clay runs hurdles and wins medals. And he must have moved to get here today, right? Although, if I can use this as an excuse to get out of going to trig next, then I might just shut up."

The class laughs, and I tell Ms. Steck that I am happy to move on from Zeno and his dumb theory. "I understand what he was doing, but I still think it's stupid," I say.

During free time at the end of class, while most people are writing their short paper on Zeno or finishing their homework for other classes, I hit the Internet, and I find someone who has something more important than "motion is impossible" to offer from around the fifth century BC.

Hippocrates. Father of Western medicine. He said this: "There are in fact two things, science and opinion; the former begets knowledge, the latter ignorance." Now tell me *motion is impossible* seems remotely important next to that shit.

▶ ▶ ▶

After I make it to fourth-period trig (because I moved my legs to walk there, and motion is totally possible), I realize this is what trig sounds like to me: "Hgdj gehuoidah zdkgj szhd-gouij fhhhf ldldfuhd. Ujfrekuhjd fhdy. Ksdihfh. 54 46 34 23. Iuhfg."

I realize I only took trig because everyone else takes trig. I realize that I took trig because Mom said, "Well, of course you're taking trig. You're going to college, right?"

I tune out everything that Mr. Trig is explaining, and I walk through my options. I can change this. I have a choice. I decide to see the guidance counselor after lunch to set myself free. I decide to schedule something cooler for fourth period. Maybe I can still get into a yoga gym class, or maybe there's still a spot in ceramics. Worst comes to worst, I can always take a study hall.

The bell rings. I don't take down the nightly reading or homework assignment from the board. I leave my textbook and graph paper on Mr. Trig's desk. I have mentally just quit trig. This makes me so happy, I smile through the rest of the day.

▶ ▶ ▶

Eighth-period European history. I am still so happy about just dropping trig, it is impossible to stop smiling. But we are watching a documentary about the Holocaust. There are dead bodies piled up everywhere. Starving people in concentration camps. Gas chambers. This isn't right, me smiling like this.

They'll say: *Did you see Astrid Jones in EH today? Smiling at those Holocaust films?*

The film footage stops, and a youngish guy with an English accent appears on the screen. He seems to be sitting in a room of Holocaust artifacts. Skulls, hair, teeth. He's telling us how the Nazis killed more than just Jews. Yes, six million Jews were exterminated, but five million other civilians were, too. He says we often overlook these five million. I think he's right. I'd never heard of them before right now.

He lists them. The Poles, the Ukrainians, the Yugoslavians, and the Russians. The blacks, the Gypsies, anyone of mixed race, the mentally or physically disabled and the homosexuals.

"At least the Nazis had that right," Kevin Herman says from the back row.

The rest of the back row laughs. The film goes on. Mr. Williams either didn't hear Kevin or has become really good at ignoring him.

The man explains the imprisonment and murder of Jehovah's Witnesses, and how they were forced to wear purple armbands. The footage is black and white, but I can see armbands. I imagine they are purple. He explains that while we might know that Jews were forced to wear yellow stars, we may not know that homosexuals were forced to wear triangles. Pink triangles.

It occurs to me here that though I am no longer interested in triangles, I am interested in pink ones. I'm just still not so sure how interested I am.

"The gas chamber was too good for them," Kevin says.

The back row sniggers again.

▶ ▶ ▶

I read books about schools that have gay/straight alliance clubs. These are fictional books. And so I believe gay/straight alliance clubs must also be fictional. We certainly don't have them here. We have a sign in the entrance hall that says THIS IS NO PLACE FOR HATE, but that doesn't actually make it no place for hate.

If we have anything, we have Holocaust deniers. We have neo-Nazis. We have the Ku Klux Klan. They leave invitations in our mailbox every few years with mints—individually packaged melty mints with the KKK symbol on the wrapper. It's 2011 and we still have them.

This whole town is frozen in time. Stuck in one place. Motionless. Except for me, because I just quit trig, which proves motion is totally possible, even if it means I now have to go home and tell my parents and listen to my mother talk about how quitters never win and winners never quit.

▶ ▶ ▶

"Look at me!" she says. "I wanted to quit art school in my first semester, but did I? No. I carried on and went all the way through and got my master's. And that master's is feeding this family now!"

The only good thing about this conversation is that Friday is pizza night and I get to eat slices of white pizza with broccoli and garlic and drink a birch beer while I listen.

"Couldn't you get a tutor or something? I don't think it

will look very good on your school records that you quit something, will it, Gerry?" She pours herself another glass of red from the bottle next to her glass.

Dad sighs. "You're not heading for the sciences, are you, Astrid?"

"Nope," I answer. I've told them my plan a hundred times: Move back to New York City and be an editor.

"It was only pissing you off, dropping your GPA and making your life harder. It's senior year. You're supposed to be having fun."

"Oh, my God," Mom says. "You sound like a hippie!"

"Pass me the wine," Dad says. He rarely joins her, but it's Friday and the stapler-stealing-and-breaking person at work hasn't come out to apologize yet and it's driving him crazy.

He pours himself a glass and looks her straight in the eye. "Just because you don't know how to have fun doesn't mean the kids can't," he says. "Astrid knows what she wants to do. Who gives a shit if she dropped trig? She was never going to use it!"

"It's quitting," she answers. "And quitters never win."

"Oh, my God, you're like a broken record, Claire. You know, some quitters *do* win. Plenty of them." He adds, "Why can't you just be nice to her for once?"

The question hangs in the air for a minute. Ellis gives me a jealous look. As if it's my fault that this whole family doesn't revolve around her. Sheesh.

Mom looks at Ellis and me. "Go upstairs."

We sit there for a second because we don't know what to do. We're not done eating yet.

Ellis quietly says, "But I'm not done eat—"

"Go upstairs!" Mom yells.

We go upstairs. But the two-hundred-fifty-year-old walls and floors are thin, and we hear the fight from our bedrooms. All the usual stuff. She can't have fun because Gerry is a loser. Gerry doesn't understand her *needs.* Gerry can't even hold a steady job. Gerry never *listens.* Gerry cares more about "your fucking stapler than your wife." Gerry is the perfect example of "quitters never win" because he quit law school.

After ten minutes of this, we hear Dad's chair move. He doesn't say a word and starts running the water for the dishes as she clip-clops up to her office because, you know, "someone has to work around here."

I don't like how pot has taken my dad away from me, but I like how it's given him the balls to stick up for me like that. I send love from my bedroom. *Dad, I love you for saying what you said at dinner. I know it was hard because Mom has chopped off your balls and baked them in a testes casserole, but thank you for trying. It means a lot.*

Ellis comes to my door. Sometimes she's like a real sister— the way we were when we were little when we'd watch *The Wizard of Oz* and she'd curl into my side when the flying monkeys would come. Sometimes she needed me, I guess. Not very often anymore.

"I'm sneaking down. Want me to bring you back some pizza?"

"Nah, I'm good," I say, even though I'm still kind of hungry. "Thanks anyway."

5

I WORK WEEKENDS.

I COULD HAVE PICKED any job—the usual fast-food places or playground summer positions. I could have stayed with friends of the family and interned in New York at some publishing house, as Mom suggested. But in June of junior year when Mom pushed (*if you don't get a summer job now, I'll get one for you*) I chose Maldonado Catering. Juan and Jorge (neither of them a Maldonado, for what it's worth) are both really nice. Jorge interviewed me and gave me the job in about twelve seconds.

"Want to know why?" he asked in a thick Puerto Rican accent.

I nodded.

"Because you didn't bullshit me and tell me that you know what you're doing. It means we can teach it to you *our way*, man."

Now it's October, and I know three things. I know how to devein shrimp really fast. I know how to open clams really fast. I know how to do inventory. (Okay, I know a lot more than that, but some days I feel like that's all I do. Especially the shrimp-deveining part.)

▶ ▶ ▶

I start my day at 5:35 AM with inventory for next weekend's jobs, which are listed on a roster next to the inventory clipboard. The walk-in freezer is full of boxes, and I sit on the one in the back corner and relax. I wish I could live in here. *I'd put the bed there.* It's the only place I feel comfortable anymore. *And a bookshelf there.* I'm not nervous about what Mom would think. *A dresser with a few T-shirts and jeans in the corner.*

There is nothing else like the sound of a walk-in freezer's door opening. It's a loud clunk of the huge handle followed by an air-suck sound. It's a big sound. Like something circus equipment would make. Logger sounds. Or those science-fiction bay doors on spaceships with air locks.

I pretend to look for a box of frozen pastry shells in case it's Juan. But I feel my stomach twist because I know it's not Juan.

"Need help?" Dee says.

"Just checking the dates to make sure I get the right ones.

Damn, there are a lot of shells here this month." I say this in case anyone is outside, listening. In case anyone knows.

Dee lets the door slam behind her, and it sounds even bigger than it does when it opens. The swirling white air dances around the caged freezer lightbulb, and she pushes me right up against the dappled stainless-steel wall and kisses me with both her hands braided into my hair.

This is not our first kiss.

▶ ▶ ▶

Dee is my real best friend, I guess. Kristina doesn't know about her, and Dee doesn't know the truth about Kristina, and that's the way I want to keep it.

Dee is the funniest person I have ever met in my life. Her laugh is big and confident. She's laid back and doesn't like to gossip. She's also kissing me. A lot. And I'm kissing her back.

Before I met her here at Maldonado's, I only knew her as the neighboring school district's badass hockey star who would periodically get mentioned in small-town gossip. I think the first thing I ever heard was from Ellis. I'm pretty sure she used the word *dyke* in her description, too. Because if you want to be a small-town girl in U. Valley, that's what you say.

The first time I saw Dee was at one of Ellis's hockey games last year. She smiled at me, and I never forgot it. Or more accurately, I always remembered it. And I checked the hockey schedule and went to the away game at her school, too, just to see if she'd smile at me again, and she did.

I smiled back. That was right about the time Tim Huber broke up with me, too, so smiling wasn't something I did very often.

I didn't know she worked at Maldonado's when I interviewed. Believe me, my first day of work was some sort of proof that everything happens for a reason. I'd thought about her smiles for eight months at that point. Probably every day.

On my second day of work, she said, "Anyone ever tell you that you're gorgeous?"

I didn't answer, but I asked myself the question for a whole month. She must have thought I was ignoring it or just thought she was joking around. But I wasn't, and I didn't. I was considering it. Astrid Jones. Gorgeous. I'd never really thought about that. Tim Huber said things like *cute* or *sweet* or, one time, *hot*—which turned me off completely because I knew he was only saying it to see how far he could get me to go with him.

But when Dee said I was hot a month after she'd asked me if anyone had ever told me I was gorgeous? She meant it. "I've said it before. I'll say it again. You're hot!"

That was the day of our first kiss.

Now she's laughing while she kisses me. "You're not going to tell me to back off again, are you?" she asks.

"Mmm. Hmm," I manage while still kissing her neck, her ear. "Back off," I say. I bite her earlobe.

So far in my life, Dee is the only person who wants to totally ravish me. I have to stop her all the time. I swear she'd do it right here in the walk-in freezer if she could. Right now. Before six AM. With morning breath. Next to a box of frozen taquitos.

"I dream of this all week," she says.

"Me too."

"We have to find more ways to see each other," she says.

"I know," I say, but the best I can do is go watch Ellis play hockey for the one game where Dee's school is the visiting team. Or, well, the go-to-Atlantis-with-Kristina-and-Justin daydream, but I haven't told her about that yet. Because it's stupid.

At the moment, we talk twice a week outside of work. Between her hockey schedule and my paranoia, that's about all we can manage. Plus, her mom is a bit of a stickler about phone minutes, and Dee only gets fifteen dollars' worth a week.

Anyway, not being constantly connected makes the whole thing more intense. It's better that way.

▶ ▶ ▶

Dee and I are washing fruits and vegetables.

"You done with the mushrooms yet?" Juan asks.

"Almost," I say. I finish them, put them in a container and take them over to him. I stop for a minute to watch him slice them. He is like ballet with a knife. "You're a natural, you know that?" I ask.

He says, "Natural? What the fuck? Nobody is born this good, man. Takes years of practice. Now get back to work."

Either way, it's beautiful to watch, even if he is a dick sometimes. I send love to him. My brain says: *Juan, you are a wonderful, awesome human being and a complete natural at cutting mushrooms, and I love you.*

An hour later, Dee is washing and prepping the strawberries and cherries while Jorge melts dark chocolate in a double boiler. I will spend the next half hour sticking the pieces of fruit with toothpicks, dipping them and laying them on waxed paper. Then, when the tray is full, I will take it to the walk-in freezer. I find myself wishing I were a strawberry. Imagine that: washed by Dee's soft hands, dipped in chocolate and left in the freezer, where no one bothers you for an hour and a half.

If I were to explain to you how she really makes me feel, I'm not sure I could. Do I love her? I don't know. Maybe. I love kissing her. I love the way she smells, and I love her lips. But Dee scares the shit out of me, too. Because she *knows*. And I *don't* know.

We punch out at noon and walk to the parking lot, which is now full of cars. It was empty at five o'clock this morning. We want to kiss each other good-bye, but instead we wave like awkward dorks and get into our cars and drive away in different directions. She goes left. I go right.

6

DO WHAT FEELS RIGHT.

THE CLOSER I GET TO MY HOUSE, the less I want to go home, so I stop at Kristina's house. I park in back so Mom won't see my car.

"Oh, God. You smell like fish," she says as I arrive in her room. The sun is pouring through the windows, and as I bounce on her bed to annoy her, dust rises and sparkles in the sunrays.

"And that's just my hands," I say.

"Ew. No, seriously. You stink."

I continue to bounce and watch the dust dance. "It's probably the brassicas."

"Brassicas? What the hell?" Now she's cranky. My arrival—and my bouncing—means that she can't stay in bed all day.

"You know, brassicas? Broccoli and cauliflower? The cabbage family?"

She's squinting at me now.

"Come on. Get up and talk to me. I'm bored. I'm hyper. I don't want to go home to Claire and her hellish Saturday mood swings."

"How long have you been up?" she asks.

"Four forty-five."

"Oh, my God."

"How late were you out?" I ask.

"Like an hour before you got up," she answers.

"Sweet."

"Justin's mom thinks he stayed over here. He's probably still out before Chad has to drive all the way home." Chad lives about an hour away. He and Justin met online at some photography forum. It's not as creepy as it sounds. "Justin said he'd call me when he was going home so I could call his house and pretend he left something here."

"And how's Donna?"

She smiles. "Awesome." She sits up and sighs. "We're going back to Atlantis tonight. You should come. You could drink. You could dance. It'd be fun."

Dancing and drinking. Two things very low on my list of priorities, along with sex, kickboxing and becoming a rodeo star.

"Sounds fun," I say. "But I need my beauty sleep if one day Prince Charming is going to gallop down Main Street and sweep me off my feet."

"Wow," she says. "You've been listening to Claire again." Kristina is allowed to call her Claire, so that's what we call her when we talk about her. I have to call her Mom to her face. "She's so jacked up on that these days."

She reaches for her phone and brings up a text message. It's so Claire. *Kristina, WHEN r u going to find a good boy like Justin 4 Astrid?*

"I wish she'd just mind her own business," I say.

"Right?"

"Last time I dated anyone, she just nitpicked me about him anyway."

"Yeah. That was Huber, wasn't it?"

I look at the message again and wonder how many moms text their daughters' best friends behind their backs like this. I wonder why she uses text-speak. It irks me so much that I almost want to reply. *Hi Mom. Y r u being so creepy n txting my frnd?*

"Yeah. Huber," I answer. I don't like to think about Tim Huber.

"She thinks you're not over him yet."

"That was a year ago," I say. Sometimes it feels like yesterday, though.

"Yeah," she answers. "Isn't it hilarious that she asks for a boy just like Justin?"

This should be when I tell her about Dee, but I can't. Even though she'd totally understand, she might tell *just one person*. And that would be *just one person* too many.

"Shit," I say. "I'd better go. The world will explode if I don't have my room clean by three."

"Thanks for waking my ass up for nothing," she says. "Tell my mom to bring me some coffee on your way out, will ya?"

▶ ▶ ▶

It's four o'clock. My room is clean, and I'm out on my table looking at the sky. I'm thinking about Dee. About how inadequate I feel. About how her hands know what to do but mine don't. About how I always have to stop her when she wants to keep going.

My brain people say: *Astrid baby, it's because you're not gay.*

They say: *You're not strong enough to be gay.*

They say: *Mom would never forgive you if you're gay.*

I try to stop thinking about it, which is easier on weekdays when I'm distracted by school stuff like Zeno of Elea, lit mag, and the dirty looks I still get from Tim Huber's friends. But now all I can think about is Dee and how this all started. How she told me how gorgeous I was. How flattered I felt. How exhilarating it was to be *wanted*. This is why I doubt. It's the loophole. It's the question no one ever wants to ask.

Am I doing this out of desperation? Is it some weird phase I'm going through? And why, if any of the answers are *yes*, does it feel so right?

There is a 747 high, leaving a crisp white line through the cloudless autumn sky. I ask the passengers: *Am I really gay?*

But they don't answer me. They are reading their in-flight

magazines and sipping ginger ale. I send them love—as much as I can gather. I ask them: *What do I do now?*

PASSENGER #54627563
ELAINE HUBBINGTON, SEAT 3A FIRST CLASS
FLIGHT #4022
CLEVELAND TO PHILADELPHIA
MEMBER OF WINGS ELITE CLUB #HU3456

I know about two hours into the flight home that I have to leave John. Call it a moment of clarity. Call it a message from God. I stare out the window at the sky and feel this smack of reality right in my heart.

He hasn't done anything to deserve it. He's loyal and sweet. He still buys me thoughtful presents on my birthday and on our anniversary. I just don't love him. It's not fair that he's wasting his life on me, a person who will never return his feelings. And it's early. Married only five years—no kids yet.

Yet.

Our last discussion was groggy. I'd set the alarm for four and was pulling on my socks when he rolled over and lightly stroked my back.

"When you get home, let's talk about a family again."

"Mmm hmm," I said.

"We have the space."

Is that the most important factor for deciding to have kids these days? Space?

His comment echoed the whole flight to Chicago. *We have the space.*

What I should have said was, "Why don't we go shopping for antiques? That would fill some space."

What I should have said was, "How about a home gym? Or a flat-screen TV with surround sound?"

When did I go from human being to baby machine to fill your space? That's what I wanted to say to him. But instead, I just held off calling until after dinner. Each sticky-sweet thing he said made me want to puke. "I miss you" vomit. "I'll keep the bed warm for you" gag. "I love you" heave. I wanted to say, "I think I loved you, too, once, but I don't anymore. Find yourself another uterus to fill your goddamn space."

Instead, I said, "I miss you. Keep the bed warm. I love you, too."

Lies.

The blue sky at thirty thousand feet asks me uncomfortable questions. It asks: *Why did you marry him? Did you ever love him? Will you?*

It asks me: *What do you do now?*

The blue sky at thirty thousand feet gives me answers. It says: *You never loved John. You hit thirty and panicked. You're too selfish to admit you made a mistake.*

The sky says: *Stop being so selfish. Everybody deserves a chance at real love. Only once you let him go will you find yours. Do what feels right.*

7

ASTRID TO HOME PLANET: PLEASE RESCUE ME.

"IT'S SATURDAY...let's go somewhere fancy!" Mom says after galumphing downstairs from her office at ten after five.

Dad, Ellis and I are in the den. I'm reading the beginning of Plato's *Republic* for humanities class. Ellis is watching a documentary about triathlons. Dad is in his Saturday stoner clothes. He has white paint on his dark brown hiking shorts. His T-shirt gives the illusion of having been sweaty and dried out again. His hair is Hollywood windswept. He's got a graying goatee, and if you look close enough, you can see Cheetos dust in it. The only thing he did while he was "cleaning out the garage attic" was take a few hits from the pipe he hides up there and exhale out the exhaust fan toward Bob's house.

Technically, my father is The Dude from the movie *The Big Lebowski*, only he's totally in the closet. (Jones closet tally: 2)

Mom looks at him for an answer.

Dad says, "Nothing fancy for me. I'm beat."

"What do you have to be beat about?" she asks. "You didn't even work today."

Dad says, "Weekends off. The perks of working for the man."

"Sorry," I say. "I have to read this, and I have to get up early for work."

I don't even know why we answer. Dad and I both know she wasn't really asking us. She looks to Ellis and puts on an annoying high-pitched voice. "A Mommy and Me night?"

As always, mere mention of this tradition makes me want to throw up in my mouth. Ellis chews on her lower lip for a second. I think she may roll her eyes to herself as if she knows how annoying this is to the rest of us. Then she claps her hands together and says, "Let's get *really* dressed up, too!"

"Fancy!" Mom chirps, and the two of them go upstairs in a fit of adolescent bliss.

▶ ▶ ▶

An hour later they're gone, and Dad disappears to the garage again on some vague errand, which means he's going to toke up. I wish he didn't act this way. He's like some kid, and I'd much rather he knew that I know and I don't care.

I'm the only one who'd be halfway cool about it. Ellis

would probably cry and turn him into the D.A.R.E. cops. Mom would freak out. My mother has never held back on how she feels about stoners. Hippies. Do-nothings. Druggies. "All those brain cells!" she'd say. "What a waste!"

Frankly, the more I read about the philosophers of ancient Greece, the more I think *her* life is a waste. What's she learning? What's she questioning? She knows everything, which means she doesn't know anything.

I mean, yes, at the beginning of humanities class, I thought most philosophers were a bunch of entitled Greek guys sitting around thinking up crazy shit (like Zeno) while the women and the slaves did all the work. But then this week we started to learn about Socrates.

Socrates lived in the fifth century BC in Greece. He didn't write anything, which means most of what we know about him comes from what other people said (a little like living in Unity Valley). His favorite thing to do was to prove to people that what they thought was truth might not be true. This did two things for Socrates: (1) It earned him the label "one of the founders of Western philosophy," and (2) it eventually annoyed enough people that they put him to death by making him drink hemlock.

A lot of what we know about Socrates comes from his most popular student, Plato, who wrote many things, including *The Republic*, which is an imaginary discussion between Socrates and a few others in order to demonstrate the Socratic method. The Socratic method is what Ms. Steck wants us to practice most during this class.

She said, "This will be a time of asking questions and not rushing to answer them. A time of poking holes in your own theories. A time of *thinking and not knowing.*"

Perfect for me right about now. I am the *not knowing* queen.

What I *do* know is that the original idea I had about philosophers is somewhat accurate. Women had it pretty bad in ancient Greece. Married off at puberty by their fathers. To older men. So they could bear sons. But Socrates thought women could be educated and should be included. While many of his peers owned slaves, Socrates said, "Slavery is a system of outrage and robbery."

But he didn't have a job. He was poor. He didn't even write down his own amazing ideas. All he cared about was truth and living a good life—while trying to define what *a good life* meant.

So if we go by Mom's standards, Socrates was the biggest loser of all time.

▶ ▶ ▶

I put my coat on and go out to my picnic table. The sky is lit up with streetlights, so I can't see many stars, but I can still see the planes blinking overhead. I can hear the bar down by the fire company. I can hear the traffic on Route 733—the road that links this small town to the next, and the next, until it meets with a road that might lead somewhere bigger.

I think about Kristina and how she's at Atlantis—the only

gay bar in the nearby city. I think about why I haven't gone yet.

I stare at the first plane that's cutting the sky in two. I stare and I send my love. I send it to the woman in seat 5A who is worried about something. I send it to the man in first class who's not feeling well. I focus on the stars, and I send love to the aliens flying millions of miles from me in outer space. My brain people like to think that one of these days, they'll be coming for me.

I concentrate back on the plane and gather more of my love. I send it to the pilot, who is tired and who misses his family. To the flight attendant and to the crying baby whose ears hurt. To the guy tapping away on his laptop computer.

▶ ▶ ▶

Am I asleep? Am I still outside? I can see blue. Blue like in the deep end of a swimming pool. Blue like if I lived in a bubble in the sky. I say to the approaching creature, "Thank you for coming to rescue me. I knew I didn't belong here. Please take me to my real family." Instead, it pulls out a long metal bar and sticks it into my belly button.

▶ ▶ ▶

I wake up to Ellis standing right above me, saying something. I jerk up and instinctively guard my abdomen. I nearly head-butt her in the process.

"Jesus!" she says.

"Sorry."

"Out here long?"

"I don't know. What time is it?"

"Eleven thirty." I can smell wine on her breath.

"She let you drink again?"

"They didn't card me."

"They don't card people like you in fancy restaurants, Ellis." I look at her. She's wearing Mom's prized jewelry—the diamond teardrop earrings and pendant. Stuff Mom saves for bigwig parties and award ceremonies in the city. Ellis is wearing a black velvet dress most people around here would wear to prom. But she looks sixteen. No doubt about that.

"Wanna stay up and watch a movie or something? *SNL* is on in a minute," she says.

"I have to leave for work at five."

She lets out a judgmental chuckle through her nose.

"What?"

"You could have quit after summer."

"It gets me out of here, doesn't it?"

"Your loss."

I get up and hop off the table. "Well, we can't all have Mommy and Me nights out at the club, you know."

She smacks my arm. "You have no idea what it's like to get drunk with Mom and listen to her bitch the whole time," she says.

I want to ask her *bitch about what?* But I know what. There are always inside jokes during the week after a Mommy and Me episode. About Dad. About me. About girls on the hockey team. "You could always say no," I say. "No one has a gun to your head."

"I couldn't," she says. "Then I'd be just like—uh."

"Just like me?" I say.

"Yeah. I guess."

I feel bad for perfect Ellis. She thinks she has it all figured out inside her safe little bubble. She doesn't realize yet that one day she's going to fail at something, and our mother will be there to critique exactly how she failed, step-by-step.

▶ ▶ ▶

In the bathroom, I look at myself in the mirror for a long time. I don't know what I'm looking for, but I know I'm different. I brush my teeth. Wash my face. With my hair pulled back like this, I look again. And I can see it. Behind my eyes. Something is in there. Something Ellis doesn't have. Something Mom and Dad don't have.

I close the door to my room and I turn off the light. I pretend I'm in an airplane. I pretend I'm drinking orange juice in seat 23A and I can feel a stream of love shooting right through the body of the plane from some lonely girl lying on a picnic table in a small town no one has ever heard of before. I send love back to her, but I'm not sure if she can get it.

I think: *If I'm on an airplane, then where am I going?* I come up with answers. *New York City. Los Angeles. Paris. Melbourne. Far enough away that this is okay. Far enough away that no one here will ever know.*

8

MOO.

THE WALK-IN FREEZER DOOR sucks the frosty air out into the kitchen hall when it opens. Dee has her hair in braids today, with a bandanna on her head. She slept late. I can still see sleep lines on her beautiful brown face.

"You hit snooze, didn't you?" I ask after the door closes with a thud behind her.

"Yep."

"How many times?"

She holds up three fingers. I want to tell her that I never hit snooze.

▶ ▶ ▶

Dee's main objective for the day seems to be making Juan laugh, which she achieves in less than two hours.

"Hey, Juan! Knock knock!"

He rolls his eyes. "Who's there?"

"The interrupting cow," she says.

He answers, "The inter—"

"Moo!"

He laughs genuinely, as if he never heard the interrupting cow joke before. Then I go back to deveining shrimp.

It's a short morning, and Dee and I are out by eleven. When we leave, we drive up to Freedom Lake and climb the hill path to our favorite spot.

Before we can have any sort of conversation, which is what I'd really like to do, Dee leans over and kisses me. Then, as always, she goes too fast. I take her hand out of my shirt and place it on my hip. She says, "Jones?"

"Yeah?"

"I think you're scared of me."

"Who doesn't know this?" I ask.

"Why?"

I don't know what to say. I want to tell her that she's too pushy—like everyone else in my life. I want to tell her that I'm not ready for intimacy. I want to tell her to stop looking at me with those lovesick eyes. Instead, I do what any awkward geek who wants to avoid the topic of sex at all costs would do. I look at her and say, "So—uh—what do you know about Socrates?"

"He was Greek, right?" she answers.

"Uh-huh."

She nods her head and puts her hand up my shirt and leans into my neck. "That's what I know about Socrates," she says.

I want to remove her hand from my belly, but I know she'll get mad again.

"Did you ever hear of Zeno?" I ask.

"Nope."

"He said motion was impossible."

She doesn't say anything.

"Like—moving. He said it was impossible to move because time stands still inside each little split second."

"That's stupid," she says. "Watch me now." And then she slips her hand under my bra. "I'm moving."

"Too fast," I say. "As usual."

She doesn't stop, so I roll on my front. "Okay. Okay. I get it!" I say.

She sighs and rolls onto her back. "So what's the big deal about some philosopher who said motion was impossible? Philosophers said all sorts of crazy shit. Wasn't that their job?"

"Their job was to find truth."

"And did they?"

I look at Dee and I think that Zeno was totally right, even though that's not what he meant: For people, motion is sometimes impossible. For Dee. For my mom and Ellis. For nearly everyone.

9

HOMECOMING
FRIDAY IS JIGGLY.

THE GIRLS WHO TALLY the Homecoming votes walked around with smirks on their faces all week. They got out of classes for half the day on Wednesday to count, and now it's Friday morning and I bet they couldn't sleep last night.

Kristina isn't even thinking about it. All she can talk about on the way to school is her double date tonight and how cute Donna is and how she thinks she might love her.

"The real deal," she says. "She *gets* me, you know?"

"That's awesome," I say.

I wish I could tell her about me. About Dee. I feel like every minute I spend with Kristina is a lie. I've been practicing a sentence in my head. *Kristina, don't kill me, but I'm gay. I think. I mean, I think I'm gay. I mean, I think I'm in love with a girl. I mean*... The sentence isn't quite worked out yet.

Ever since European history last week and those damn pink triangles... it's as if quitting trig opened up a channel of thinking I was pushing away. I freed myself of something I was faking, and now I want to free myself of all my faking.

"You okay?" she asks.

"Sure." I'm not, though. I'm a little angry or sad or something. Impatient. I am sick of it not being Saturday. I want to fast-forward to tomorrow morning, please. While I'm at it, I want to fast-forward to next year. College. Leaving Unity Valley.

"You don't look it."

My eyes dart to the rearview, where I can see a pickup truck full of senior boys speeding toward me.

"I always wonder if the people driving behind me are texting and are about to kill me. That's all."

"They'll outlaw it soon," she says.

"That never stopped anyone from driving drunk, did it?"

I can tell Kristina is looking at me with that face. "What's your damage?"

I shrug. I pull over to the curb and let the truck pass me.

"Come on. Don't be pissed. It's Homecoming Day! No matter how the day ends, I'll be a princess or maybe even— could it be possible—your *queen?*" She forms her hands into a finger tiara and pretends to place it on her head and says, "What they don't know will never hurt them, right?"

▶ ▶ ▶

My replacement for trig, fourth-period study hall, is pleasant. No one all that recognizable in here. Stacy and Karen Koch, twins, sit next to me and smile occasionally as if they know something I don't. Probably Homecoming results. As if I care.

I read a little bit of Plato's *Republic* as well as the chapter in our textbook about the trial of Socrates.

Can I admit I'm a little freaked out that Socrates only has one name? I know that's how it was done in those days, but it bugs me. I can't tell if it's his last name or his first name or what. And it can't be shortened—except to *Sock*, which is completely stupid. I want him to have a more familiar name— something laid back and modern, so I can relate to him better. So I stare at the picture in my book of the curly-bearded guy with the pug nose, and by the end of study hall, I name him Frank. Frank Socrates. Makes him more huggable.

Makes his clothes easier to label for summer camp. F.S.

▶ ▶ ▶

After sixth-period lunch is over, the entire school population empties into the football stadium. The band plays soft numbers down in the band area.

Without Kristina and Justin, I don't have anyone to sit with. I know a few people from classes, but most of them play in the band. I'd rather sit by myself anyway. I pull out Plato's *Republic*, but the minute I do, Jeff Garnet sits down next to me and stares, nervously, until I look up.

I know he's nervous because Jeff is always nervous. He's a

leg shaker—you know, the bouncy kind that rattles entire rooms and makes you want to toss up your lunch? I see his knee bouncy-bouncy-bouncing there until I close the book around my bookmark and look at him.

"Do you know who won?" he asks.

"No."

"Do you want to know?"

"Not really," I say. Jeff bounces his leg so much, I want to put my hand on it and make him stop. I want to tell him to relax.

"I guess you'll find out soon enough," he says, acknowledging the band director giving the signal for the band to fade out.

"Yeah."

Jeff has been staring at me for two months. Every day in third-period AP lit, I feel it as sure as I feel him shaking the whole room with his leg, making the heating unit jangle.

"Astrid?" he says.

"Yeah?"

"You want to go out sometime? I mean, no big deal or anything, but you know—just you and me?"

"I don't know," I say. "I mean, yeah, sure, maybe. I'm pretty busy at the moment, but I guess I'd like that." I have no idea why I said that. I do not want to go out with Jeff. Not because of the leg thing, but because I'm—uh—*taken* already.

"No pressure," he says. "You can get back to me about it."

"Sure. I'll get back to you," I say.

An hour later, all is right with the world—the football captain and cheer squad co-captain are crowned Homecoming king and queen. The cars drive the losers and winners out of the stadium while we applaud their collective greatness, and then we're all sent back into school before final bell.

▶ ▶ ▶

Kristina calls me at seven because she already heard Jeff asked me out.

They say: *Why would she snub a nice boy like Jeff Garnet? It's not like she has other options.*

They say: *She's just like her mother. Thinks she's better than us.*

"Why didn't you say yes?" she says. "You *do* want to get Claire off your case about dating, right?"

"I didn't *not* say yes. I said I'd get back to him. That I was—uh—busy for a while."

"Oh, sure. All that Plato and Aristotle."

"Seriously, Kristina. He's not my type."

"You really should hook up with someone this year, Astrid. It's depressing. Plus, I feel guilty. You spend so much time with me and Justin, I feel like it's our fault."

"How's it your fault?" I ask.

"How can you date anyone if you're so busy keeping our secrets?"

She has a point. Except she's missing the biggest piece of information in the equation. My secret is bigger than her secret, because nobody knows it yet.

Not even me.

At dinner, the subject comes up again. Me and Jeff Garnet—talk of the town.

"I don't know," I say when Ellis asks me if I'm going to say yes.

"I hear he's a really sweet boy," Mom says. "I hear he's at the top of your class, too. Do you two share some classes?"

"Just lit class. And lunch," I say.

Ellis says, "You know, if you don't start dating again, people will think you're still not over Huber. Or they'll probably say you're gay."

I smile at her and give her death-ray eyes. And anyway, I already had my gay rumor. Tenth grade, December. Right before Christmas vacation.

I think if we kept a calendar of who gets called gay in high school, there would be a new person on every single day of the 180-day school year. Gay, dyke, fag, lesbo, homo, whatever. Every single one of us has heard it somewhere along the ride. It's more common than the flu. More contagious, too. Nobody gossips about whether you have the flu or not.

Then, as if on cue, Claire blurts out, "That reminds me. I was at the printer today, and Luanne said that there are only *lesbians* on the school hockey team, which I took to be an ignorant attempt to insult Ellis. What decade are these people living in? I mean, that might have been true back when I was in school, but in the twenty-first century, all kinds of girls play sports. Why do these small-town people have to have such small minds?"

Ellis looks at Mom as if she's reading from the wrong script.

"I knew plenty of girls who played sports when we went to school who weren't lesbians, Claire," Dad says. "My sister, for one. Hell, my mother played sports in the fifties. Last time I checked, she wasn't a lesbian, either."

"Well, it's no big deal to us, girls. Your father and I lived in New York for a long time. We knew plenty of gay people." That's Mom. Friend of the Gays. FOTG. Wait. Her FOTG badge is around here somewhere. Let me find it. "I just don't understand why people here talk about it like it's leprosy," she says. "I hope you're nice to them, Ellis."

Ellis gives her an insulted look. "Of course I am! Geez, Mom. Stop being so weird."

"Some people around here think you can catch it, you know."

All three of us look at her as if she has just landed from space.

"Well, they do!" she insists. "I've heard them say you can catch gay off gays. Isn't that ignorant?"

We keep looking at her. She drinks more wine.

I'm happy to see that Ellis is as annoyed as I am, but I'm working really hard not to get paranoid about why Ellis said anything about people thinking I'm gay in the first place.

I look at her. "So you'd rather have me dating Tim Huber again than happily single?"

"God!" she says. "No!" Then she chews and swallows. "Anyway, he doesn't talk to you anymore, does he?"

No. Tim Huber doesn't talk to me anymore. Not since I completely fell for him and Ellis and Mom started bugging me to break up with him because he's fat. Then, when I wouldn't, somebody (most likely the somebody to my right, or to *her* right) started the rumor that broke us up.

They said: *She's only dating him because he's fat.*

They said: *It's a pity thing.*

"No," I answer. "He doesn't talk to me."

"But Jeff Garnet is a nice kid," Ellis says.

"I know. Look. Why can't you all just butt out of my life?"

Claire holds up her wineglass. "If we butted out of your life, you'd still be in diapers. *And* dating that fat boy."

10

I DO NOT LIKE THE PLAN.

"YOU'RE GOING TO CALL JEFF, and you're going to get him to cover for you," Kristina says.

"Were you talking to my mom?"

"No, why?" she asks. She's not lying. I can tell when she lies, and she's genuinely clueless about the rally cry at dinner last night about how badly I need a boyfriend.

We're in my room, and until she started talking, I was completely blissed out after a morning at work with Dee where we worked side by side and spent the entire time pretending to talk in our own language of clicks and weird robotic animal sounds until we cracked everyone up and I nearly peed my pants. We spent a half hour "taking inventory" in both walk-ins (fridge and freezer) for a huge job we have next week. Some big reception and open-house event for the Hispanic Center in town, the biggest job Maldonado Catering ever got.

"Dude? Did you hear me?" Kristina says. "You're going to call Jeff."

"Why?"

"So we can go out."

"I think I can go out without having to drag Jeff Garnet into my life," I say.

Kristina is lying on my bed, dressed in sweats, looking awesome, even though I know she probably rolled out of bed five minutes ago, hasn't showered and probably hasn't even brushed her teeth. I'm sitting on my windowsill because I'm still in my shrimp-flavored catering pants.

"We have to come home a little later than the Claire and Gerry Jones curfew," she says. That's eleven thirty on Friday and Saturday nights. And I've never used it due to my work hours...and the fact that I don't have anyone to go out *with*. "That's why Jeff is the perfect cover. Claire's been bugging me all year to find you a boyfriend. So, now we've found him."

"Can't we find a guy who talks? All he ever does is stare and say things like 'hi' and 'hey,' and he jiggles his leg. I don't know. I mean..."

"Can you just listen? This is the only way we can get you out late enough for the plan to work. Trust me. I have Claire wrapped around my finger."

"Then why can't *you* be my cover?" I ask.

She thinks about this for a millisecond. "Jeff would work better. I mean, even just at the beginning. Plus, it would keep Claire quiet for a minute."

"If we're doing all this conspiracy stuff to get me out of the house, can you at least tell me where we're going?"

"You know."

I'm looking at her like she's stupid. "If you want to drink, can't Justin get anything he wants from his brother?"

"It's not about drinking."

"What other reason is there to go to a bar? And to get Jeff Garnet to lie for me?"

"It's not just any bar," she says. "You know that."

We hear Mom moving around on her office chair two rooms away. Kristina makes the motion for *get dressed and let's get out of here*. So I shoo her to the stairs, take off my catering clothes, throw on some clothing and pop my head into Mom's office. "We're taking a drive. Back in an hour."

"Where are you going?"

"I don't know. Probably to the lake."

"Fine. Just make sure your room is clean by three," she says.

▸ ▸ ▸

"Why do you want me to come to a gay bar with you?" I ask. Maybe she already knows. Maybe I already show up on gaydar, even though I don't clearly show up on my own.

"With me and Donna and Justin and Chad," she corrects.

I glance at her with suspecting eyes. "I don't get it."

She raises one eyebrow. "What's there to get? I already told you there are straight people there."

So when she says that, I think maybe I do get it. I mean, she's not implying I'm gay, right? She's just trying to get me to go out.

"I don't know," I say. "Seems like a big risk for me to take when I don't really want to drink or anything."

"Dude, it's not about drinking. It's about letting loose and being around people who don't give a rat's ass about you. It's ... like ... the *opposite* of Unity Valley."

I pull into the parking area of the lake, and we sit at a picnic table. The place is empty except for the pickup trucks and trailers at the other end of the parking lot that belong to the horse people who come and ride the trails on the weekends.

Kristina has her thumb on Jeff's number, but I still don't feel right. I say, "Can we just chill for a minute before you call? I want to think it over."

What if we can't get in? What if Jeff says no? What if we get caught? What if I get hit on by women who are old enough to be my mother? What if Dee goes there and all my worlds collide? What if people see us? What if I get an answer?

What if I get an answer?

What if. I get. An answer?

I laugh to myself, and Kristina asks, "What're you laughing at?"

"Nothing."

"Not fair."

"I was thinking about getting hit on by old ladies the same age as Claire," I say.

She laughs. "Could happen."

I ask, "Aren't you afraid we'll get caught?"

"Cops are busy solving real crimes. A bunch of underage queer kids is the last thing they care about. Not to say you're queer or anything. I meant the rest of us," she adds.

I say, "What if someone sees us? What then?"

"Don't you think they'd be equally concerned that we don't tell people we saw *them*?"

I sigh. I know Kristina isn't going to take no for an answer.

"Exactly what are you going to tell Jeff that will make him cover for me?" I ask.

"It's easy," she says. "I'm going to promise him beer and a double date with me, you and Justin at the diner next week in exchange for telling Claire that he's taking you to the midnight movies tonight."

I sigh.

"Leave it to me," she says. "I know what I'm doing."

She pulls out her phone and presses some buttons with her thumb, and we both look up, watching clouds—or, in my case, planes. When Jeff answers, she cons him into calling my mom later and telling her a few lies in exchange for liquor.

Then she hands the phone to me but keeps her ear close so she can hear what Jeff says.

"Hey, Jeff. Thanks for this," I say.

"Sure. I'm really glad you're taking me up on my offer."

He sounds like a happy puppy. I feel horrible. I'm reminded of Tim Huber, and my stomach churns.

Kristina makes the motion for me to pass it back to her.

"Hey, Garnet," she says. "Just remember—you can't tell

anyone. I hear one word on the street about this, there's no more booze and no date for you. Dig?"

She hangs up.

I say, "Wow, you're all connected to shit I don't know anything about, man."

"Oh, he's just a boy who wants booze," she says. "He heard Justin got a bottle of gin for Tyler and Vince, and now he wants some, too. Quid pro quo, you know?"

I'm watching a high-flying plane, and I send some random love to it. I'm wondering if any of the people on the plane say *quid pro quo*. I'm wondering if any of them live in a small town like we do. If they've ever snuck out on a Saturday night. (To a gay bar.) If they've ever wondered what making love to a girl must feel like. I ask them: *Is it okay to lie in order to be happy?*

PASSENGER #5654
HELEN OBERLIN, SEAT 27F
FLIGHT #103
DETROIT TO PHILADELPHIA

"Ha!"

I bust out laughing so hard that I spit my ginger ale into the seat in front of me. It fizzes through my nose and burns like bad cocaine. The guy next to me makes a disgusted face, and I give him my napkin. As I reach into my purse for a tissue to blow the ginger ale out of my nose, I can't figure out what just happened. Did someone ask that out loud? Where did it come from? Am I hearing voices? Hallucinating again? And who doesn't know that nearly *everyone* lies at some time in their lives in order to be happy?

In my case, I thought happiness was a lot of stupid shit. Drugs. Guys. Telling my parents off. More drugs. More telling my parents off. More guys. More drugs.

That shit isn't happiness. But I thought it was. And I kept lying to get it.

What I also got was: two divorces, a kid who won't talk to me, herpes, three stints in rehab and so much debt I went bankrupt.

What I have now is: nothing. So much nothing that at my age, I am flying to Philly to move back in with my mother. It's pathetic.

To her, I'm the biggest loser who ever lived. And Mom never held back telling me that, either. Asking me, "Why couldn't you be more like Robert?" Meaning my brother, who married his high school sweetheart and had three perfect kids. She can't seem to stop telling me about them.

Truth be told, I'm scared shitless to move back in with her. I'm hoping she can see the good in me.

Just thinking this makes me so sad I look out the window and hold back tears. And I realize that *I* can't even see the good in me. How can I expect Mom to see it? It's twenty-nine years since I lied and left and made all those mistakes, and I still feel as bad about it as I always did. I run through the twelve steps of recovery in my head. I remember asking everyone else in my life for forgiveness, but I realize I never asked myself.

I ask the man next to me to get up so I can go to the bathroom.

He does, still with that look on his face like I might have given him a disease from my ginger ale spitting. As I slowly walk down the aisle, I look at the people, and I wonder what they lied about in their lives. I want to ask for their help. *How do I forgive myself?* I have an imaginary conversation with them, and then they tell me: *Just do it.*

A minute later, as I wait in line for the bathroom and stare out at the beautiful Pennsylvania landscape, I get that feeling again—like I want to bust out laughing. I can't control it. It's worse than any drug giggles I ever got. I'm fifty years old and moving in with my mother, and I'm laughing my ass off. When I look to the other passengers, they don't think I'm some junkie. They smile. I can almost hear them asking, *What took you so long?*

11

IT IS *WAY* TOO EASY
TO GET INTO ATLANTIS.

LOOKING CONFIDENT and looking twenty-one are two entirely different things.

Right now, I'm pretty sure I look like a very nervous seventeen-year-old. And it's cold out here, and we left our coats in the car. It's a short line. Maybe three people in front of us. By *us*, I mean Kristina and Donna, Justin and Chad, and me. I am the fifth wheel.

"You have your money ready?" Kristina asks.

I nod, my five-dollar bill getting soggy in my palm.

"Don't look so worried!"

"I'm not worried," I say.

Kristina gives me the look. "You look scared shitless."

"I'm not. Seriously. I was just thinking about something. That's all."

Yeah. I was thinking about getting caught. At first I was scared the bouncer might say, "Sorry, kids, I need ID," but then I realized that would be fine. Then we could go home. Kristina could go back to meeting Donna at McDonald's or the parking lot out by Freedom Lake and double-dating with Justin and Chad on Fridays like always, and I could go back to keeping my secret love for Dee stowed away in the deepest regions of my baffled heart.

We move forward, and we all hand him our five bucks. Donna says, "Hey, Jim. How you doing?"

Jim says something I can't hear because the music is too loud and I'm concentrating on not passing out from fear. He smiles at me, and I know that he knows I'm seventeen. Then... we're inside. Just like that.

It's small. Maybe as big as the floor plan of my house. The bar itself is a big oval, packed two people deep. There's about four feet between those placing orders and the walls. Donna and Kristina lead us past the bar to the dance floor, which is tiny. There are mirrors on two sides, and they skew my ability to figure out square footage, but I figure it's twenty feet by fifteen feet, tops. It's packed with dancing people. Dancing gay people. People letting loose and not giving a shit what other people think about them, just as Kristina promised. People who aren't thinking about small-town bullshit or, say, the humanities homework they have yet to complete. People who I wish I was.

We follow Justin and Chad into the back room, where they find a darkened corner and immediately set to work gnawing the faces off each other. Donna says she has to pee, so Kristina and I are left standing in the back room of Atlantis, looking around at the arcade games and vintage pinball machines, trying to pretend that we're not seventeen. I pull my phone from the pocket of my jeans and check to see if anyone has called. No one. I check the time: 11:15. I am abruptly pissed off that all it took was a phone call from Jeff Garnet to convince my mother to let me break curfew. I'm pissed at how she said "Knock 'em dead" before I left the house. Let's not urge our teenager to go and get laid quite yet, Claire.

They say: *All normal teenagers are doing it. As long as they don't come home with a disease or a baby, what's the big deal?*

They say: *She hasn't met the right boy, is all.*

Donna comes out of the bathroom and looks ready to dance. She grabs Chad and Justin from the corner by the small coatroom and pulls them with her. The DJ puts on something techno and upbeat, and we head out to the dance floor like a tiny mob.

This is around the time when I remember that I don't really dance.

12

TURNS OUT ASTRID JONES IS A ROBOT.

I LOOK AROUND THE DANCE FLOOR and see other people who are good dancers, and then I see myself in the mirror, and I see I am a nervous dancer. A barely dancing dancer. A robot. I don't move anything below my waist. I look like I'm about to do a defensive drill during basketball gym class.

Upon noticing this, I become so self-conscious that I can't stay on the dance floor, so I gravitate toward the edge, where people are standing around drinking, talking and watching. I turn to watch the people on the dance floor. There is a lot of grinding and shaking and virtual humping. Kristina is there by herself while Donna goes to the bar for two beers, and she's really moving. Justin and Chad are nowhere to be seen. Probably back in the corner by the coatroom making out again. They get two nights a week to see each other, so they use them well. I get it.

"Why'd you stop?" someone says. I don't think she's talking to me until she tugs on my sleeve and says it again. "Why'd you stop?"

She's about a foot shorter than me, about fifty—maybe older. Yeah. Older than Mom, for sure.

"Better to leave the dance floor to people who can actually dance, you know?" I say this in the most nervous seventeen-year-old voice I ever heard. I think I'm shaking.

"I thought you were great," she says.

I say, "Really?" because I have no idea what else to say. There is no doubt this woman has hit on at least three million women in her life. And though she looks a bit leathery and is dressed like the biker from the Village People (leather vest, boot-cut jeans, leather biker cap and engineer boots), there's something attractive about her because she's *her*.

"Really. You looked great."

I nod and send her love. *Biker Lady, I love you for talking to me right now. Time is moving so much faster because you're talking, and I need that because I just discovered I am a robot.*

"You here with someone?"

I look to make sure Kristina and Donna are still far enough away not to overhear. "My girlfriend had to work," I say, nodding.

She smiles at me. It's not a creepy smile or a flirtatious smile. I can't describe it. It's like a supportive smile. Friendly and happy for me. Happy that I have a girlfriend. Behind her, edging in like he's about to order a drink, is Frank Socrates.

He's smiling, too, because it's my brain that put him here. I dressed him in a toga and made his hair extra frizzy because it's humid outside. He puts me at ease, which is better than how I felt up until now as a robot.

The music morphs into another song, and Biker Lady turns to me and says, "Come on! Show me what you got!" and grabs my wrist and drags me out to the floor. I look over my shoulder, and Frank's still there, smiling. I'm so glad I brought him. I need the moral support.

So I dance with Biker Lady. It's an old song, "Boogie Wonderland," and I start my robot not-dancing dancing again while she dances around me and blows a whistle periodically and claps. She's got biceps twice the size of Dad's.

Halfway through the song, I get a little glimpse of what it's like not to care that people might be looking at me. Not to care what they might say about me. I smile, and the biker lady smiles back and blows her whistle and then starts a victory lap around the bar.

All the people at the bar put out their hands for high fives, and some pat her on the ass or hug her and some duck down and kiss her. It occurs to me, as I stand on the edge of the dance floor out of breath, that people here are nice to each other.

It occurs to me that Atlantis *could be* the exact opposite of Unity Valley, just like Kristina said it was.

"New friend of yours?" Kristina asks.

I nod.

"You sure this isn't weird for you?" She points to two women kissing.

I shrug. "I've seen you and Donna do that before." I want to add that I don't see one straight person here, but I don't think it's relevant. Plus, I guess we both know Kristina was lying to get me to do what she wanted me to do. Which is what she does sometimes.

"Who said my name?" Donna says as she dances into our conversation.

"I think we should make this a Saturday night tradition," Kristina says.

I pull out my phone again and see it's one o'clock. I realize that I have to leave for work in four short hours.

Kristina points. "Here comes your friend."

Biker Lady comes up on my right side and puts her strong arm around me. "You coming back to see us next week?"

Kristina and I nod.

"You bringing your girlfriend next time?"

"I don't know," I say.

Kristina hears this and has that look on her face, so I wink at her to let her know that this was a lie I had to tell to cover my ass on my first night in a gay bar. It doesn't stop her from looking at me in a new way, though. As if maybe I do have a girlfriend.

"I hope to see you then," Biker Lady says. "And your lucky lady." Then she walks to the back of the bar and blends in with the regulars who all stand by the DJ booth.

We hold our laughter in until she is completely out of sight. Then we crack up. Kristina says, "Lucky lady! Oh, my God!"

Donna brings us two beers, and we crack up again when I say, "Speaking of lucky ladies!"

You know what this is? It's fun.

You know the last time I had fun? I can't remember.

13

ASTRID JONES JUST ISN'T READY YET, OKAY?

MY ALARM GOES OFF AT FIVE. As in five AM. Oh-five-hundred hours. Like, about an hour after I fell asleep. I can still hear the music pumping in my ears. I can still feel the crispy hair at the base of my neck from dancing until I sweated. I manage to brush my teeth, put a bandanna on over my insane hair and get dressed in my catering standard: checked pants and a white men's T-shirt. The idea of food—eating it or preparing it or touching it—is just so far from what I want to face right now. I feel like during the night, a family of raccoons built a nest in my head and then got diarrhea there. I think this is called a hangover, but I can't be sure.

Dee is waiting for me in her Buick, and she smiles when

she sees me round the corner of the parking lot. I park in the space next to her and put my forehead on my steering wheel to indicate that I am still technically asleep. I hear her car door slam shut, and then there is an aggressive knock on my window.

"Hey, sleepyhead. Come on."

I pretend to sleep more. I slouch. I slide to my right and lump myself on the passenger's seat. She opens the door and climbs in on top of me.

She kisses my neck and my cheek and my head, and I instantly get giggly, and then she turns my head and kisses me and time stands still and I don't care how late I am to punch my stupid time card.

When she moves to put her hand between my legs, I stop her.

"Whoa there. Just where do you think you are?"

"I know where I am," she says, moving to my fly. "I know where I'm going."

"Where are you?"

"I am in a big parking lot that only has two cars in it. Yours and mine. And no one can see or hear us." She kisses my ear. "So why waste it?"

I escape by rolling onto the floor and crab-walking my way toward the open driver's door. She pouts like this is a joke. It irks me that she thinks this is fine. It's not fine. It's pushy. Annoying. Not to mention borderline creepy that I had to escape my own car.

Seconds after I stand up outside the car and straighten my

shirt, Juan arrives at the deliveries door and says something to me. I have no idea what he says. I think he's speaking Spanish.

If I spoke Spanish, I think a little part of me would want to say, "Thank you for saving me, Juan. I owe you one."

▶ ▶ ▶

Today we make five pounds of shrimp, some clams on the half shell, four vegetable trays with broccoli, cauliflower, celery and carrots, and three trays of mushroom vol-au-vents. I pretend to have fun with Dee singing our shrimp-deveining song and stuff like that, but I don't go into the walk-ins. I don't even help her do dishes. Before we go our separate ways after work, we sit in my car. And before I say anything, she says, "You're going to tell me to back off again, aren't you?" She pouts.

"See? You're a maniac."

"I'm a fiend for you. I can't help it."

"You can't or you won't?"

"I don't know. I just—" She moves in closer. "I just want you so bad, Jones."

I grab her approaching hand. "If all you want is sex, then why don't you find a girl who just gives out? I want to get to know you better."

"What's there to know?" she asks.

"I don't know." I reach past her into the glove compartment for my Rolaids. "What's your favorite meal?"

"Seriously?"

"Seriously." I reach over and hold her hand. We slink down in the car seats, and I put my feet on the dash.

She shrugs. "I like roast beef and mashed potatoes with homemade gravy and…hmm…carrots? No. Peas. No. Carrots."

"You can have both, you know."

"Yeah, both."

She looks bored. It's as if she's never talked about her favorite foods and held hands before.

"What about your favorite thing to do?"

She looks at me with that pout again. "Not allowed to say," she says.

"I mean, before you did that—what was your favorite thing to do?"

"Hockey."

"Oh yeah. Of course."

"And running. I love running."

"And you love washing cauliflower, right?"

"As long as I'm with you, I love it."

I look at her and cock my head. "I think that's the sweetest thing you ever said to me."

"All true," she says. "So why were you so tired this morning? Up reading some crazy book? Writing poetry about how much you love my fine brawny ass?" she asks.

I chew my Rolaids and take an extra second to consider my options here. It's Dee. She no doubt knows about Atlantis. She may have even been there before. I think about Kristina and Justin and their secrets that I've sworn to keep. I think about how I have different secrets hidden from different people in different areas of my life. I think about how that might be the reason I'm chewing on Rolaids all the time.

She leans in to kiss me good-bye, and when she does, I wish I lived on the right planet where kissing Dee Roberts wasn't a big freaking deal. Where it didn't mean I have to affix a label to my forehead so people can take turns trying to figure out what *caused* it or what's *wrong* with me. And I wish I didn't have to lie so much. I don't think Frank Socrates would approve of all this lying.

I think Frank would want me to cause a lot more trouble.

14

I THINK THE RACCOONS NOW HAVE DYSENTERY.

THE CLOSER I GET TO HOME, the worse my hangover gets. My head aches, and my gut feels horrible. Especially when I walk into the house and have to face the smell of my mother's paella. Oh, God. It's her crazy ultimate paella with every shellfish known to man in it. Why can't I have a normal mom who wants to make American food? Burgers and fries. Something from the freezer section? Grilled cheese sandwiches and canned tomato soup?

I change out of my work clothes and take a shower. Then I check through my backpack for any homework I can get a jump on so I can avoid going into the land of ultimate paella. I have to write a paper about one of the stories we read in lit class, so I lie on my bed and wait for an idea to come to me, until I get dangerously close to sleep, and then I make myself get up.

"Will you give me a hand?" Mom says as I walk through the kitchen.

"Sure."

"Can you fill glasses?"

I grab the pitcher full of water and start filling glasses.

"Shit!" she says. I look over and see her wrestling with the huge stockpot, trying to tip the contents into a large serving bowl. I put down the pitcher and help her. Not without catching a whiff of the mussels and pimentos.

"Thanks," she says. I am amazed at how normal this whole exchange was. I'm impressed that she didn't critique my serving-bowl-holding abilities or something.

Twenty minutes later, I'm pretending to eat paella but really eating more bread dipped in olive oil than paella. So far, no one notices.

"We play Holy Guardian on Tuesday, and then we're at home on Friday against Frederickstown again. Over halfway through the season already," Ellis says.

"I'll make it to the Frederickstown game. Can't do Tuesday, though," Dad says.

Mom stays quiet.

"Awesome, Dad. You rock," Ellis says.

Does anyone else in the room hear the *not awesome, Mom—you don't rock* part? I do.

"Doesn't look like you guys will make it to the postseason, though," Dad says. "I know you really wanted to."

"It's cool. I have next year to try again, right?" Ellis smiles at him.

"What about you, Astrid? Anything happening this week?"

I dip more bread into the oil and pick up my fork as if I plan to eat paella. "It turned out that Zeno is right," I say. I still haven't told them about Zeno, so we'll see if they bite.

"Really?" Mom says.

"Yep."

"Which one is he again? The history or the American lit teacher?" Mom says. She pours herself another glass of wine.

"Isn't he a philosopher?" Dad says.

I point at him and shoot a finger gun. "Bingo."

"Oh," Mom says. And when I don't say anything else, she says, "Which one was he again?"

"The guy who said motion is impossible," I say. I take one pseudo-bite of the paella, and it's pretty good except for the pimentos. And the fish. I try to get forkfuls of rice only. Then I go back to just the bread.

"Like *moving* motion?" Ellis asks.

"Yep. Like all motion."

"He said it was impossible?"

"Him and a lot of guys before him. But he proved it in new ways. Mostly to disprove it, I think, but still, yep. That's what he meant."

Mom and Ellis look at me like I'm weird. Dad says, "How'd he prove it?"

I explain the arrow theory.

"That's stupid," Ellis says. "That's like saying that I'm not eating paella." She eats paella. "See?" she says with her mouth full of paella.

"I know."

"So didn't you say he was right?"

"He is," I say. "But not in the way he meant. In other ways."

"Are you getting graded for learning this stuff?" Mom asks. "Because I can't see how this will help you get a job." Ah, there's the Claire that was missing half an hour ago. *I missed you, Claire.*

"Come on, Claire. This is what college kids learn in Philosophy 101. You don't remember Zeno?" Dad asks.

"Nope."

"Didn't they teach philosophy in art school?"

She glares at him. "They taught it. I didn't take it. I had more practical things to learn so I could one day support my family."

I dip more bread in more oil.

"So when are you moving on to the Socrates part of the class?" Dad says. "I was talking to a mom at one of the hockey games, and she told me that it's awesome. Her son took the class a few years ago."

"We started last week," I say. "But this week we'll really get into that part—the project."

"Stuff like that makes me wish I could go back to high school."

I'm about to say something lame like "yeah," but Mom talks over me. "You *can* go back to college any time you want, Gerry."

He stops and looks at her. She said it to cut him down, but he took it as a real suggestion. His eyes dart around. "You know, Claire, you're right. I could," he says. "What do you think of that, girls? Imagine going to college with your dad. Freaky, huh?"

"I don't think so," Ellis says. "I'd have a built-in on-campus fan for hockey games."

"And I'd have someone to go to wood shop with who won't make a bong," I say. Although I know there is a great chance that Dad would probably make a bong.

Mom puts her fork down loudly. "No one wants to go to college with me? I was fun in college, you know."

She throws a sad look at Ellis, who says, "Aw, I'd go to college with you, Mom. I bet you threw some great parties."

15

THE 135.

IT IS ONLY 135 HOURS until we are all standing at the door of Atlantis again with our cover charge in our palms. Only 117 hours until I see Dee again in the parking lot of Maldonado's. The school week is like a holding pattern. It is the invisible man. It is a black hole. It is the Enso of Zen—the big zero. All I can hear are the ticking of seconds, each one a notch in the 135. For the record, that's 486,000 notches.

On Tuesday in humanities we learn about Socratic paradoxes. Here's one of Frank's: *No one desires evil.* Of course, that's an insane thing to say. One look around Unity Valley will prove the guy dead wrong. One look at *anywhere* will prove the guy certifiable. Especially in fifth century BC Greece.

Geez. So for him to say *No one desires evil* is about more than just challenging the obvious fact that plenty of people desire evil.

When I raise my hand and Ms. Steck calls on me, I say, "It was about making people think. Because the only way to disprove something that defies common sense is to ask why. Why would people desire evil? Why are people evil? Don't they think they are doing good from their perspective? What is evil, then, anyway? That's exactly the type of thing Socrates was after. Making people think so they could find the truth."

"And do you have any answers?" she asks.

"No. Only more questions," I say. I have come so far from my Zeno-denying arm-flailing only two weeks ago.

They say: *Astrid Jones is such a kiss-ass.*

They say: *Ms. Steck will give her an A just because of lit mag.*

They say: *You know about Ms. Steck, right?*

Anyway, our final assignment for the unit is to create our own paradox and be ready to argue it Socrates-style. This is the Socrates Project. Every year we've been in high school, the day before Thanksgiving break, senior humanities students dress like Greek philosophers and argue throughout the halls all day. It's the reason people fight to get into this course, and the reason some people wouldn't touch it with a barge pole. I fluctuate between being shit-scared and totally geeked out with excitement. I'm even going to go barefoot. I haven't figured out my paradox yet, but I have a month, so I'm not going to push it.

▶ ▶ ▶

All week, Kristina is weird.

Monday: *Are you sure there wasn't any truth to that thing you said about a girlfriend? You know you could tell me, right?*

Tuesday: She squints at me a lot and whispers something to Justin right in front of me. Justin shrugs, then pulls up his camera and snaps a picture of me. When I complain, they claim it's just a funny joke.

Wednesday: *I thought we were best friends, dude. You're not keeping secrets from me, are you? Justin and I can help, you know.* Justin nods.

Thursday: Silent treatment. Or at least that's what it seems like. Plus, she's overly friendly with her plethora of more popular friends. The Homecoming Court people, the majorettes, the two lead actresses in our fall production of *The Miracle Worker*. I even see her talking to Aimee Hall—enemy of many, thanks to her knack for making shit up and spreading it like mulch so the weeds of sanity can't poke through and doubt her.

Friday: Kristina's all perky and nice at lunch. "Maybe you'll tell me the truth tomorrow night?"

"You know the truth," I say.

"That's not what I heard," she says.

I try not to look panicked. I call Frank S. to rescue me. Bad idea. He slides into the booth behind Kristina and looks right into my eyes. He knows the truth, too.

16

AM I WEARING A
"BE PUSHY WITH ME" SIGN?

THE HISPANIC CENTER CATERING JOB is hard core. We work from five thirty to three thirty. That's a long day here in the land of shrimp veins. Dee and I meet in the walk-in only once. We don't even have time to talk except catering-teamwork talk, so while we wash and sanitize big pots and pans, she occasionally hip-bumps me and I hip-bump her back.

▶ ▶ ▶

My quid pro quo double date with Jeff, Kristina, and Justin is at the Legion Diner on 773. It's a popular place to get anything with fake mashed potatoes and gravy. I'm in love with their grilled cheese sandwiches. I don't know what they do, but they make them taste better than any grilled cheese sandwich I've ever eaten in my life. I think they dip them in grease first or something.

I decide to walk because it's five minutes from my house. Justin and Kristina drive there together and are ten minutes late, as always, and to avoid being stuck with Jeff by myself, I wait in the alleyway behind the diner until I see them park. When we get inside and sit down, Justin squeezes Kristina's ass all the time and they kiss and hold hands, and you would never ever know that they are not two teenagers in love. I think they could both embark on serious acting careers just based on this behavior. At the same time, I wish they'd stop. They're giving Jeff ideas, and I don't like it.

He tries to nuzzle my ear before our food comes and it gives me a chill and I jump. Then he puts his right hand under the table and on my thigh a little too casually, and I kick Kristina under the table.

Our food comes and my grilled cheese is greasy and cheesy and crispy on the outside and I eat it in about three minutes and excuse myself to go to the ladies' room. I hear the bathroom door open while I'm peeing, and Kristina comes in, sits on the toilet in the stall next to mine and once she releases her pee, she says, "Oh, my God, Astrid. He is totally in love with you."

"I know. He keeps squeezing my leg under the table."

"No, I mean he's actually in love with you. He said it. Just now," she says.

I feel my cheeks warm.

"He said it?"

"Yep."

I flush and zip, and while I'm washing my hands, Kristina joins me and gives me a sympathetic look.

"How can he be in love with me when he doesn't even know me?"

She shakes her head. "I don't know."

"Do we really need to string him along like this?" I ask. "I mean, I don't mind being the bad guy and telling him to go away."

She's touching up her eyeliner. "Claire will want to know why."

I sigh and think about it.

"Anyway," Kristina adds, "if you keep being cold, he'll get the picture. He wants in your pants in a big way. Maybe you can tell him that you're gonna wait until you're married. That'll probably scare him off."

"Oh, God. Imagine if Claire heard that," I say. I look at myself in the mirror and adjust my hair to its perfect position across my forehead.

"Are you sure you don't have anything to tell me? Because I hear things, you know?"

"What would I have to tell you?" I ask. "And who's telling you things about me?" But I know I'm really bad at lying, which is why I've never really lied before.

She shrugs and gives me a half-disappointed look and pushes the bathroom door open.

I look into my eyes again in the mirror. I can see her there—the me who's waiting to come out. The me who doesn't have to send her love away. The me who loves Dee Roberts and isn't afraid to say so. I stuff her back inside my Unity Valley suit and go back to the table.

As I walk between the tables, I notice a toga at the counter, sitting on a stool. I should have never named him Frank. He was fine for 2,400 years as just Socrates without me conjuring him up to help me out of dumb messes like fake double dates with Jeff the leg jiggler.

When I get back to the table, Justin has a look on his face that's a mix of pain and laughter or maybe fear. Kristina leans over him and jiggles her boobs in front of his face and then plants a huge kiss on his lips. Then she whispers something to him, and he looks at me in that way—like he's disappointed, too.

I sheepishly slide in next to Jeff, who immediately puts his hand on my knee.

"I was asking my man Justin where you guys are going tonight," Jeff says, mouth half full of roast beef and mashed potatoes.

"And I told him we go different places," Justin says. He kicks Kristina so hard, the table wobbles.

Kristina says, "Private party for a friend of mine who goes to Mount Pitts."

"And I can't come?"

Justin lets out a disappointed chuckle. "Not just you, bro. No guys allowed, apparently. I'm out, too."

"All you hot girls in one place?" Jeff says. "I wish I could crash *that* party."

Kristina and I look at each other. I have no idea what to say.

"You're just going to have to be a gentleman and wait your turn, dude. Plus, it's a sober party...and in an hour, I'm hooking you up, right? So, that's, like, two strikes against you."

"Yeah," Jeff says. "I guess." I can sense his skepticism. It's a seed. But it's there. I want to distract him before he waters it or lets in any sunlight, so I kiss him on the cheek.

Outside, a half hour later, he has me pinned up against his car and is trying to get his tongue in my mouth, and I choose to nuzzle into his neck instead. I accidentally find the spot where he must have slopped on his nasty cologne, and my eyes water instantly. I have to keep myself from gagging.

Kristina yells for me to hurry and I kiss him on the ear, say good-bye and squeeze out from under him right before he squishes me that tiny bit too hard. Which is creepy and makes me promise myself never to fake-date him again.

17

WE HEAR THINGS.

"DO YOU HAVE ANYTHING you want to tell us?" Kristina asks from the front seat as we drive to Atlantis the long way because we have some time to kill.

"No."

"We hear things," Justin says.

"Will you guys stop saying that? If we all believed what we hear, then you two would be screwing each other in the backseat right now. And there'd be barking. But that's not true, is it?"

"You seem so distracted lately," Kristina says. "We just want to help."

I sigh. I'm sick of lying, so I pick something true to say. "I hate that I'm lying to Jeff like this. It feels wrong. I think Claire would be fine with you guys covering for me. You could tell her that you're trying to find me a soul mate at the movies or something. It would totally work."

"We could do that," Justin says. "But that's not what we're asking."

"Yeah. I'd be happy to do that. I mean, that's what friends do, right? And we're best friends," Kristina says.

"Which is why you should tell her," Justin says.

"Because something is up, and we know it," Kristina says.

Oh, God. I feel like this is the worst time ever to tell her anything. She's been mad all week about it, and she doesn't even know what *it* is yet.

She turns around in the passenger seat, and she looks at me. I look at her. She isn't smiling. "Dude. What the hell? You know everything about me! You're my best friend," she says. "Aren't you?"

I'm speechless, which makes me look more like something is up.

"Seriously. What the hell is up?"

"I—I can't tell you."

She gets concerned. "Are you okay? Did something bad happen?"

"God no. I'm just—oh, God. I don't know. I'm—kinda seeing someone. So this whole Jeff thing isn't going to work out."

She tilts her head. The look on her face is a mix of girlish excitement and some sort of pain. "Who is it? That guy from your humanities class? What's his name? Kyle? Ken?"

"Holy shit, no. Clay? Blerg. No. Not a guy. I mean—"

"Not a guy?" she says. "Not a guy." She stops and looks more pained than excited. "Not a guy?"

"I don't know," I say. It's only hitting me now how hurt she's going to be about my keeping this a secret.

"Dude—you don't know who you're going out with?" She hits me nicely on my arm. "Oh, my God, Astrid! Just tell us!"

"I don't know. I'm still not even sure, I don't think. I mean, how do I know?"

"It's not a guy?"

I shake my head.

Justin hoots. "Dude! You're one of us!"

I keep shaking my head, and I add a shrug, but I'd be lying if I told you that his excitement and invitation into *one of them* isn't making me cringe. Because I'm not in this to be a member of some club. I'm not going through this so I can lock myself in the *one of them* box.

"So, you're questioning?" she says.

"I guess."

"If she has a girlfriend, she's not questioning," Justin says.

"Shut up," Kristina says. Then she turns back to me. "That's completely normal. Especially with me and Justin around. Seriously. Totally normal."

That's not what they'd say.

They'd say: *I think she likes girls.*

They'd say: *I bet one night with me would make her change her mind.*

"So who is it?" I am so not ready to tell her this and I am

so afraid she will be pissed if I don't. But I can't. She sees my pain and says, "No rush. These things take time."

▶ ▶ ▶

Kristina is three beers into her night, and she says, "I can't believe you didn't tell me, dude."

I feel guilty and make a face to show it.

"Were you scared?" Justin asks.

Chad says, "I remember being scared." This makes me smile at him.

I pretend I want to dance to escape the conversation, but Kristina comes with me. Donna joins her and the two of them get all touchy-feely with each other and it makes me uncomfortable, so I dance my way over to the corner and then stand off to the edge and try not to watch them.

When Kristina sees I've escaped, she dances toward me, Donna right behind her.

"Why don't you call your girlfriend?" Kristina yells. The music is really loud.

"Nah," I say.

"Why not?"

"Just because," I say. God. Life was a lot simpler a few hours ago when she thought I was just an asexual sea sponge.

"It's me, isn't it?" Kristina says in her nervous three-beers-in babbling. For all her pushy, ponytailed U. Valley girl confidence, she sure does have weak spots. "Why you won't call her?" she says, pointing to her chest.

"You're drunk."

"No. Think about it, Astrid."

She's right. It's her. How can I be myself around Dee and Kristina in the same room? I'm not ready for that yet. I only just told Kristina tonight.

I say, "What happened to 'these things take time'?"

She stops at that and nods. "Yeah, but you should tell me who it is."

"I'll tell you later. It's not the right time or place."

"Is she from school? Do I know her?"

I give her an annoyed look.

"Come on. Just a hint," she says. I look at her again and roll my eyes. "Okay, I'll just guess then. Is it Briana? Lisa? That chick who homeschools but plays in the band—what's her name? Kelly something?"

I cock my head and look even more annoyed than I looked a minute ago.

"It's a hockey player, isn't it? That's why you went to a few of Ellis's hockey games this year," she says. I stay poker-faced. "Is it Kira? Kelly? Michelle?" Multiple choice. Hmm. Maybe it's not the worst way for this to come out. Not something Frank S. would be proud of me for, but it could work. "Am I getting warmer? Colder?" she asks.

"No," is all I say. "All you're getting is annoying."

"Colder. I can read your mind. If it's not one of our hockey players, then maybe..."

My face twitches. Darn it.

"Another school. Yes. How about—Dee Roberts?"

Shit. I try to give her a shut-the-hell-up look.

"Oh, my God! It's Dee Roberts, isn't it?"

I say nothing and try to keep looking annoyed.

"It *is*! Hah! No way!"

"Stop. Let me just tell you when I'm ready."

"You don't need to tell me. I already know. I totally should have figured that out. You've been working together for months. I'm slipping."

I sigh.

"Oh, come on. It's not a big deal that I know. Dee's been out for years anyway. It's not like you just outed her or anything."

"I didn't tell you it was Dee Roberts."

"Yes, but you didn't *not* tell me it was her, either," she says. "You should call her and tell her to get her ass out here," she says.

"Why? So you can gloat about how you guessed?"

"I don't gloat."

"Anyway, you'd have never known if I didn't tell you in the first place. You'd think I was still an androgynous bookworm."

"Hold on. You're not an androgynous bookworm?" she asks, and pulls out her phone. "Shit. I need to update my files."

▶ ▶ ▶

The drive to the Superfine parking lot is fun. We blast a few songs they play at Atlantis, and we sing along out of tune. I watch the scenery go by—the occasional farmhouse and the cornfields. Then the Legion diner, where I remember Jeff pressing me into his car too forcefully.

When Donna and Chad exit the car, Justin says, "I'm so happy for you, Astrid. I wish I would have known before so I could have helped you."

"Me too," Kristina says. Not completely convincingly. Almost like she might be a little mad or something.

"I guess I had to find my own time. I dunno. I'm still not really sure, you know?"

"That'll change," Kristina says. Which is warmer than the last thing she said.

I don't say anything else the whole way up Main Street, and when Justin stops in front of my house to let me out, I say good-bye and close the car door quietly. I walk in the front door, lock up, turn off the lights and then walk out the back door and lie on my table. I don't have any thoughts, because I'm not sure what thoughts to have. I know I just changed things, but I'm not sure if the change is for better or worse. So, I just send my love up. Away from here because love shouldn't hang around confusion like this. It deserves a full commitment.

Then I wish it were as easy to send myself away from here as it is to send my love. I think I deserve a full commitment, too. From my family. From my friends. From my girlfriend. From myself. And for some reason, I think starting over somewhere else would be the best way to do it.

So I send my love, and I ask the passengers: *Where are you going? Can I come with you? Maybe where you're going, I could finally feel at home.*

PASSENGER #338790
BILL DERRINGER, SEAT 12F
FLIGHT #795
LOS ANGELES TO PHILADELPHIA
BUSINESS CLASS UPGRADE

Going home again isn't something I thought I'd ever do. Not for their weddings or their babies or their graduations. Not even for their funerals. The idea was: *Get out and never go back.*

But the idea changed when I heard Nuna got cancer.

Cancer. My little sister. I hadn't even met her husband yet, and they're married seventeen years. Three kids. A little house by the river, right down the road from where we grew up. Right down the road from all those assholes who gossiped me out of town.

I Googled them. Most of them still live there. Until cancer, I cared about this.

Until cancer, you care about a lot of bullshit that doesn't really matter.

When I left, I called *them* cancer. I said their gossip was *like* cancer. I realized too late that gossip can't kill you unless you let it. But cancer? Cancer doesn't give a shit how much you want to live. If it wants to kill you, it will.

Cancer killed my father. I didn't come back for his funeral because I'd made my mind up to never go home again...and because he never understood my need to move away, and took it as a personal affront. Then I missed my mother's funeral because I was on business in Japan, and I didn't think she would want me there after the letter she sent after Dad's funeral. She said I'd broken her heart. She said my alienating the family would one day seem foolish to me, as it did to her. She said: *One day it will hit you.*

Last week. Last week it hit me. Cancer. Nuna. My final good-bye.

Now she's gone. And I've packed my black suit, and Anne will meet me for the funeral in two days so I have someone to hold my hand.

I stare from seat 12F into the dark sky, and I see the moon. It's not quite full, but it's big. And then Nuna appears outside my window. She's healthy. She has her hair. She has that smile. We stare at each other for a long time. She sends me this feeling—like she's telling me she loves me. Like she's telling me it's okay that I left. Then she takes off and flies around the moon, and I get that feeling like I've just gone over one of those hills in a car, at just the right speed.

I laugh at her and feel like I did when we were kids and she'd show off doing handsprings in the backyard. I keep my eye on her and she keeps flying around the moon and I keep laughing.

This is how I want to remember her. Nuna flying around the moon, smiling.

18

THE BIG BANG.

I CAN'T KEEP THIS SECRET from Dee, too. That's the thing that hits me as I drive to work.

So when Dee asks me a few times, "Why are you so tired on Sundays?" I tell her that I'll tell her later, which isn't lying, so that's good.

When we walk into the parking lot after work, I say, "What are you doing for the next hour?"

She shrugs and shakes her head.

I tell her to drive to Freedom Lake and that I'll meet her there in ten minutes.

I call Kristina on my way to the lake to make sure this will be okay with her. "First, I'm sorry again about not telling you sooner. Second, I want to tell Dee everything so she can come with us next weekend. Is that okay with you guys?"

She pauses. I know she's having the same conversation with herself that I've had with myself about how *even one person* might tell, and that would be just enough to ruin everything.

"It's fine," she says finally, but I hear something in her voice that sounds like it might not actually be fine.

"And asking her to come with us to Atlantis next Saturday. That's cool, right?"

"Oh, shit. Yeah. Next Saturday. Look—before we go out, I promised Jeff another date."

"Ughhhh. I told you I wouldn't do this anymore."

"I know. But Justin and I will be there, and Jeff will cover for you again, and that's good, right?"

"You promised."

"I know, but the kid is lovesick, dude. Just once more? It's the perfect cover. And Claire is buying it and everything."

"Ughhhh. Okay. Good-bye!"

"Make Dee come with us next week!" she says before I hang up.

It's official.

I am about to make two worlds collide.

▶ ▶ ▶

Dee is on the phone when I park and walk up to her driver's side window with the picnic blanket draped over my arm. She gives me the wait finger, and I lean up against the back of the car until she's done. She looks angry when she hangs up.

"Whoa. Who was that?" I ask.

"Jessie," she says. Ellis's teammate and running partner, and Dee's old friend from hockey camp.

"What'd she say that made you look like that?"

"I'll give you a hint," she says. "Starts with a *J* and ends with *eff*?" I realize that Jessie heard that Jeff and I double-dated last night. "Now I understand why you're so tired on Sunday mornings. Shit!"

"Ughhhhh. This Jeff guy. Jesus!" I say.

She perks up a little at seeing my genuine annoyance at the mere mention of his name.

"Look. I have a shitload of stuff to tell you," I say. "When we're done, you'll understand all of it. Even this stupid *date*." I bring my fingers up to air-quote the word *date*, and the blanket slides down into the crack of my elbow. I start up the trail to the clearing, and she follows me. We're both still in kitchen garb. I'm pretty sure I smell like shrimp veins.

When we reach our favorite picnic area, I spread the blanket out and lie on my back. "I'm not sure where to start. I mean, first, you have to promise everything stays between us."

"Duh."

"No. I mean it. This has to stay between us," I say. "Even if we break up or hate each other one day or whatever," I say.

"Break up? Are we in a relationship?"

I put my middle finger up so she can see it. "Promise."

"I promise," she says.

"Okay. First I want you to go out with me next Saturday night."

"Uh, with or without Jeff Garnet?"

"Without. We'd be going after that *date*." I use air quotes again.

"That's called two-timing where I come from," she says. But she's smiling, so I know she isn't mad anymore. "Hold up. Did you say *after*? Like—how late?"

"From about eleven to two thirty?"

"That's late." She stops and realizes and love-smacks me on the arm. "Hey! Is that why you're so tired today?"

"I would call this exhausted," I say. "Thanks to Atlantis."

She turns her head to look at me and makes me turn my head, too. "Are you kidding me? You went to Atlantis?" Then she looks concerned. "By yourself?"

"With friends."

"Now you have gay friends?"

"Actually, a long time before I met you," I say.

"You're full of surprises," she says. "Do I know them?"

"I'm pretty sure."

"And?"

"And here's the thing you have to never tell anyone. You still promise?"

"Uh-huh."

"Between us?"

"Oh, my God, just tell me."

I take a deep breath. "Kristina and Justin."

She totally doesn't get it. Blank stare.

I say, "Kristina *and Donna* and Justin *and Chad*."

"Who the hell is Chad?"

"Chad is Justin Lampley's boyfriend."

She sits up and stares at me. "You mean Kristina Houck? Your friend?"

"Yep."

"Wow," she says. I watch a plane fly west above me—just a small sparkle in the sky. I send my love to it just for a second because I feel guilty leaving all those people up there all alone.

"But I hear all these rumors about those two!" she goes on. "How she's into all sorts of weird stuff. Last week I heard she likes to bark when she does it."

I raise my hand. "Guilty. She made me spread that one. All I had to do was tell Shelly Anne, and my work was done. Shelly Anne has a three-district-wide spread."

She says, "Jessie always says she's like the hometown girl over there." She takes another minute to grasp it. "People would freak out if they knew this, wouldn't they?"

"True. So? Saturday? Will you come?"

"Isn't your curfew midnight or something?"

"That's where Jeff comes in." I roll my eyes. "Apparently, my mother takes the word of a boy she's never met when it comes to important things like extending my curfew. Jeff says we're going to a midnight movie, and Mom says, *Fine, be home by two thirty*, and there's your answer to the Jeff question."

"Yeah, but Jessie told me that he's really into you."

"He *is* really into me." I make the gag face. "But Kristina promised him liquor, and so when we go out, he covers for me. Sadly, this means I have to endure another *date* with him next weekend. But it's a double date with Kristina and Justin, and it's the last time, so it'll be totally okay. Then I get to go to Atlantis with you, right?" I take her hand in mine and watch another airplane enter my field of vision from the east. "So, I could cover for you if you want. I mean, we can say we're all going to the movies together or something."

It's a big jet—probably a 747. I want to ask the passengers if they can see us lying here holding hands. I want to ask them if we look happy.

"My mom is pretty cool about stuff like that," she says. "So, what you said earlier. About breaking up. You never answered me."

"What?"

"Are we in a relationship?"

I ask the passengers: *Are we in a relationship?*

"Yes. I think we are," I say. "But it's a secret."

"I know," she says.

"I'm sorry."

"Don't be," she says.

I ask the passengers: *Why am I still sorry?*

"It doesn't seem very fair to you. I mean, I wish there were other places we could meet and hang out," I say.

She rolls herself to the space above me. "How about here? And now?"

When Dee kisses me, the taste of her is enough to make me die right here on the spot. I don't care if some mountain biker zooms through on the path. I don't care about anything. Not Zeno or Socrates. Not motion or truth. When Dee kisses me, I am alive. I am moving. I am the truth.

19

THIS IS NOT POLITE DINNER CONVERSATION.

AT DINNER MONDAY NIGHT, Ellis is a complete douche.

"So it turns out the whole front line is like a dyke picnic," she says. "I thought it was just Kelly and Kira, but now I hear it's Michelle and Gabby, too."

Mom says, "Ellis, that's ridiculous."

"I know, right? Jesus! It's, like, spreading."

Mom says. "You've been hanging around these small brains for too long."

"Yeah," I say.

Dad just eats. I can't believe no one else can smell the pot wafting from his core. At this point, I think we could scrape off his epidermis and smoke it for a buzz.

Ellis laughs. "How about lesbian luncheon? Is that better?"

"No," Mom says.

"Uh, gay garden part—"

"Stop it," Mom says. "Don't be so small-minded."

"Yeah," I say.

Mom reaches over and rubs Ellis's forearm. "I think you need a Mommy and Me night."

Oh. Of course she does. Because nothing spells parental discipline for homophobic slurs like dressing up fancy and underage drinking at some faraway country club where larger minds are present.

"I'm running with Jess this week," Ellis says.

"Come on. One night away from running won't kill you."

"I'll go," I say, seemingly out of control of my own mouth. Why did I just say that?

"I think I can do Thursday," Ellis says.

"Great," Mom answers. "We'll go Thursday." She doesn't look at me when she says this. Her hand is still on Ellis's arm. This was like a private conversation they had. My offer to go along stayed in another dimension.

Dinner conversation drifts, and Dad mentions his stapler and how he now uses Diane's (the alleged thief) every time he needs to staple something. No one responds to him, either, as if he's in the same dimension I am.

"I made dessert!" Mom says as I'm clearing the table. "I had too many eggs, so I tossed together a bread pudding."

"Oh," we all say, because the Joneses don't eat dessert

unless it's a holiday. We all sit back down, and she serves us each a bowl of warmed bread pudding with ice cream.

When she sits down, she turns to me. "How'd your date go on Saturday night? Kristina said it was a lot of fun."

"It was."

"*Fun* fun, or just fun?"

I think back to Saturday. I look forward to this Saturday. "Just fun, but with the possibility of becoming more fun," I say.

"You should go out more often. You know, you can see Jeff on Friday nights, too, if this is getting hot and heavy," she says.

Bleh.

"I want to know if it gets hot and heavy before it gets hot and heavy," Dad says. "It's my right as a father. Plus, I'll have to sit him down and give him the talk."

"It's not getting hot and heavy," I say. "And who says that anymore?"

Ellis says, "Hot and heavy. Hot and heavy. Hot and heavy."

"Shut up," I say. She sticks her ice cream–covered tongue out at me.

"You have the rest of your life for that stuff anyway," Dad says.

"Gerry, you know nothing about teenagers," Mom says. She turns back to me. "Unlike your father, I know everyone is doing it. You don't have to talk about it, but just promise me you'll be safe." Oh, my God. I need an invisibility pill right now. I need the ring from Frodo Baggins. Precious! Where is the ring?

"Can't we go back to talking about the lesbian luncheon or whatever?" I say while I get up and leave my half-eaten dessert in the sink. I am suddenly paralyzed by the truth. *I have no control over my life.* Now that I've made worlds collide, I'm in less control than I ever was before.

▶ ▶ ▶

Thursday night when I get home, Ellis and Mom are already getting dolled up for their Mommy and Me night, and Ellis is in the red dress that is too low cut for a sixteen-year-old.

"I love it!" Mom says.

I close my bedroom door and read more Plato. Today's humanities class was the day I was waiting for. Penny Uppergrove, the über-valedictorian who has a photographic memory, finally freaked out. She drives Ms. Steck crazy. *But what's the* answer? *How can any of us pass a test if you don't give us answers?*

Today she shouted, "I give up! How am I supposed to study anything if there are no answers?" Then she burst into loud, obnoxious tears. It ended with two of the Zeno-lovers talking her down in the back of the room along with Ms. Steck promising that the class wouldn't hurt her GPA.

I hear Mom and Ellis clip-clop their way down the steps after sufficient makeup application and jewelry adornment.

"I say we make Thursday the new Friday," I hear Mom say to her on the way out the door. "Who needs school?"

And for sure, Ellis doesn't go to school on Friday. Neither

does Penny Uppergrove. But her father comes to see the principal, which is the talk of sixth-period lunch.

They say: *That Ms. Steck is letting the kids run her class.*

They say: *What kind of class doesn't have tests? Is this where our tax money goes?*

We start our unit on the Allegory of the Cave. It's a part in Plato's *Republic* where he wrote a dialogue between his brother Glaucon and his teacher, Socrates. The short version: People chained in a cave are only able to see a wall. The wall has shadows cast from a fire they can't see. They guess at what the shadows are. Their entire reality becomes these shadows.

Clay has read it before. Of course. Knows *all about* the Allegory of the Cave. "The only life these prisoners know is the sounds and shadows of the cave. Imagine living like that!" he says. "Or maybe we are living like that, right?"

Ms. Steck stops him before he can spoil the rest. Apparently there is more excitement to come for the prisoners in the cave. For now, all we have to worry about is a three-hundred-word essay from the point of view of one of these prisoners exploring the realm of belief versus the realm of knowledge.

Which, if you think about it, is a really funny subject to explore around Unity Valley.

20

CONFESSIONS OF A DANCING QUEEN.

COMPARED TO LAST SATURDAY, work is a breeze. I am sent into the freezer to do inventory for the second big job next week. I see Dee a few times—out in the kitchen from a distance. She smiles at me and I get that feeling again, like the first time she smiled at me at the hockey game.

Before we leave the parking lot, she says, "I'm really stoked for tonight."

"Me too." I reach for her, but she pulls away a little—like she's trying to make me want her more by keeping her distance all morning.

She fiddles with the zipper on her sweatshirt, then looks up and has a weird expression on her face. "What's it like, Jones? I mean—what should I wear?"

She's clearly nervous. I smile and say, "Whatever you wear will be perfect. You're beautiful. You'd look good in anything."

"You really think I'm beautiful?"

"Would you rather I said you're hot? Sexy? Hot *and* sexy?"

"Beautiful works."

"Good. Wear whatever you dance in. You do dance, right?"

"I dance."

"Good. Then tonight will be our first dance. I can't wait," I say. Only when I hear it come out of my mouth do I remember that I am a robot.

"Have fun on your date," she says, which reminds me I have to see Jeff and lie to him for a few hours before I go to Atlantis. "I want a full report."

"See you in the parking lot at eleven?"

She nods. No kiss good-bye. We just keep staring at each other and grinning.

▶ ▶ ▶

The Legion Diner is particularly busy tonight, so we go early for once. Justin, Kristina and I wait for Jeff to show up, and we talk.

"I really can't string him along like this anymore. Everyone knows he's really into me, and I don't want to hurt his feelings. I mean, he's an okay guy. I hate lying to him."

"You didn't hate lying to us," Kristina says.

God. I wish she could just pick a side and stay there for a minute.

"Meow," Justin says. He winks at me.

Then Jeff walks in, so we can't have the rest of the discussion.

Here are the stats from dinner:

- ❧ LEG SQUEEZES: *21*
- ❧ COMPLIMENTS ON HOW I LOOK, WHISPERED TOO CLOSE TO MY EAR: *6*
- ❧ USES OF THE TERM *BRO* WHEN CONVERSING WITH JUSTIN: *13*
- ❧ ASS PINCHES (WHEN I GOT UP TO GO TO THE LADIES' ROOM): *2*
- ❧ FRANK SOCRATES SIGHTINGS: *0*
- ❧ MINUTES I FELT GUILTY FOR LYING: *approximately all 110 of them*

▶ ▶ ▶

Dee is waiting in the bar parking lot when we arrive in Justin's car at 10:56. We are eager. I see the lights of a passing plane above me. *You'd be eager, too*, I tell it.

I hop into Dee's car and jump on her like a lonely dog after a day at home alone. This is probably the most forward I've ever been with her, and while I'm doing it, I try to figure out why. I think it has something to do with Jeff Garnet.

She slips her hands into the waistband of my jeans, onto my hips. I kiss her as if we are not in a parking lot surrounded by a bunch of other people. Someone raps on the window.

"Break it up, lovebirds. Let's go!"

Though Dee knows Kristina and Justin vaguely, I introduce them as if they have never met before. And oddly, they interact as if this is the case. I sense a respect toward Dee. She's out. We aren't.

Getting through the door only causes me minor heart palpitations this time. Jim the bouncer seems to recognize us from last week, and he takes our five-dollar bills and stacks them atop the other five-dollar bills in his little cashbox.

Dee stays close, and I hold her hand as I lead her from the back of the bar to the border of the dance floor.

"Is it always this loud?" Dee screams into my ear.

I hold up two fingers and say, "I've only been here twice, but yeah. I think so."

She nods.

We're both dancing in place—just a little. Dee's arms are wrapped around me from behind like a blanket, and I feel myself relax. After a half hour of watching other people dance, Donna asks me if I want something to drink, and before I can ask for a bottle of water, Dee orders us two hard lemonades and hands Donna ten bucks.

Donna brings the bottles, and Dee takes them both and hands one to me and holds hers up to toast. The music is a particularly loud techno song, and she has to nearly scream, "To us!"

I clink. I drink. It's not half bad. Tastes like lemonade.

A half hour later I am feeling really loose. And happy. Loose and happy. I know this has something to do with the hard lemonade. As I look around the bar, I see people smiling at me. One of them is Biker Lady with her whistle. She waves, and Dee asks me if I know her.

"Kinda." I wave back and blow a kiss, which makes her point at me and blow her whistle.

▶ ▶ ▶

I'm dancing like I am not a not-dancing robot. I don't know what's happened. Suddenly, I can dance as if I've done it a million times before. Like I am a dancing *queen*. Dee is right here, rubbing up against me. We are two parts of the same animal. People are hooting. We're on fire. Every time Dee gets her face near mine, we kiss. Right there on the dance floor. After the song is over, we stand to the side and I gulp water and she gulps more lemonade and she has her hand in the back pocket of my jeans. It's as if someone has taken the real Astrid Jones and replaced her with one who is okay with intimacy in public places. *It's like I'm the anti-Astrid.*

"You two are hot," someone says. When my ears hear it, it's fuzzy.

Biker Lady is doing her bar circles with her whistle, and she stops once to grind with the two of us. It's not as naughty as it seems. It's not real grinding. We're just being funny.

And I am pretty sure I'm gay.

I mean, not just by default because I am in love with Dee, but I feel like these people are *my people* or something.

By the time the bartender calls for last call and the lights flicker, I'm too tired to dance anymore. I'm still soaked, but I'm no longer tipsy. The same can't be said for Dee.

"I'm going to drive you home in your car," I say. "Then I can meet up with everybody at the Superfine parking lot."

"I'm fine," she slurs.

I take her keys—proof that her reaction time is lame. "I'm finer."

In the bar parking lot, Kristina and Donna fall into Donna's car for a few minutes, and Justin and Chad are in Justin's car. We agree we can leave in five minutes after some *alone time*.

Dee looks at her watch. "Shit, man. We have to be at work in three hours."

I kiss her on her neck. "Totally worth it."

"True." She kisses me sloppily and it makes my insides twist up and we make out for a few minutes and everything is going great until she jams her hand into my pants and I have to stop her from going too far because I don't want to go that far.

She slaps the car seat and says, "Dammit, Jones! Just shit or get off the pot!"

I decide Dee is now fine to drive home.

How's that for getting off the pot?

21

LIFE OFF THE POT IS QUIET.

I GET INTO JUSTIN'S CAR, and we all take off for Unity Valley. I don't say good-bye to Dee and I don't cry and I don't feel anything but numb indifference. Part of me scolds myself for ever bringing her here. Part of me knew this was a bad idea.

Maybe part of me wonders if I'm even gay, though only an hour ago, I was about 99.9 percent sure. It's like I just walked in a big circle.

But what's the difference between Jeff Garnet and Dee Roberts right now? Last week, Jeff's pressing me up against his car like some big jerk and tonight Dee's doing the same damn thing.

"You okay back there?" Kristina asks.

"Yeah."

"Something happen with Dee?"

"Nah. Just tired."

"You danced your ass off!" Justin says. "It was awesome!"

"Yeah," I say. I think: *But what does it matter now? I can't just dance. I can't just have fun. If I start having even a little bit of fun, I have to shit or get off the pot.*

▶ ▶ ▶

My alarm goes off at five, and I hit snooze. It goes off again at 5:09, and I hit snooze again. Finally, at 5:18 I get up and get dressed. I don't do anything to my hair except run my fingers through it.

By the time I get to Maldonado's, I think I may have fallen asleep while driving. Twice. I don't remember at least four blocks of Washington Street. Dee is already inside, which means I must really be late.

I smile and pretend I'm not heartbroken. *Shit or get off the pot.* I can barely keep my eyes open, so the I'm-too-tired-to-talk routine is 100 percent believable. The morning goes by slowly. I devein six hundred thousand million shrimp, and Dee chops broccoli and cauliflower into twelve million trillion perfect little trees. We wash and chop fruit together and grunt occasionally.

I avoid all contact with both walk-ins until a quick inventory check while Dee is doing dishes. I'm sure she notices, but she doesn't mention it.

The only conversation we have all day that isn't about food is this:

HER: Hey.
ME: Hey.
HER: Wanna go to the lake after work?
ME: Yeah.
HER: I don't have to be home until three.
ME: Great.

▶ ▶ ▶

Dee and I are on our blanket in our usual spot at Freedom Lake, and we're just lying here on our backs watching the sky. It's cold today, and we're both wearing our scarves and hats. I spot a small commuter jet descending to land at the local airport, and I send it all my love. All of it.

Dee doesn't have much to say, and neither do I. We're both tired—or maybe she's more tired and I'm more pretending I'm tired so I don't have to talk.

I ask the passengers: *Are you shaking your heads with disappointment? Are you yelling* shit or get off the pot *from your reclining first-class seats patterned in neutral-colored propellers and airplane silhouettes? Are you sick of hearing me say it?*

As if she's reading my mind, she says, "Are you pissed off at me for last night?"

"Nah."

Silence.

"That means yeah, doesn't it?" she says.

I sit up and cross my legs and look at her. "That thing you said. It pissed me off."

"Thing I said?"

"Shit or get off the pot." When I say this, I hear her say it all over again, and this huge, out-of-proportion anger fills me.

"Oh. That," she says. She sits up, too. "What's wrong with saying that? You say it all the time."

"I say it to people who take their time at red lights or who can't make a decision about a subject for their next research paper. I don't say it about important things like this!" I'm yelling a little. "How can you be so calm and act like it was nothing?"

She stares at me.

"Is that how you want to make love to me the first time? Forcing yourself?" I'm crying. I know I'm crying about everyone who's trying to control me, but I can't explain that to Dee right now.

"I wouldn't have ever done something that made you feel horrible. Jesus! You make me out like a date rapist. You know I'm not like that."

"You were last night."

"Stop saying that. I was not."

"Dude, I had to stop you. If I hadn't stopped you, what would have happened?"

"What the fuck?" she yells, throwing her hands up. "I can't figure you out, Jones. One minute you want me, and the next minute you don't."

"That's bullshit. I want you all the time, but I asked you to be patient."

"I was patient!"

"For two weeks. That's how long you were patient!"

She chews on the inside of her cheek. "I just don't get what the big fucking deal is. I mean, we've been together for over five months now. I'm pretty sure I love you!"

Wow. That was ... gutsy. Not romantic, but ... wow.

"Oh," I say.

"Oh? That's all you're going to say?"

"No," I say, trying to be gutsy, too. "I'm also going to say that if you—if you think you love me, then shouldn't you treat me like you love me and respect me? And be patient with me?"

I realize that I'm saying this not just to Dee but also to my mother. And Kristina. And Ellis. And Jeff. And maybe even myself.

Dee sighs and squeezes my hand. "I'm really sorry, Astrid."

We look at each other for a whole minute. I trace her high cheekbones down to her full lips and wish I wasn't attracted to them at all. I think about going back to being an asexual sea sponge, and I cry more.

She says, "I'm really sorry, okay?"

"Okay," I say.

"It's just really frustrating for me. I've never had a person hold out so long, you know?"

"Can't you see how even *that* hurts?"

"Yeah. Sorry."

We're quiet for a while. I dry my tears. "Look. I didn't want to get all loud and mad. I've just—just been under a lot of pressure from everyone, and I need a break."

"From us?"

"What?"

"You need a break from us?" she asks.

"I don't know," I say. "I don't think so. I mean, I don't know." I watch a plane zoom across the sky, and envy the power and control of it. I simultaneously realize that without a pilot, it would crash. "I need to be my own pilot," I say. "And I don't understand why my copilot is saying stuff like *shit or get off the pot*. It just doesn't seem like a good team."

Dee looks at me softly. "I don't want you to get hurt, you know?" She picks a long piece of grass and scars it with her thumbnail. "Do you remember Deanna Klinger?"

"Yeah." I vaguely remember her. I think she ran cross-country.

"We dated for a while, you know?"

I feel my whole face go hot. "Oh." Reason number 543 Dee Roberts was a bad first choice. She has dated a lot of girls, and I haven't dated any.

"She—you know—chose the wrong side. It wasn't pretty."

"Chose the wrong side?"

"Yeah. She found some guy she really liked, and now she's all hetero."

I sigh deeply and lie back down to look at the sky. No airplanes. No passengers to ask. So I ask the clouds. *Did you guys know there's a wrong side and a right side? Why didn't you tell me?*

The clouds don't answer.

"So when you said *shit or get off the pot*, you didn't mean for me to make up my mind," I say. "You meant for me to just come out, be gay, and be done with it."

"Well, yeah. I don't see what the holdup is."

"You wouldn't understand," I say. "Obviously, this was a piece of cake for you."

"Are you saying you might not be gay? That this is all just some kind of joke or something?"

"It's not a joke."

"So what is it, then?"

"It's a question. And I'm answering it. But I don't know the answer yet, and I'm sorry."

She lies back down and crosses her arms.

"And you shouldn't dis Deanna Klinger. Maybe she realized she wasn't what she thought she was," I say. "People change, you know?"

"Are you gonna change?" she asks.

"How am I supposed to know? I can't see the future," I answer.

We lie there, and when a plane finally appears in the sky, I picture a cabin full of fliers getting excited about their destinations, and I ask: *Isn't it enough to be in love with Dee's amazing eyes and the smell of her hair? Isn't it enough that she thinks I'm funny? That we have fun when we mess around at work? Why does everything come with a strict definition? Who made all these boxes?*

PASSENGER #0098
JOHN KIMBALL, SEAT 22B
FLIGHT #1209
CHARLOTTE TO ALLENTOWN

Jenny is asleep, and I watch her breathing in the seat next to me. I think about what she said last night. I think about what I said last night. I can't figure out if we were having the same conversation or what.

All I know is that I asked her to marry me and outlined my plan. I told her that we should wait until we're done with grad school. I told her that we should stay in the area because she has a good chance of getting that job at U of P.

I'd practiced the speech for weeks. I made reservations at the resort for our weekend vacation. I bought the ring in March. *March.* I never guessed in a million years that she'd give it back to me. I touch my pants pocket from the outside and feel the ring there against my leg.

I stare at her beautiful sleeping head and try to extract her reasoning. She wouldn't answer my questions last night. *Don't you want to get married? Don't you love me? Is it the ring? Did I do something wrong? Why aren't you talking to me?*

As I look out the window, I get a feeling of dread in my chest. Like someone is poking me in the throat. *Maybe she doesn't love you, John. Maybe she's using you for your car.* That's my mother. She's said that all along. And other stuff. But as I look out the window, all I can think is how wrong my mother is about this. Jenny has always loved me. We're soul mates. It was love at first sight. I know it.

So why'd she say no?

She didn't even say *maybe* or *let me think about it*. She just said no.

I pretend to cough, and jostle my elbow so she wakes up. This only makes her turn over a little. I do it again and then stroke her head and tell her that we're landing soon. I give her a minute to stretch and do some neck rolls, but that's all.

"Can we talk about this?" I ask.

"Here?"

"I can't drop you off and then drive to my parents' house without knowing why," I say. "It's not fair that you won't tell me."

When she looks at me, she looks heartbroken. "I can't. It's too hard to talk about," she says, and tears roll down her face.

"Why are you doing this to us?" I ask. "Why can't you just say yes?" I reach into my pocket and retrieve the ring. "Just say yes." I'm sobbing. This would be a first for her—seeing me sobbing—and it seems to flick a switch.

She stares at me seriously. "My mom told me that a Jewish boy marrying a non-Jew is like a mini death for his family. I can't do that to your family."

"What? That's completely insane. Anyway, who cares? It's not like either of us goes to church, right? Is that all this is about?" I shake my head and feel relief. It's so good to know that it's not me or the ring or anything else. It's just something stupid her mom said.

"That's not what your mom said to me the last time we were at your house for dinner," she says. "In fact, your mom seems to agree a hundred percent with my mom. I think that's where my mom got the idea."

I say, "What?" but it's rhetorical and she knows this. She hugs me, and though I have a small feeling of wanting to scream at my mother when I get home tonight, I hug Jenny, and all I can think about is how much I love her and how out of control I feel after all the work I did to make this the most perfect engagement ever. I have no idea what to do. And then…I suddenly know what to do.

My chest tightens with nerves. "Look," I say, holding the ring up. She has a pained look on her face. Then I stand and face all the people behind me. A planeful of strangers. I hold up the ring. "I am madly in love with Jennifer Ulrich, and I want her to marry me. She is the kindest, smartest, most beautiful woman I have ever met, and I want to live my whole life with her. All she has to do is say yes."

I look down at Jenny, and she's partly smiling and partly mortified.

"She's all freaked out that I'm telling you this, but I want to make something clear. I don't give a crap where she came from, and I don't give a crap what my mother said to her. I want to marry her, and I'm not going to let anyone stop us."

The people on the plane smile at me. Jenny stands up.

I face her and ask again. "Will you marry me?"

When she says yes and I slip the ring onto her finger, the plane erupts with yelling and applause, and it's as if all of us are possessed by something we will never understand.

22

MY NAME IS CLAIRE, AND I'LL BE YOUR PILOT TODAY.

CLAIRE IS IN ESPECIALLY ROTTEN FORM when I get back. When I walk in, she's mincing Dad into tiny pieces about putting a knife in the wrong drawer. When she sees me, she barks, "Astrid, come here." I can't even send my love to her, she's that bad. *Claire, I am not sending any love to you because you are a horrible person right now. Who made you eat bitch for lunch? Who poured you a tall bitch beer float? Who sprinkled bacon bitch on your salad?* I nearly crack myself up with these but keep a straight face for the interrogation.

"What time did you get in last night?" she asks.

"Just after two."

"Are you sure?"

"Yes," I say. "Why?"

"Because sometimes teenagers lie, that's why." Picture Elizabeth Taylor in *Who's Afraid of Virginia Woolf?* That acrid, biting, accusatory tone she takes every time she speaks.

"What movie did you see?" she asks. The second she asks it, my brain goes numb, and I can't even think of one title of one movie ever made. Like, ever. Not even my favorites. All movies are titled *Untitled* in my brain.

"I only saw about half of it. We were late getting there because Jeff's car broke down, and Justin had to help him get it to the garage."

Where the hell did that come from? I seem to be a natural liar. Who knew? Up until two weeks ago, I'd gotten by on doing nothing exciting and telling the truth all the time.

"What was wrong with his car?"

"I don't know," I say. Then I head up the steps so I can change out of my shrimpy-smelling work clothes, and once I do, I sit on my bed for a minute and stare into space. I don't feel right about Dee. I don't feel right about lying about Jeff. I don't feel right about anything.

I make Frank S. appear. This time he's on the flat roof outside my window, so I have to open it and let him in. When he gets in, he hovers over the warm radiator a minute and then looks at me and smiles and sits down on my vanity bench.

"Are you ever going to say anything?"

He just looks at me.

I sigh. "I wish more people would be like you, Frank. I need quiet people in my life."

He keeps looking at me.

"That said, I could really use some advice, you know? Got any advice?"

He doesn't have any advice, so I ask myself the same question. *Hey Astrid, got any advice?* And the only answer I have is to tackle the problems I *can* tackle. Like lying to Jeff.

I take out my phone to text Kristina about how I can't do this to Jeff anymore, and when I flip it open, there's a message waiting for me. From Dee. It says: *I'm sorry for being an ass. How about we agree on a signal? When you're ready to take it further, you say "Abracadabra" or something. Until then, I'll be more patient, and I will shut up right before I'm about to say something stupid.*

A huge part of me wants to text back *abracadabra* because that would make such a great line in a movie, wouldn't it? It would be so romantic and make everything perfect.

But this isn't a movie.

▶ ▶ ▶

Ellis arrives at my door a few minutes later.

"Hey."

"Oh, hey," I say.

"Everything okay?" she asks.

"Sure. You?"

"Yeah. I guess." She shrugs. "Some stuff could be better."

I think she means Claire's mood, but in case they're about to go off on a Mommy and Me wine binge/country club buffet/shopping trip or something, I keep the speculation to myself and continue to reorganize my closet, which is what I've been pretending to do since she showed up at my doorway.

"I saw Jeff last night," she says.

"Oh yeah?"

"He was walking around Main Street. You weren't with him."

"So?"

"So you're lucky Mom and Dad didn't see him, too."

I sigh. "God. That kid."

Ellis sits on my bed, and I sit on my vanity bench, where Frank just was. She says, "You need to watch out because Mom is getting all buddy-buddy with his mom, and they're, like, joking about weddings and shit."

At times like these I wish I was a passenger.

At times like these I need an air sickness bag and an oxygen mask and a chair cushion that doubles as a flotation device.

"I think I need to throw up," I say. We both think I'm joking until I catch a whiff of my shrimpy catering pants on the hamper and I jog to the bathroom and puke. Twice.

When I finish brushing my teeth and go back to my room, Ellis is still sitting on my bed.

"Wow. So I take it you don't like Jeff Garnet?"

"Yeah." She smiles at me a little—like she feels bad for me. "Were you serious about Mom talking to his mom? Because that's just gross. What's wrong with her?"

"She thinks it's cool," Ellis says.

"Would you want her being like that about you?" I ask.

"It's her way of caring without leaving the house." She rolls her eyes. "Which is more important than, you know, *everything*."

Ellis baits the hook, and I know she genuinely wants to talk, and she's bummed, probably, that Mom can't make time for her hockey games. But though she's pissed off right now and needs me to save her from the flying monkeys, there's the "Mommy and Me" Ellis. The one who might drink too much wine while wearing Mom's fineries and spill out whatever I say.

"Shit, man. I have to get this load of wash in, or I'll have nothing to wear this week. You have any whites?" I ask. My brain says: *Ellis, you're a great kid, and at the moment you are perfect. Enjoy it while it lasts and know that I love you, even though you can't be trusted. One day you will know the truth, and then we'll talk.*

"Yeah. I have a few whites," she says, and goes to her room to get them. She puts them in the basket, and we both go downstairs. I go to the laundry room and start the machine, and she flops herself on the couch and flips through the channels.

I see Mom at the kitchen table, her empty lunch plate still in front of her, banging her phone keyboard with her thumbs. She giggles. She texts again. It makes me realize that maybe this is her back door to being accepted in Unity Valley. If she doesn't leave the house, the gossips-in-charge won't have anything to say about her. But she can still be involved somehow from her handy smartphone.

I put on a sweatshirt and my coat and my gloves, a hat and

a scarf, and I go to my table and lie down. The sky is biblical today—rays of sun forming straight lines from behind rounded, fluffy clouds. The planes shine like gold stars up high. I ask: *If I unzip my Unity Valley suit and let my happy person out, will she still be happy?*

The back door slams, and I look and see it's Ellis.

"What do you do out here all the time?"

"Just watch the sky, I guess. Think. Dream."

"Can I talk to you? About stuff?" she asks.

"Sure."

"Why doesn't Mom come to my hockey games? Or go anywhere, really?"

I think about this. "She goes out with you all the time on your Mommy and Me trips, right?"

She's silent. Probably wasn't a good time to say that. But I really don't want to talk to perfect Ellis. She should be happy in her bubble. And let me be happy out here on my picnic table.

"Mom says you lie here because it's what you do to feel normal."

"What's normal?" I ask.

"I don't know. Moms who watch their kids play hockey, for one thing." She frowns in thought. "And I don't think you're that abnormal," she says.

"Thanks."

"So? What do you do when you lie here?"

I sigh. "Nothing really. Just watch the sky, like I said."

"Huh," she says. She looks at the sky for a minute and then goes back inside.

23

JEFF THE LEG JIGGLER TALKS, TOO.

MONDAY MORNING SUCKS. I mean that specifically—not a general comment about how all Monday mornings suck. I've always been a fan of Mondays because Mondays get me out of the house and away from Claire. Claire-who-is-beginning-to-make-me-paranoid now that Ellis told me she talks to Jeff's mom.

The minute I see him, I ask Jeff what movie he told his mom he saw.

"She didn't ask," he says.

"Well, I told my mom your car broke down."

"Why?"

"I don't know. I panicked."

"But my car didn't break down," he says.

"Yeah. I know. But if your mom talks to my mom, she might say something about it, and I wanted you to be prepared."

"Okay," he says. He has a goofy look on his face—mixed with annoyance. Thank God. Maybe he wants out of this as much as I do.

"I had a lot of fun on Saturday night," he says. "Are we on again for next weekend? Midnight movies? For real this time?"

"Can't do it. Next weekend is out for me." A sad smile forms across his lips. I feel instantly guilty. "But maybe the weekend after that?"

He smiles. Why do I do this to him?

▶ ▶ ▶

It's been two weeks since I dropped trig, and I'm still aware of it every minute of fourth-period study hall in the auditorium. I stare into space and picture those poor students still stuck up there in room 230, learning about triangles. I think about the theorems and the equations I will never have to do. I think about the way Mr. Trig's ass looked in those plaid suit pants—how flat it was. How I used to picture it as some sort of foam insulation sprayed atop his blocky pelvis.

Seriously. I think of all those things. And I smile and smile and smile.

"You thinking about your boyfriend?" Stacy Koch asks.

"What?"

"I said are you thinking about your boyfriend? You look all happy and shit."

Stacy has never talked to me before, so I have no idea what to say. She and her twin sister, Karen, are grinning at me. They are cheerleader types. Not real cheerleaders, but close. I think Karen might twirl a baton.

"Oh. No. I was, uh—" I can't tell her I was thinking of Mr. Trig's ass in plaid suit pants. "Yeah. I was. Can't help it."

"He's a catch," she says. "Isn't he, Karen?"

Karen leans forward and nods. Stacy adds, "He's like a little brother to us."

Before lunch, I hear two interesting tidbits.

Astrid Jones is a prude. Jeff Garnet says she doesn't even kiss yet.

I hear one of the Koch twins has it bad for him, too.

Life was so much easier being an honest nerd who didn't do anything.

▶ ▶ ▶

On Tuesday I realize I am a horrible person. I am a horrible person for doing this to Jeff Garnet. And to whichever Koch twin is in love with him. I should set him free.

But I don't.

I tell Kristina at lunch about how Ellis saw Jeff walking around Unity Valley on Saturday night, and she says, "So?"

"So didn't you make him promise not to blow the cover?

Why are we using him if he's just going to mess every-thing up?"

"I don't know."

"Well, it was your plan," I say.

"You don't have to do anything you don't want, dude. You are the master of your own destiny and all that," she says. She's a little cold or something. I can't put my finger on it.

"What's that supposed to mean?"

"I don't know. Isn't that what you learn in humanities?"

I think about what Frank S. would say. But I say nothing.

▶ ▶ ▶

It's Friday. I'm reading Plato's Allegory of the Cave during lunch.

This week kinda sucked all the way through. From hear-ing rumors about prude Astrid Jones and being the only reader who showed up for lit mag on Wednesday and doing all the work myself to having to take a European history test yesterday that I forgot to study for. Plus, Kristina is still acting weird. So, now is not really the time for me to see Jeff Garnet.

He sits across from me the minute I'm done with my Cae-sar salad. I made it four whole days avoiding him—taking dif-ferent staircases, using different hallways, only going to my locker during lav breaks.

"Are you avoiding me?" he asks.

"No, why?" I ask, completely nonchalant, as if I wasn't hid-ing in the girls' room two periods ago, waiting for him to pass by.

They say: *I don't know why she's stringing him along. Maybe it's a pity thing, like Tim Huber.*

"Astrid?"

"What?"

"Did you hear what I said?"

"No. Sorry. I was spacing out. What did you say?"

"Stacy told me that she heard you were avoiding me."

"Huh." I shrug. "Well, she's wrong. I'm not avoiding anyone," I say.

"Oh," he says. "Okay. Uh. Still not free this weekend?"

"Nah. I gotta do some family stuff. Bleh, you know?"

"Sure. So, how about you, uh—you know—just, uh—" he says as he awkwardly half stands so he can lean across the table to kiss me. As he's doing this, I pretend I don't see it, and I turn to my stack of books, pick them up and walk out of the cafeteria.

▶ ▶ ▶

When I get home, Mom is at the kitchen table. Never a good sign.

"Astrid, I need to talk to you."

I sit down and pretend for a minute that she actually cares about me and is going to say something normal Unity Valley mothers say to their normal Unity Valley daughters.

"Kristina told me that you and Jeff are having problems."

I think of all the things I could say to this. I say nothing.

"Look. You can talk to me if you want. I can tell you what

you need to know about—you know—sex, or whatever the problem is."

The problem is I'm dating a girl. I say nothing.

"Hmm. Well, Kristina called me today and told me she wanted to take you out this weekend, but you said no, and really, Astrid, the time you need your friends is now. I mean, if you and Jeff are going to break up, you shouldn't take it out on Kristina."

This is ridiculous. This is Kristina trying to get me to go out when she knows I don't want to. My brain people remind me: *This is also Kristina trying to help you stop jerking Jeff around. She's lying to Claire to help you.* I remind my brain people that this is also Kristina talking to my mom behind my back, which I don't like. They reply: *But it's for your own good, and you know it.*

"Anyway, just know I'm here for you," Mom says.

"Okay."

"And those people calling you a prude were prudes once, too," she adds.

Great, I think. *That's just great.* On the way up the steps, I tell my brain people they can just shut up now.

24

I AM A PUSHOVER. THAT'S WHY THIS SHIT HAPPENS TO ME.

I'M TEN MINUTES LATE to work because I wanted to be. Last I heard from Dee was her *abracadabra* text message last Sunday, and I didn't answer, because I'm not sure what I'm supposed to do now.

Juan says, "Big day today. Same as last time, but even bigger."

"Grande!" Dee sings, high-pitched and with plenty of extra cartoonish vibrato. The guys laugh. I don't even smile.

Dee and I are awkward by ourselves. We don't talk or joke while we work, and I ignore her when she asks, "So, are we on for tonight or what?"

We don't finish the dishes until four. I don't punch out

until 4:10. That's a ten-hour workday. Juan tells us we don't have to come in tomorrow, and Dee says, as we toss our aprons into the laundry box, "Come on. Let me make it up to you. You got my text, right?"

"Yeah."

"You still mad?"

"Yeah. I'm mad at all of you."

She laughs. "All of me?"

"No," I say, smiling a little. "All you people who think you can boss me around."

"You *are* a pushover. That's a fact." She starts dancing a little and smiles at me, and when we get to the parking lot, she says, "Come on. You know you want to. Let me make it up to you, and I promise, no stupid pushy shit."

I admit I could use a night out away from my house, and I wouldn't mind a hard lemonade after the cruddy week I had. We get into her car and brainstorm my cover. We totally suck at brainstorming, so I call Kristina.

"I'll cover you for tonight," she says. "Claire owes me one."

"I don't even want to know what that means," I say. "Text me with whatever I'm supposed to tell her." Dee is dancing in place to imaginary music, making a bass sound deep in her throat. I admit I'm excited to go out to Atlantis again. An hour ago, I wasn't going anywhere tonight. I think: *Maybe it's okay that people talk you into things. Maybe if they didn't, you'd never go anywhere.*

▶ ▶ ▶

Claire is locked in her office, talking on the phone with a client. You can tell she's talking to a client because she puts on her New York City accent and talks about three decibels louder.

I find Dad in the quiet room, dozing with a book on his chest. I dust quietly around him, and before I leave, he says, "How's my favorite daughter?"

"Dad," I say in that exasperated way. "You can't say stuff like that."

He sits up and blinks his eyes hard a few times and stretches. "You know what I miss? Making birdhouses. What are you doing now? We should go make one."

"I'm doing stuff," I say. I wiggle the feather duster. "Waiting for her to get off the phone so I can sweep the upstairs."

"You going out tonight?"

"I hope so."

"Ah."

"Yeah."

"This guy a serious thing? Shouldn't you bring him here to meet me?"

"Nah. Don't tell Mom, though."

▶ ▶ ▶

At seven thirty the doorbell rings.

Claire fast-walks to the door to open it, and I stand up because I can hear Kristina giggling outside, and then Kristina and Donna drag me out the door.

"Have fun, girls!" Mom says.

They lead me down the walk and into a car. Kristina seems to be my best friend again. She even loops her arm through mine rather than Donna's.

"Where are we going?" I ask.

"We're heading to a clean, fun and safe college sorority party. Which is what I told Claire, and it's actually true." She deposits me into the backseat of Donna's car and then gets into the passenger's side.

"Are you and Dee okay now?" she asks.

"We're fine," I say.

"I'm glad to hear that," she says in the weirdest voice ever—like she's not glad to hear it.

"You okay?" I ask.

"Sure. Why wouldn't I be?"

"I don't know. It's been a weird week," I say. "I'm just all over the place, I guess."

"Bummer," she says. That's it. Just "bummer."

For the rest of the drive, Kristina and Donna talk as if I'm not there, and I try not to feel like Kristina's socially retarded dumbshit friend again.

When we get there, a Lady Gaga song is playing so loud, it's bouncing the road outside the house. Kristina has talked about spending more time at Donna's dorm room, but her roommate is a douche, and if she knew Donna was gay, she'd probably freak out and call an exorcist. So Donna has joined a not-so-official sorority called Gamma Alpha Psi (ΓΑΨ), which is a GLBT hangout with an off-campus house. This is Kristina's first time here, too.

"We've got two hours before we leave. Have some fun.

Mingle," Kristina says as she disappears up the stairs with Donna.

Mingle.

I look around the room. This is not like Atlantis. Most of the people are keeping to themselves, and there are no leathery biker ladies with whistles who were sent from the gods to make me smile. There are just strangers. So I go out the back door past the two smokers, and what do you think is in the farthest and darkest part of the backyard?

A picnic table.

▶ ▶ ▶

There are tall trees obstructing most of my view, but I can see the occasional plane, and I send it my love. Then I have a conversation with myself about Kristina.

ME: You know, you're going to have to say
    something to her about this up-and-down shit
    she's been doing.

ME: I know. But if I say something, she'll just
    ignore it.

ME: Doesn't that make her a shitty friend?

ME: Yes and no. Yes, she should listen to me and care
    how I think, and she doesn't. No, she's not a
    shitty friend, because she's my only real friend
    in Unity Valley, so if I didn't have her, I'd be on
    my own.

ME: You'd have Dee. You'd have Ellis.

ME: Ha-ha ha-ha ha-ha. Ellis. You're hilarious.

ME: She's your sister. You have her whether you want her or not.

ME: She may have me, but I sure don't have her. Mom has her. You know it.

ME: Well, then, you have Dee.

ME: Thank God.

ME: You're getting closer to answering all the questions, aren't you?

I sit up and look around. A few more women are outside smoking now. They are facing me but looking up to the stars. I look up too, and I get up to try and make conversation and not be an antisocial nerd. Plus, I have to pee.

I walk past them and say, "Hi," but all I get is a series of grunts in return. Inside, I smile at people and ask where the bathroom is, and when a woman tells me, she says, "I think it's out of paper. You got a tissue?"

I laugh at this, thinking it's funny—whether it's true or not.

No one else laughs.

Do I not show up on their gaydar? Or is this just how they are here at Gamma Alpha Psi? Either way, I don't have a tissue, so I look around and go back to the kitchen, where the back door to the picnic table is, and there I find a napkin, so I grab it and put it in my pocket in case the woman is right about the paper.

I go up the steps and pass a couple coming down the steps and say hi, and they half-smile. Everything feels territorial—like I'm trespassing.

I pee, and there are several rolls of toilet paper on a holder right in front of the toilet. I use the napkin anyway because I feel an intense paranoia that if I use their toilet paper, they will be even more pissed off with me than they already seem to be.

I look at myself in the mirror above the sink, and she is more visible here—the girl inside my Unity Valley suit. She's telling me to go out there and be myself and talk to people. I hear my dad's voice: *You have to let people get to know you before you decide they don't like you.*

I plaster a big fat smile across my face and go back downstairs. I say hi to a few people and then I find a girl who's standing on her own reading the back of a CD cover and I say hi to her and she looks up and smiles at me.

"Never saw you here before," she says.

"First time."

"Ah," she says. "That explains it."

"You go to school here?" I ask.

"Yeah. I'm a poli-sci major. Here to change the world," she says. "You?"

"My best friend is dating someone from here. We're only visiting tonight."

"Who?"

"Donna?"

"Oh! So you're in high school, right? Her girl's from high school, isn't she?"

"Yeah. We're seniors."

"You the one who was lying on the picnic table for the last hour?"

I nod and try not to blush.

"What were you doing out there?"

"Just looking at the sky. And at the airplanes. It's what I do, I guess."

"Huh," she says. "Wanna show me how you do it?"

I look around, and I see the others looking at us. Still, no one is really smiling or being all that welcoming. I don't get that. These are supposed to be my people. I didn't think they'd be douches at all. *Note to self: Not all gay people will be cool. Not all straight people will be not cool. When did you get so us-and-them, Astrid?*

As we walk out to the table, I ask my new friend, "Is it me, or is everyone at this party kinda standoffish?"

"That's just how they receive strangers."

"It's weird," I say.

"Not really. It's hard. You'll understand soon," she says. "Plus, it's early. In another three hours, the place will be packed and everyone will be drunker and the mood will lighten considerably."

"Good. Because it's a little like a funeral in there."

"What's your name?" she asks.

We get to the table. I sit on the bench. She sits next to me. "Astrid."

"I'm Kim. My ex should be here any minute, and I'm kinda not okay with it."

"Bummer."

We both spend half a minute looking up into the sky.

"Have you told your family yet?" she asks.

I laugh. "God no."

"Anyone?"

"Just my two best friends. And my girlfriend," I say.

She laughs. "I hope so!"

"Yeah."

"Are they going to be okay with it, do you think?"

I nod. "I think so."

"I thought mine would be cool. They are now, but they weren't at first. I think it's a shock."

"Yeah. I guess."

"You know, you're really cute," she says.

I let out a shy laugh. "Thanks. You too."

She steps onto the bench and sits on the table and then lies down. "Is this how you do it?"

"Do what?"

"Look at the planes."

"Well, yeah, but those trees don't help," I say, pushing her over so I can lie next to her.

"There's one!" She points. "Can you tell what kind they are from here?"

"Sometimes. Not at night, though." I spot the blinking white taillight. "Did you know that every plane has a red light on the left wing and a green light on the right for navigation?"

"So you're cute *and* smart," she says.

"So the white strobe you see"—I point—"is the tail."

She softly pulls my hand down and onto her chest and holds it with her two hands.

We don't say anything for a while. I can feel her heart beating.

"Do you mind if I kiss you right now?" she asks.

And my mouth says no, even though it knows I am dating Dee. (It also knows that Dee has never been polite enough to ask me anything before she does it.)

As we kiss—and Kim is a spectacular kisser—I begin to think about what this means. This means I've kissed two girls in my life. Which is one more than the one boy I've kissed—if you don't count Jeff Garnet, who I'm not really kissing. It means I am more of a lesbian than I was only a minute ago when I was just looking at Kim and thinking about how cute she is. It means that one day I will have to tell my parents. And Ellis, who says things like *lesbian luncheon*. It means that maybe I will finally drive my pseudo-agoraphobic mother into full-fledged hiding.

Or maybe I will save her from Unity Valley, and this will finally get her to move back to New York City, where we belong.

They'll say: *Good riddance to her. She thought she was so damn special.*

"Wow," Kim says.

Then we go back to kissing, and I clear my mind of all those thoughts and I just feel stuff. I feel aroused and happy, and kissing becomes harder when I smile a little, and when she feels me smile under her lips, she smiles, too. I bring my hands up to run them through her hair.

We stop and look at each other in the dim light. And then I hear "Asteroid!"

And I say, "Shit." I roll off the table and sit on the bench for a second, and Kim follows me and sits next to me, and I can tell we're both trying to look innocent and failing.

"Should have known I'd find you here," Kristina says. She looks at Kim, who moves her hand in a wave. "Are you ready to go?"

"Sure," I say.

Donna looks at her phone. "We'll be really late if we don't leave now."

"And Dee's waiting, right?" Kristina adds.

"Yeah," I say.

Kim walks with us to Donna's car. We fall behind them, and she says, "It was nice meeting you. Come back any time you want." She slips her number into my back pocket and then says, "See you guys!" as if we had just played on the swing set in fourth grade together.

"She seems nice" is the last thing Kristina says to me.

ME: I just kissed someone else.

ME: True. Not very cool.

I bring my hand up to my face and see if I can smell Kim on my hands. I realize how stupid I am for doing this.

ME: You know what this means, right?

ME: No. Not at all.

ME: It means you're gay, Astrid.

ME: Oh. That.

ME: Yeah. That.

Since Donna and Kristina are talking and listening to music up there as if I'm not in the backseat, I summon Frank to sit next to me. He winks as he arrives. Then he gives me a thumbs-up.

I have no idea why he's so happy for me. I could have just ruined everything.

25

WELCOME ABOARD FLIGHT ATLANTIS.

BY THE TIME WE PULL INTO the bar parking lot, it's 10:42. Earliest we've ever been. Dee is here, in her car, waiting for me. I make my exit while Donna and Kristina start making out in the backseat and Justin texts Chad because he's not here yet.

When we kiss, it overflows into a longer kiss and then a longer one and then a passionate, sink-down-in-the-seats kiss, and I feel a blanket of desire over me like I've never really felt before. Not ever. She grabs my hair and twists it. She squeezes my hip, and I put my right hand up her shirt and touch her through her bra and then slide my index finger around her waistband. Just a little.

▼ FACT: I WANT MORE THAN ANYTHING TO SAY
ABRACADABRA RIGHT NOW.

▼ FACT: I'D RATHER STAY HERE IN DEE'S CAR THAN
GO INTO THE BAR.

▼ FACT: NEITHER OF THESE THINGS IS GOING TO
HAPPEN.

So I nibble on her ear and whisper other words. "Aba-lone," I say. "Abercrombie."

She chuckles and slips her hands into my jeans and down the sides of my legs. Under my panties, and then aims them around my ass and holds it like someone would hold a water balloon. Carefully. Skillfully.

"What were you saying?" she asks.

"Ab...dominal external oblique muscles."

She removes her hands from my jeans and lifts my shirt a lit-tle. She kisses my lips. My chin. My neck. My collarbone. My belly. My ribs. She says, "I'm sorry. I wasn't paying attention. Were you trying to say something?" She begins to unbutton my fly.

"I think it was abrasion," I say. "Or maybe abridgment."

She lifts my bra, and my breasts spill out. "Are you sure? I thought you might be trying to say something else."

Brutally loud knock on the window. We lie and breathe for a second.

"Abrupt, abominable abuse. That's all she's good for at times like this."

Kristina keeps knocking.

I sit up and sigh. "Did you ever wonder if what you believe

is reality? I mean, that beyond this is a real reality that's more real than the reality you know?"

"Shit, Jones."

"But did you? Did you ever get pulled in so many directions you weren't sure which one was real?"

She bear-hugs me.

I say, "I love you."

She kisses me on the forehead.

Kristina knocks again and says, "We're leaving you here if you don't come now."

We straighten ourselves and get out of the car. I feel the cold more than I usually do. I realize that I was sweating. Parts of my body are damp. The right parts. I shiver. Dee and I cross the street and get in line and press ourselves together. Neither of us can stop smiling. I know this sounds stupid, but it's like no one else is here. Justin's and Chad's lips are moving, and they seem to be having a conversation, but I can't hear them. Same with Kristina and Donna. Blah blah blah. I feel 100 percent ready to say *abracadabra*.

Maybe even tonight. Claire would be so proud.

▶ ▶ ▶

We are now experts at getting through the door. My heart rate doesn't increase. My palms aren't sweaty. I don't even have exact change. I smile at Jim the bouncer and hand him my twenty-dollar bill. I say, "For two," and hold up two fingers. Dee thanks me as he hands me ten dollars in change.

As I step over the threshold, I feel I am entitled to happiness, even if my best friend is acting weird and making me paranoid. Even if I just did what I did with a complete stranger named Kim. Even if I feel like an occasional dumbshit. I am in my own personal happy jet—in a wide seat and with the perfect mix of cool and warm air and the little pillow positioned perfectly in my lumbar region.

I look around at the other passengers. Biker lady is here. She is a leather-clad flight attendant. She brings me a bottle of water and says, "I know that's the kind you like." She takes Dee to the dance floor and dances with her during an old disco classic. Dee is probably more beautiful than I've ever seen her. It's not just her clothes or how she's put her hair back. It's the cabin pressure in here. It's making us worry-free. Timeless. Funny. Grown up.

The pilot puts on some more disco and says, "We're playing your favorites until midnight! Drop by the cockpit and give me a request!"

It's all so good, I don't have time to feel guilty.

▶ ▶ ▶

Dee and I drink lemonades and find a place in the back corner of the dance floor. Atlantis is particularly crowded tonight. There's a line for the ladies' room that stretches to the bar doorway.

When the techno comes on at midnight, more people crowd onto the dance floor, and Dee and I start to kiss again in the corner while our hips are pressing into each other and our hands are touching places that should not be touched in a public place.

We are right by an amplifier, so she has to yell. "You want to go back to the car? Maybe you could find that word you're looking for."

I really want to say yes, but I'm afraid of leaving now and what Kristina would say. "I do, but I . . . I don't want to do it in the car," I say. I don't like quite how that came out, but she nods.

"Maybe you can remember the word tomorrow? I've got a free house."

We pull away from each other and lock eyes. She nods. I nod.

We dance until we're twice as damp as we were when we arrived.

I see Kristina and Donna over by the bar. Kristina waves at me and smiles. I wave back. After a brief rest, Dee grabs me for a slow dance, and we dance so close I think I'm losing circulation in my torso. Nothing ever felt more perfect. I think about telling Mom and Dad again. I think that it would be easy to tell them if they understood that I'm happy. All parents want their kids to be happy, right?

Right when I think this is when everything changes.

First, a loud voice. Then the music goes off. Then the lights come on.

26

OHSHITOHSHITOHSHIT.

THOSE OF US IN the middle—halfway between the street entrance and the back parking-garage entrance—start a surge toward the back door. But then we're pushed back toward the bar by those who were in the back room, because there are cops coming in that way, too.

"Oh, shit," Dee says.

I don't know what to say.

"Can they arrest us?" I ask.

Justin and Chad whisper a few things to each other.

"They're checking IDs," Dee says.

"I don't have an ID," Kristina says. "Except my school ID."

Donna says, "Babe, I don't think that's what you want to say when they get to us."

I reach to my back pocket. I have my driver's license and a ten-dollar bill.

Dee puts her head in her hands. I can see the color drain from her face. This might kill her hockey scholarship chances. Or maybe all of our everything chances.

The cop goes to Chad first. Chad reaches into his wallet and pulls out his license.

"Looks like a long drive for your folks tonight, all the way from Allentown!"

"Am I going to jail?" Chad asks.

The cop smiles and shakes his head. "Just a trip to the district justice with your parents. Go give them a call." He points to the phone on the bar.

Chad nods. What a mixed-bag answer. No jail, yes district justice. What the hell does that even mean?

As the cop moves on to Donna, who has, unbeknownst to all of us, a fake ID, it begins to dawn on me that I am completely up Claire Creek without a paddle.

And then Kristina starts laughing. Like a crazy person. Just laughing and laughing. Donna tries to shake her out of it, but she can't. The cops look disturbed. One of them asks if Kristina is on drugs. Instead of this making her stop laughing, it makes her laugh more. She even snorts a few times. Tears are pouring out of her eyes.

"Did she have a lot to drink?" the cop asks.

None of us answer because we can't figure out what's happening to Kristina.

It's Justin who snaps her out of it. He makes her sit down

on the bar step. "Kris, stop it. You're freaking out. Breathe with me."

They breathe together. She has to giggle in between. Then she gathers herself and stands back up, no longer laughing.

"Are you okay?" a cop asks.

She laughs again—through her nose—and says, "Yes, sir." Another giggle. "I'm fine."

She's smiling so big you'd never know she was getting busted along with the rest of us.

27

OHSHITOHSHITOHSHIT
PART TWO.

"HELLO?" Oh, thank God it's Dad.

"Dad? I'm really sorry about this," I say. I give him a minute to wake up. It's now two thirty AM.

"Is everything okay?"

"Yes. Everyone is fine, and nothing bad has happened. Buuuut. Uh. I'm gonna need you to come pick me up."

There's silence.

"Dad?"

"Did that jerk just leave you there?"

"No. No. Nothing like that. Except, well," I stammer. "He *is* a jerk." I realize that Dad is so asleep/stoned/out of the loop that he thinks I'm out with Jeff tonight.

"Okay, which theater are you at? I'll come get you."

I hear him get out of bed and breathe heavily as he puts on his pants. He says, "You know, I'm really proud of you for calling. I'm glad you took us seriously when we told you that you could call if you ever needed help or if anyone was drunk or any of that." He pauses. I can hear him zip his pants. "He didn't drive drunk, did he?"

"No, Dad."

"Good. You're so smart. Thank God for that," he says. "So are you at the mall or over at the Multiplex?"

I sigh and look at Dee. Kristina is still standing next to me.

"I'm actually in the city," I say. "On Chestnut Street."

I hear him put on his coat. "Chestnut Street? Is that where they put that new IMAX? I thought that was farther downtown. Huh."

"No. Uh, Dad, I'm at a bar. The cops just busted it, and I'm not allowed to leave unless you pick me up."

Silence.

"Dad?"

"A bar?"

"Yeah."

Huge, heavy sigh. "What the hell, Astrid?"

"Look. It's at the corner of Chestnut and Fifth. Just get here."

"Jesus Christ."

"I know, Dad. Believe me. Just get here."

"What's the name of the place?"

I take a deep, jittery breath. "Atlantis."

"Atlantis?" he says. Like he knows. Like he knows exactly what Atlantis is.

So I hang up.

28

THE END OF THE WORLD AS WE KNOW IT.

DEE'S MOTHER IS THE FIRST ONE TO get here. Well, the first one we know. There are at least fifteen other underage people here who we don't know, and some have already been picked up.

She looks around and exhales in deep disappointment, signs the ticket and takes Dee out the front door without a word to her. I feel like following them out and apologizing and telling Mrs. Roberts that it was all my idea and my fault for dragging Dee out. But my feet don't move.

Five minutes later, the door opens, and it's Dad and Kristina's mom at the same time. Dad looks around and gets a look on his face like he's disgusted. Not sure why. There is nothing in here that looks too different from any bar, I don't think.

Chad is waiting alongside Justin. Kristina says something to both of them before she goes toward her mother, who slaps her right across the face like in the old movies. The Houcks have a knack for that sort of thing. It's like *Gone with the Wind* or something. Strictly the 1939 brand of slapping. It only works because the slapper loves the slapee, and the slapee knows it.

This wouldn't work in my family.

My dad doesn't say a word and just stuffs my ticket into his coat pocket and grabs me by the elbow and pulls me out the door.

I wiggle free when we're outside and go to get into the passenger's seat.

"Sit in back," he says.

"What?"

"Sit in back. I don't want to talk about this."

I close the passenger's door and I sit in the back.

About halfway home, he says, "Do you have any idea what your mother is going to say?"

I stay silent and think about how I can lie my way out of this, because tonight is not the night to make this decision. Not under these terms. Not under interrogation.

"She's going to lose her mind."

"There's no way we can keep this between us?" I ask.

He's quiet for long enough that I think he might actually agree. Then he says, "Do you know who you're dealing with?"

I let that question echo and look out the window into the

quiet night. Dad doesn't have the heater on and I'm freezing, but I'm afraid of what he might say if I ask him to turn it on. I am his prisoner, in the backseat, trapped by child locks. I deserve to be cold and uncomfortable, I guess. I look out my window, and I see a plane high in the sky, its taillight flashing.

I ask it: *Do you know who you're dealing with?*

I ask myself: *Do you know who you're dealing with?*

Yes. I know who I'm dealing with. I'm dealing with the fire that sends flickering shadows. I'm dealing with the Claire-plane on which I've been a passenger for seventeen years. I look at Dad and I know he's a passenger, too. Even Ellis, up in first class. We're all passengers.

I ask us: *Do you know who you're dealing with?*

29

THIS IS NOT HOW
I EXPECTED IT TO UNFOLD.

NOT AT FOUR IN THE MORNING. Not with my mother sitting in the kitchen waiting. Not with a fight between her and Dad first when Dad tells her the whole story about where he picked me up. And certainly not with Ellis being woken up on purpose to hear my "news."

She says it so smarmily. "Sorry to wake you, but your sister has some important *news* and I think you need to hear it."

I sit at the table and hear her say this upstairs at Ellis's bedroom door.

Ellis clomps down the stairs behind Mom and sits in her chair in the kitchen, then flops her head down into her arms and tries to continue to sleep.

"Well?" Mom says. "We're ready for you to tell us *the big news!*"

"I don't have any big news."

"Your father says you do," she says.

"He didn't even talk to me on the way home."

"He knows where he picked you up," she says. "Why don't you start there?"

"I made a mistake. I went to a bar. I got caught. I'm sure it will be fun for you to watch me reap the consequences." This answer makes Ellis look up. We make eye contact for a millisecond.

"You think this is fun for me?" Mom asks.

"No. Of course not. If this was fun, then you'd make sure to wake up the whole family and put me on some sort of mock trial at four in the morning."

Just as Mom is about to tear into me for being a smart-ass, Ellis asks, "What the hell is this about?" She yawns. "You went to a bar? Why is that a big deal?"

"I know, right?" I say. "She takes you out drinking all the time, and you're a year younger than me."

"Yeah," Ellis says before Mom yells over us both.

"But I don't take her to homosexual bars!" she says. The way she says *homosexual* is...*not* standard FOTG issue at all.

"Who calls them that?" I ask.

"Who?"

"Who what?"

"Who's them?"

I look at her. "I mean who calls bars for gay people *homosexual bars?*"

"I think the proper nomenclature is *gay club*, Mom," Ellis says.

"Did you know about this?" Mom asks Ellis.

"She didn't know about anything," I say. "Only me, Kristina and Justin knew. And maybe a few of their friends." I figure invoking Kristina might help me.

But it's as if she didn't hear it.

"So do you want to tell your family why you were at a *gay club* tonight, Astrid? And do you want to tell us how long you've been lying to us about where you are on Saturday nights? Because don't think I won't call Dana in the morning."

"Who's Dana?" Ellis asks as she shuffles across the kitchen and gets herself a glass of juice from the fridge.

"Jeff's mom," I say.

"Well?" Mom presses.

When Ellis gets back to the table, I sit forward. "Look. The last few weekends we went to this gay club in town. We did it because we heard we could get served there. No one cards you at the door. And like most normal high school kids who live in"—I look right at Mom when I say this—"small-town America, we are bored out of our minds sitting around this stupid little town and doing nothing. It's our senior year. We figured we could find a way to have some fun. So yes. We went out. We had fun. We danced. I had one drink."

Ellis cracks up.

"It's not funny," Mom says. Then she looks into Ellis's eyes. "You knew about this, didn't you?"

"She didn't know. No one knew," I say. "Anyway, if you're

expecting some big news about how I'm some lesbian or whatever because I got busted at a gay club, then you're fresh out of luck."

I look over and see Frank S. sitting in the corner. He's not smiling.

"So how come you didn't go to one of a hundred normal bars to dance and drink, then?" Mom says. See that? *Normal bars.* As opposed to, you know, *homosexual bars.* I think we might have to revoke that FOTG badge, Mom.

"Because I didn't," I answer.

"You woke me up for this? On a weekend?" Ellis complains. "Jesus!" She gets up and slams her chair into the table and goes back upstairs.

Mom and Dad look at me. I look at the clock. It's 4:03—exactly two minutes since the last time I looked at it. Dad looks tired. Guessing from his usual Saturday night routine, I'd bet that he only went to bed at one o'clock, after *Saturday Night Live.* He was probably a few notches over too stoned, and I most likely called him and woke him out of a near coma.

"I hope you're happy," she says. "This will ruin our reputation."

"Oh," I say. I thought we all knew that our bad reputation has been building in this town, birdhouse by birdhouse, but hey, I guess we can blame everything on me now. World hunger. War. Apocalypse. Mom's unpopularity in a town her ancestors helped found.

"You can't just think of yourself, you know. Think of Ellis.

She's going to be a target now, too," she says. "And do you know what this means?" She's waving the ticket. She slaps it on the table.

"I think it means I have to go to court."

"It means you're going to lose your license for a few months," Dad says. "And you're going to have a record."

Mom sighs. "How do you think that will look now that we're about to choose a college?"

"I don't know," I say. I look at Frank. Still not smiling.

We sit in silence for a while.

"Can we go back to bed now?" Dad asks. "I'm sure Astrid will realize what this all means as it slowly bites her in the ass. Right now I just want to sleep."

"No one is keeping you here, Gerry," Mom says. "I guess I'll go back to bed and try to sleep, too. I hope you had fun tonight, because you're completely grounded with no car. And I'm sure once Jeff hears where you were, he's going to break up with you, and I can't say I blame him."

I put my head down and hold back laughter.

Poor Claire.

▶ ▶ ▶

On the picnic table everything is quiet.

All of the adrenaline from getting caught has clogged in my muscles, and I'm exhausted. Frank S. is still with me. He's sitting on the bench by the back door.

I wave. "Hi, Frank."

He waves back. "Hi, Astrid." He still isn't smiling. "Shame you had to lie."

"I just didn't think it was the right time," I say.

He nods. "Is there ever a right time?"

I don't like him right now, so I look back at the sky. There's a plane making its way west, and I mentally put myself on it. Where would I be going on that little thing? Pittsburgh? Cleveland? Would it matter? Wouldn't any of us catch a flight to *Anywherebuthere* right now?

I ask the passengers: *What does the airport look like at four o'clock in the morning? Did they even have coffee brewing? Was there toilet paper in the stalls?*

And why don't I feel ashamed right now? Is that a sign?

PASSENGER #1298
JANE TILBERTS, SEAT 2A
FLIGHT #9321
NEWARK TO CLEVELAND

I sit bolt upright in my seat and suck air as if I'd been drowning. The flight attendant immediately offers me a drink of water.

"You were sleeping," she says.

I nod.

She offers me water again. I say, "Okay."

I remember the dream I was having. I was me, the teenager. I was in the backyard of our summer house by the lake, lying on an old quilt my mother used as a beach blanket. I was watching an airplane up so high, and wondered where it was going. I did that a lot. Until I moved closer to the city, I only ever saw airplanes up high.

In the dream I was lonely. And I was ashamed—probably about what happened to me and Jenny that night at Mike's party. We should have never gone. Those boys only invited us to take advantage of us, and so we arrived innocent and we left broken.

Even though it wasn't my fault, I've never told anyone about it. Not even my own husband. Not even my therapist when I had a therapist. It's old. I should be over it by now, right? It was just past the free love of the early seventies. It was just boys being boys.

But I don't think I'll ever shake that night. It's been almost forty years, and I haven't come close to shaking it yet.

I wonder if Jenny has.

I lean up against the window and close my eyes. I have a daydream. It's a warm day and I'm a teenager and I'm happy and I'm wearing that great pair of red corduroys I had in eleventh grade. As I sit on my back porch the way I did the day after, I know in my heart that I did everything I could. I know in my heart that what happened to me wasn't my fault, no matter what those boys said.

That's the way it has to be, so that's the way I see it.

And the warmth I feel is real. For the first time since it happened forty years ago, I feel okay about it.

I finally feel okay about it.

30

CLAIRE MAKES SHADOWS.

MOM STANDS INSIDE MY ROOM and annoyingly knocks on my door until I drag myself from REM dreams.

"You missed work!" she screeches. She's a pterodactyl.

I look at my clock and I do the math. Eight AM minus five AM equals three. I've had about three hours of sleep. "I have off today," I say. "Did that long shift yesterday, remember?"

"You didn't tell me that."

"I did. Yesterday when I got home."

"No you didn't."

"Well...I have off," I say.

She clip-clops down the upstairs hall and slams the door to her office. After a few minutes, she turns on her stereo and I can't sleep.

I get that ringing in my ears, the kind you get when all the blood rushes to the anger center in your brain. If this was reversed, she'd insist I have respect for the rest of the people in the house. It would rate at least an hour on the lecture scale.

Dad would have to sit there and nod every time she asked a rhetorical question. "Do you think we raised you to be rude?" Nod. "Are you ever going to grow up and think about other people?" Nod. "You know you're never going to make any friends in college with this attitude, right?" Nod.

Ellis beats me to the shower. Mom turns up her stereo even louder with her horrible eighties music, and I give up on sleeping. I lie in bed and pick up Plato's *Republic* and skim the Allegory of the Cave as I seethe.

I replace the words with my own words. Instead of it being a conversation between Socrates and Glaucon, I make it a conversation between Ellis and me. A fictional Ellis who talks to me—and not just when she needs something.

ME: This family is an illusion.

ELLIS: You think?

ME: All we can see is the wall Mom wants us to see. On it she's drawn the people we know in shadow. For me, she's drawn you and Dad and the residents of Unity Valley. For you, she's drawn me and Dad and the residents of Unity Valley. Based on Mom's shadows, I see a sister who will always be better than me. A sister who will always win because I am a loser. She has cast this same shadow for Dad. We are the losers in the Jones family illusion, and you and Mom are the winners.

ELLIS: (*nods*)

ME: Now imagine we were set free from this illusion. Our chains removed, our heads able to turn and look at each other. What would I look like to you? And what would you look like to me? And what would Dad look like to us? Would we still rely on the shadows, or would we see the real people?

ELLIS: You're starting to worry me, Astrid.

ME: That's because you're still chained.

ELLIS: And you aren't?

ME: Not after last night. Not after the last seventeen years of my life in this cave. What if I told you that I am not a loser? What if I told you that Dad is not a loser?

ELLIS: He'd have to get a better job before I'd believe that.

ME: That's the shadows talking. What does Ellis think?

ELLIS: (*stops and pouts*) I love that he comes to my hockey games.

ME: And do losers go to their daughters' hockey games?

ELLIS: I guess not.

ME: I guess not, too.

ELLIS: But if I change the way I think, Mom will
stop loving me.
ME: How do you know?
ELLIS: I know because that's what she did to you.

▶ ▶ ▶

After two hours of half sleeping and half reading, I roll out of bed and shower. I hear Mom on the phone with someone, and I can't find anyone else when I go downstairs, so I grab my keys off the quiet-room desk and decide to take myself out to breakfast.

Why the hell not? What are they going to do? Double ground me?

As I drive up Main Street, I look in my rearview mirror and see Frank S. in the backseat. He's smiling again.

"Hi, Frank," I say.

"Hello," he says.

"Why are you smiling?"

"I love pancakes," he says. "Why are you smiling?"

"Because today is the last day." I say. "Before the word spreads. Before the people know. Before the people talk. Before they come for me with pitchforks and torches."

He laughs.

"I also love pancakes," I say.

I call Kristina's cell, and when she doesn't answer, I leave a message. "I'm going to the diner for a sick breakfast. Call me in the next ten if you want me to pick you up."

I call Dee's cell, but when she doesn't answer, I don't leave a message.

I drive to my favorite diner across town and order a huge plate of pancakes. Then, for dessert, I eat a sundae. As I'm digging at the bottom of my sundae dish with my long-handled spoon, my phone buzzes with a text.

It's from Dee's number. And it says: *Stay away from my daughter.*

▶ ▶ ▶

All I can think of as I drive home is what it would take to say those words. *Stay away from my daughter.* Does she think I'm some bad influence? Doesn't she know by now that I'm just a nerd who edits the school literary magazine? That I'm harmless? A lot more harmless than her daughter?

After all, it was Dee who told me I was gorgeous.

It was Dee who found me in the walk-in freezer.

It was Dee who kissed me.

It was Dee who invented the word *abracadabra*.

Not me.

It's like an accusation, that sentence. *Stay away from my daughter.* It's the kind of thing Dad would say to Jeff Garnet if he wasn't always upstairs in the garage attic exhaling out the right window depending on the wind.

It's the kind of thing Mom would say if she knew what really happened at work this summer. *Stay away from my daughter.*

And Dee has been out since she started high school. She's dated a ton of girls. Why am I suddenly the bad guy?

I look to Frank, who is still in the backseat, picking blueberry pancake crumbs from his beard. "It's about last night," he says. "It's about Atlantis."

I nod.

Dee may have dated tons of girls, but none of them got her busted at a gay club. Just me.

As I reach Unity Valley, I am distracted. I drive down Main Street, and it's like driving through a fog of gossip. I put the window down just a little to check if I can hear it. It's like that sound people make when they pretend they're whispering. *Pppssssswwwsssww.* They have heard the news here. I can feel the fog feasting on my reputation as I drive. I feel my pulse in my palms as I grip the steering wheel.

When I step out of the car, the gossip fog is like ether. I am instantly four times more exhausted than I was when I left the diner parking lot.

I get in the door, kick off my shoes and go straight up the steps and into my room. I curl up on the sheepskin rug and drape two knit afghans over my body. I think about calling Dee to make sure everything's all right, but then I don't.

The last thing I think before I fall asleep is: *Stay away from my daughter.*

31

I WAS NOT IMAGINING THE GOSSIP FOG.

MONDAY MORNING.

They say: *Holy shit! I can't believe it!*

They say: *Did you even know we had a bar like that?*

They say: *Did you hear? Did you hear? Did you hear?*

But no one actually talks to us.

They say: *I knew* something *was wrong with the Kristina-and-Justin thing. No relationship is that perfect.*

They say: *We should kick them off the Homecoming Court. Liars.*

Actually, that's the Koch twins. They are talking right to my head and not to each other here in fourth-period study hall.

"Who'd have thought they were dykes? They don't look like dykes."

"I just can't believe that Jeff kissed the same lips that were probably all over Kristina Houck's privates."

I turn to them both. "Can you stop?"

"Why don't *you* stop?"

"You're completely wrong, you know. You're completely full of shit."

"That's not what we heard." They say that in unison, like the creepy girls in *The Shining*.

They say: *That's not what we heard.*

▶ ▶ ▶

The fog is so heavy by lunch, Kristina and I go outside—totally against the rules—and walk through the parking lot toward the football stadium and sit on the empty bleachers behind the press box.

"Holy shit," she says.

"Yeah."

"So you know everyone thinks we're a couple, right?"

"Yeah."

"And they think we've been together since we were in grade school."

"Yeah."

"And I heard someone say Justin was offering favors for ten bucks a shot in the back room."

"Ugh."

"And I heard—"

"Stop!" I say. "I can't care about what the assholes in this stupid town say. I just can't care." I eat two more Rolaids. I've lost count today.

She puts her hands up in a defensive way. "No problem. Just thought I could vent with my best friend about the weekend everyone found out we're gay. Obviously not."

"Sorry. You can vent. I just don't want to hear the rumors. So stupid," I say.

She sighs. "So how was yesterday? Did they freak out on you at home? Because they sure as shit freaked out on me."

"Claire held a mini-trial from the minute I got home until about four thirty. Even woke Ellis up for it," I say.

"Wow. At least mine waited until yesterday," she says. "My mother seems to think I did it to kill her. How'd Claire and Gerry take it, though? Are they okay with the news?"

I don't say anything for a while. Then I say, "I didn't tell them."

"But didn't he pick you up?"

"I mean I didn't tell them that I'm gay," I say.

She looks at me sideways. "You mean they didn't get the hint from the whole *busted at a gay bar* thing?"

"I told them I was only there to have fun with my friends."

"And they *bought* it?" she says way too loudly. I nod. She bursts into overexaggerated laughter. Just like at the bar on Saturday night.

I give her an annoyed look. "The Koch twins totally sucked in study hall."

Kristina pretends to fluff her hair. "The Koch twins are jealous."

I sit there silently for a minute.

"What's your problem?" she asks me. "You look like you're gonna hurl."

"I got a text from Dee's mom yesterday, and it said 'Stay away from my daughter,' and I'm really freaked out because what if I did this all for nothing? What if I can't see Dee again, and I'm wrong about all of it?" I put my face in my hands.

This is all slowly biting me in the ass, just like Dad said it would.

I got caught in a gay bar. Dee's mom hates me. I am about to lose my license. I will have to go before some judge and talk about this. Everyone thinks I'm gay.

And I think I *am* gay.

I think I'm gay, and my girlfriend's mom wrote *stay away from my daughter.*

"Have you talked to her?" she asks.

I shake my head. "I'm too freaked. Her mom has her phone, anyway."

"You should call her. Her mom probably freaked out like all of our parents did, right? I mean, we did get totally busted at a bar, right?"

"Yeah. I guess."

She looks at the time on her phone. "Almost time to go back."

"Did you get my message yesterday?"

"Yeah."

"You didn't call me back."

"I was in between lectures, cross-examination and scream-ing fits. First my mom, then my dad, and then my mom again. *Oh, poor us! Our reputations are ruined forever! Are you sure you're gay? How could you lie like that? Is Justin gay, too? How long has this been going on? How could you do this to us?* Blah blah blah. And then they had a huge fight because Dad wanted to set me up with someone's weirdo son to make things all better, and Mom said nothing would make it all better and that we are all basically screwed until the end of time. And then Dad packed a bag and drove off." She shrugs.

"Shit. That sucks," I say.

"As far as I know, he may never come back. He didn't show up last night, anyway."

"Huh," I offer. For all of Claire and Gerry's fighting, I can't imagine either of them leaving and not coming back. I don't know what to say.

"Justin, too," she says, and hands me her phone with his texts on-screen. *Back after shit blows over. Don't worry about us.*

The bell rings for the end of sixth period and we start to get up and Kristina stops dead in her tracks. Her smile fades, and I can see the cockiness dissolve in waves. What's left is the friend I met when I was ten. Nice, vulnerable and sincere. The kind of kid who helps you unpack your boxes and arrange your room even though she just met you.

She starts to tear up. I don't think I've ever seen her cry about anything. "I can't go back in there," she says.

"You've lived through the worst of it," I say.

"No. There's a lot more. I can't go back in." She's shaking her head, and her lip is sticking out.

"You don't have to, I guess," I say. "You can just walk home. No one will stop you."

We look at each other. Kristina nods and starts walking toward the street entrance, and I run across the parking lot and in the side door by the industrial arts wing. We don't say good-bye.

▶ ▶ ▶

I block out everything I hear in the hallways.

They say: *Blah blah blah Kristina Houck.*

They say: *Blah blah blah Astrid Jones.*

They say: *Blah blah blah Justin Lampley.*

European history is Kevin in the back row whispering "Hey, dyke! Yo, lezzer!" the whole time. "One night with me and my crew would cure that, you know!"

▶ ▶ ▶

I walk home by myself and I think about stopping at Kristina's house, but I see her dad's car in the driveway and I don't want to make things more complicated for her. I always kinda wished Mom was more like Mrs. Houck—easygoing, not so obsessed with work, not so concerned with what people say about her. But I guess I was wrong. Maybe perfect people care more than us *unique* people do.

When I walk in the front door at home, the first thing I notice is the silence. Then, as I walk up the stairs to my room, I hear muffled talking. I walk past Mom's office, and it's empty and all the lights are off. The red message light is blinking on her answering machine.

The muffled talking is Mom and Ellis in Mom's room. I don't want to hear what they're saying, so I go into my room and close the door. I bring up Dee's number on my phone, and then I look at the text. *Stay away from my daughter.*

Can I just say *what the hell?* Only two days ago, we were in Atlantis being so free and open and in love, and everything was perfect. *Perfect. Abracadabra* was on the horizon. I was sure of everything—not to say I'm not sure now, but how am I supposed to feel about *stay away from my daughter?* I feel scared. I feel as though it's ruined. I feel like this was the final straw in a line of fails. The universe might be telling us we are not supposed to be together or something.

I try to write her a letter, but I start three of them and then crumple them up and stick them in my backpack in case Mom reads my trash while I'm at school. In the end, I decide I'll call her . . . tomorrow. I open a book and start doing homework.

Only when I cross paths with Dad on my way to the bathroom do I see into their bedroom as he closes the door behind him and realize that Mom is still in bed.

I'm shocked. I've seen Mom with pneumonia hacking up lungs while bent over that drawing table. Even that one time with that weird vertigo, she worked. She didn't wear heels, but she worked.

So maybe perfect people and *unique* people react similarly when their daughters get busted at a gay club.

▶ ▶ ▶

Ellis has gone to a friend's house for dinner, which is about as weird as Mom still being in bed. Dad has brought home lukewarm Chinese food. I can tell he still likes me after Saturday night because he's bought me crab Rangoon. Kinda soggy and cool crab Rangoon, but still. The thought counts. Mom and Ellis haven't really talked to me in two days now, so having someone give a shit around here is good.

While he changes out of his office clothes and into his Dude clothes, I crank the oven and put our Chinese food in to warm it a bit. I see Mom has ordered General Tso's chicken. I decide that she should have hers lukewarm, and I do not add it to the oven tray. He takes it to her on the wooden tray Ellis and I use for Mother's Day breakfast in bed.

When he sits down at the kitchen table and starts attacking his chow mein, I say, "Don't they feed you at work?"

"I skipped lunch."

"Me too," I say. "Thanks for the Rangoon."

"Sure, Strid." He hasn't called me Strid since I was in middle school.

"You have a good day at the office?"

"As good as can be expected. Still no stapler. You?"

"No comment."

"Yeah. I heard."

I assume he means from Mom, who heard from Ellis and whoever else said whatever made her stay in bed today. I nod.

I point to the ceiling. "Is she sick?"

He shakes his head.

"She'll be back to her normal General Tso self tomorrow?"

"Maybe," he says.

"Huh."

"We don't like that you're lying to us."

I don't answer.

"We only want to know you're okay, and if you're lying to us, then we don't know where you are." He takes a bite of his chow mein and adds, mouth full and noodle hanging out one side, "Both geographically and metaphysically, you know?"

"Yeah."

"Where are you, Strid?"

Two uses of my childhood pet name. Crab Rangoon. The two of us sitting here eating dinner together. Ellis at a friend's. Mom in bed. Only one explanation: He's been sent by the General to interrogate me.

"Geographically, I am at the dinner table, Dad. And metaphysically, I'm just fine. You know—just a rough day at school thanks to small-town living."

"It's safe to tell us stuff, okay?"

This means it's not safe to tell them anything.

"Sure, Dad," I say as I take my plate to the sink.

After dinner, I go out and lie on the table and send my

love to the sky. I can't see any planes, but I can hear them up there behind the clouds.

Exhaustion sets in as I lie here. I think about school tomorrow. I think about staying in bed like Mom. Or running away like Justin and Chad and Kristina and Mr. Houck. But I really don't feel like it. Plus tomorrow is the day I call Dee, and maybe everything will be all right.

I hear another jet above the clouds, and I whisper to it. "I love you. I love you. I love you. I love you." My eyelids get heavy, and I feel an instant urge to make today disappear by falling asleep until it's tomorrow. But I can't move.

▶ ▶ ▶

I am strapped to the table. My table. I am strapped with warm bungee cords—like octopus tentacles. Like rubber. Around my ankles, my forearms, my hips and my forehead. The needle plunges into my belly button and sucks something out. I can see it coming out through the translucent tube. They are storing part of me in a space jar—like a test tube. It is labeled, but I can't read the label.

The big one says, "You sent for us." I can't say anything because I am entirely bungeed. Even my tongue. "How did you know we were there?"

The little one says, "You are the only one who has ever found us."

The big one answers, "We love you too."

▶ ▶ ▶

The back door slams as Dad makes his way to the garage. I lie here and ask myself, *Just how many things do I have to invent in my head to survive this?*

I make Frank S. appear on his favorite bench by the back door. He answers, "As many as it takes."

I reach down to my belly button and make sure there's no wound, even though I know that there's no wound. "What are they extracting from me?" I ask, because even though these are my imaginary alien people, I have no idea what they are extracting.

"I don't know," Frank answers. "Maybe they're extracting the truth and saving it for later. Like you."

32

IT ONLY GETS WORSE, YOU KNOW.

ABOUT FIFTY-FOUR SECONDS before first period on Tuesday, I walk straight into Jeff Garnet and drop the books I'm carrying. He stops and looks at me, and his face is full of hurt and anger. Then he keeps walking, which makes me feel ten million times worse for everything I did to the kid. One of the people he's walking with kicks my copy of *The Republic* way down the hall, where Mr. Trig picks it up and hands it back to me.

"We miss you in trig," he says.

Which no doubt is weird but is meant as something positive, so I'll take it. It almost makes me want to draw a pink triangle and then measure the angles and sides and figure out the functions.

In humanities class, Ms. Steck concentrates on our previous discussion about Plato's Allegory of the Cave. She asks, "What do you think Plato meant to say when he talked about the freed people returning to the cave? Did he think they couldn't handle the outside world? Did he feel they needed to be controlled? What does that compare to in our society? Do we have places like the cave?" She glances at me when she asks this, but she doesn't call on me, and I send love to her for it. *Ms. Steck, I know you sat in that faculty room and heard every stupid rumor. I love you because this discussion is exactly what I needed.*

I will not be like Kristina and go back into the cave.

During the final five minutes of humanities, she says, "Only one week until Socrates week! Are you all ready?"

Clay shouts, "Hell yeah!" like he's at some basketball game or something, and it makes us all laugh.

"I want all paradoxes on my desk by Friday," Ms. Steck says. "If you want to change it, you'll have until project day to do that. But I want something from all of you by Friday. Got it?"

We all say, "Got it."

▶ ▶ ▶

During fourth-period study hall, I sit in the back corner of the auditorium, as far away from the Koch twins as I can, and when the teacher calls roll, I say, "Here," and no one makes me move. Students turn around and look at me. Some empathetically. Some meanly. Some just fly-catchingly, like codfish. I tell myself that the majority of people in study hall are fine people. The Koch twins are just lame. Kristina was right. They're probably jealous because of Jeff.

Speaking of Kristina, she's not here today. Which means it's just me against the world—all by myself.

Before American lit, I see a sign outside Ms. Steck's door. It reads: MS. STECK ♥'s PUSSY. Is it wrong for me to want to at least correct the misplaced apostrophe before I rip it off the wall and stuff it in my backpack?

▶ ▶ ▶

Mom is still in bed when I get home.

They say: *Did you hear Claire Jones is sick?*

They say: *That kind of news could kill a person.*

I hear the low murmur of Mom talking to Ellis through the bedroom door again—the two of them giggling and chatting about something giggly and chatty, so I knock.

I stand outside the door for a few minutes, and the two of them stay quiet. Then I slink to my room and close the door.

I call Kristina, and she answers on the first ring.

"Hey," I say.

"Hey."

"You ever coming back to school?"

"Maybe Friday. The Houcks are taking a last-minute autumn vacation to see the glorious leaves of New England," she says.

"Aren't the leaves all done already?"

"I don't know. It's all bullshit because my mother is still freaking out. Jesus. You'd have thought I killed someone."

"Have you talked to Donna?" I ask.

"We're texting, mostly. I don't want to piss off the parental units too much. But I told them that I love her, and I'm guessing it'll sink in one day. Maybe the leaves of Vermont will help them not be amoral assholes."

"So it's Astrid against the world this week, eh?" I ask.

"I guess. Believe me, I'd be there if I could. Being stuck in a car with these two for a few days is probably worse." I know it's not really worse. Mrs. Houck will probably let her drink fancy coffee drinks and eat pastries to make everyone feel better about their ruined lives. "Anything else?" she asks.

"Uh, no, I guess."

"I have to pack, you know?"

"Yeah. Of course," I say. "Have a nice trip."

She hangs up before she can even hear me say that.

Dad and I eat alone again. Pizza this time. He takes half of it upstairs, where the exclusive Mommy and Me–type slumber party is going on without us. He's too stoned to talk, and eats like a college student. I don't see Ellis until we meet in the hall outside the bathroom on our way to wash up before bed.

"You go," she says quietly. "I can wait."

"So what's with you?" I ask.

She sighs and crosses her arms. "Look, just leave me alone, okay? And whatever you do, don't talk to me in school. Let's just pretend we're not sisters for the rest of the year."

"Wow," I say. "That's shitty."

"You want to know what's shitty? Everybody in my home-room calling me a dyke!" She points to herself. "What's shitty is having to explain to people that it was you, *not me*, who was caught in a seedy gay club. What's shitty is what this whole thing has done to Mom. She can't even get out of bed. She knows everyone is talking about her."

I so want to tell Ellis that Mom can get out of bed. She's not paralyzed. She's just using this as another way to pull Ellis closer to her and farther from me. But I don't say that. Instead, I say, "She knows everyone is talking about her?"

"And me."

"And you," I say. "About her and you?"

"Yes, Astrid, I *know* the whole world is talking about you, too, but you *are* the one who chose to go out and shake your booty with your gays, you know?"

I stare at her before I turn around to leave. *Ellis, I love you even though you are a complete idiot.* It doesn't work. *Ellis, I love you even though you are brainwashed.* Nope. Still doesn't work. *Ellis, I'm sorry. I tried to love you, but right now I wish you weren't my sister, either.*

33

NOTHING MATTERS.

WEDNESDAY. I avoid looking up at school anymore.

People say: *I think Astrid Jones is gonna commit suicide.*

They say: *I hear Kristina Houck dumped her.*

They say: *She should just kill herself now.*

As I walk down the halls, I see them shackled to the waxed tile floor, ankle cuffs digging into their skin. I see how many of them need to be in the cave. I see the ones who will never leave and the ones who have to return because they can't handle what's outside. Which is: nothing. Nothing is outside. Rumors don't matter. Unity Valley reputations don't matter. Whether I'm gay or not doesn't really matter.

This is an extremely freeing thought. I smile all the way to my homeroom wing only to find some idiot has drawn this in red crayon on the block wall above my locker:

My God. Are people really that dumb? Why not Astrid and *Kristina*? Why not *Dyke* or *Fag* or some other acceptable U. Valley slur? But Astrid and *her own sister*?

Seriously. The realm of belief around here is breeding morons.

▶ ▶ ▶

In humanities class, people are starting to freak out and second-guess their paradoxes. No one shares because we all think we have the most original idea, but usually there are no original ideas. Ms. Steck told us that weeks ago.

I stare at the blinking cursor on the computer screen, and I type in my paradox and hit Send. *Equality is obvious.* I wonder what Frank Socrates would say about that.

▶ ▶ ▶

In study hall, I overhear people talking about Aimee Hall's mom. Apparently she came in yesterday and freaked out because she heard that her daughter has to sit in classes with *known homosexuals.* I try not to break out into a sweat when I hear this. I look around and realize that everyone in this room is, right now, being forced to sit in a class with a *known homosexual.*

Then the story gets worse.

Last night, Mrs. Hall and one other parent showed up at the school board meeting and complained that the Unity Valley School District has a "homosexual agenda" and made calls for three teachers to resign.

One of the teachers is Ms. Steck.

They say: *She's not married. You know what that means.*

Another is Mr. Williams because he kicked some kid out of class for denying the Holocaust. How this fits into the "homosexual agenda" is beyond me.

"That makes no sense," Clay from humanities says.

"Whatever," the blond who's telling the story says. "It's about our freedom. To be who we are, whether we recognize gays or not."

Clay just looks at her. Then he scratches his head. Then he

goes back to the novel he's reading. I sit there and play a word game in my head. I replace the word *gays* from her sentence with these other words: *blacks, Hispanics, immigrants, women, people of mixed race, Jehovah's Witnesses, Gypsies, Russians, Poles, Yugoslavians, Ukrainians, mentally and physically disabled.*

Frank says, "Bingo, Astrid Jones."

"Bingo? You say bingo?"

"Isn't it great what they teach you in school these days?" He pats my knee and adjusts his toga so it doesn't reveal too much while he sits in the low auditorium seat.

I'm so glad I have Frank. I kinda miss Kristina this week, but I also kinda don't. Either way, Frank is filling the void. I mean, as much as he can, considering he's dead and in my head.

▶ ▶ ▶

Ellis is waiting for me outside of my lit class. She's sobbing.

"Couldn't you cover it up with something?" she screams. "Couldn't you deny it or report it or do *something normal?*"

"What are you talking about?" I ask.

"That SHIT above your locker!" Next to her is Jessie, her running and hockey friend. Dee's camp friend. I give her a weak wave.

I realize I have no idea why I didn't do anything about it. I guess I figured no one would care. "I'm really sorry, El."

"It's not just *your* name up there, you know!" she says. This is like one million on the flying-monkey scale for her.

"Yeah, totally. I know," I say. "Look, I'll go report it now. I figured it would be gone first thing, like any other graffiti, I guess. I really am sorry."

She just walks off with Jessie, who gives me an empathetic look.

When I see Ellis at lunch, she's sitting up near the salad bar with Aimee Hall and her band of merry rumor-makers. I'd be lying if I said the mere thought of what could be said at that table right now doesn't make me feel sick.

I sit by myself.

I hear things.

They say: *Astrid Jones was the one who took them out to that place, you know. Must be those city roots.*

They say: *If I was the Houcks, I'd rip her a new one.*

It really is amazing what some people will say. I can't wait to tell Kristina this one when she gets back. We'll laugh until we pee, I bet.

▶ ▶ ▶

Before seventh period, I drop in and tell Ms. Steck I'm skipping lit mag this week. She nods as if she already knew this.

"Did you see those?" she asks, and points to the blackboard. There are two more signs like the one I pulled off the wall yesterday. One says DYKES NEED DICK! Same lettering as the sign in my backpack. "I'm starting a collection," she says. "Kids can be so clever."

The other sign reads ADAM AND EVE, NOT ADAM AND STEVE, which is wholly unoriginal.

"Yeah," I say. "People here are really bright."

Ms. Steck says, "Just remember it's a small minority."

I reach into my backpack and find the MS. STECK ♥'s PUSSY sign from yesterday, and I take it to the board and straighten it out. We tape it there together, and I draw an arrow in chalk to the apostrophe and write UNNECESSARY APOSTROPHE. FAIL.

▶ ▶ ▶

There are three afternoon announcements after the usual list of kids who need to report to the vice principal for disciplining. The first one is about a change in tomorrow's lunch menu—not chicken patties but turkey cheesesteaks. The second one is about how Monday's schedule will change because for third and fourth periods, the entire school will recognize a Day of Tolerance with an assembly and a "No Hate" pep rally. I don't hear the third announcement because I'm too busy hearing the blood pulse through my ears and feeling like there is a hot direct spotlight on me.

34

IRON THIS.

WHEN I GET HOME, Mom is sitting at the kitchen table waiting for me. With Dad. Ellis is upstairs playing her music too loudly. Something is really different, but I can't figure out what it is.

The letter from the district magistrate's office is at my place setting, opened.

"Hi, Mom," I say. "Glad you're feeling better."

I look past her into the living room. I make out three distinct shapes. The ironing board. The iron, on, with its little red light glowing. A pile of—what is that?

"Ellis tells me that you're having a hard time this week at school," she says.

"Actually, it's not that bad."

"Hmm. Well, *she's* having a bad time this week at school," she says.

Dad says, "And this Tolerance Day next week is something she can't do. It's too difficult for her after . . . this."

I shrug.

She adds, "You know people are saying it about her now, too, right?"

"Saying what?" I ask, even though I know exactly what she's talking about. But if we're all so New York City open-minded, then why are we making such a big effing deal out of this?

"We want to know if you're gay," Mom says. "We can't really go any further with you until we know the truth."

"You can't go further with me? What does that mean?" I ask. "As parents?"

Dad says, "We're doing the best we can, but with all your lying, we don't think we can get you back on track until everything is out in the open."

Back on track. Can't go any further. Sounds like they've been watching Dr. Phil or something. "I didn't know I was off the track," I say. I go to the cabinet and fetch a few Rolaids and chew on them.

"You didn't?" Dad says.

"For Christ's sake, Astrid, look at you!" Mom says over him.

I look at myself. I look exactly the same as I did a week ago, before Atlantis got busted. I look exactly the same as I did five months ago, before I started kissing Dee in the walk-ins. "I don't look any different than I did last week, do I?" Frank hops up onto the kitchen counter, crosses his arms and snickers.

"I think your mother means your criminal record."

"And the lying!" she adds.

"And the lying!" Frank says.

"Oh," I say. And then I notice what's different: It's the curtains. All the curtains are down. Even the privacy lace ones. That's what's in the pile next to the ironing board. Mom is washing and ironing all of the curtains.

Which is why it's so bright for a dreary November afternoon.

"Well? Can you tell us the truth?" Dad asks.

"How come you're ironing the curtains?" I ask.

"What?"

"That must have taken you all day. Why didn't you get them washed and pressed at the dry cleaner?"

Dad leans forward. "Does this mean yes?"

"Yes?" I ask. I already forgot the question.

"Are you gay?" Mom asks.

I sigh. "I have no idea," I say. Frank sighs and rolls his eyes.

Mom perks up. "So, we went from *I'm not gay, I was just in a gay club to dance* to *I don't know.*"

"Right," I say.

"So does this mean yes?" Dad asks again. I look at Frank Socrates, and he says, in my head, *Settle for nothing less than the truth. Even if the answer is* I don't know.

"No," I say. "It means I don't know. It's really not as easy as you're making it."

"Don't give me that," Mom says.

"What?"

"It's not a choice. Either you're born gay or you're not born gay," she says.

"While I appreciate your strict categorization and policies of gayness, I can't say that I know one way or the other. So, logic tells me that if I was born gay, then I should know that I am gay, which means, by your rules, no. I am not gay. Because I don't know." They stare at me. I start writing a list on a piece of notepaper as I talk. "But if it's about love and attraction to people of the same gender and a possibility of maybe being in love with a girl, then the answer could be yes. But I wouldn't call myself gay. It just wouldn't seem right to real gay people. Especially if they were born knowing for sure, like you say they were."

"Jesus Christ! Can you just cut the sarcasm and answer the damn question?" Mom yells.

"I just did answer the question," I say, still writing without looking up.

"You can't give us a yes or a no?" Dad asks. I can tell he's dying to get out to that garage as soon as humanly possible. He's nearly drooling.

"Not really," I say. "Sorry." *However, I can give you a leave-me-the-hell-alone-why-does-it-matter-so-damn-much-and-it's-none-of-your-goddamn-business. Love you.* "It's just not as simple as you're making it out to be. I don't think every gay person can be clearly defined and kept in a nifty little box, you know?"

After a minute of silence, Dad says, "So you're not going to tell us."

"I just told you."

Mom says, "Frankly, I'm even more disappointed than I was before we started."

I sigh. I'm exhausted by them. I'm exhausted by me. I'm exhausted by having to be me, with them.

I finish my list. It reads: *Here is a list of things you can put in a box: Puppies. Lipstick. Jump ropes. Jewelry. Card games. Hair accessories. Love letters. Spoons. Office supplies. Nail polish. Art projects. Leaves collected on an autumn walk. Cereal bowls. Popsicle sticks. Used staples. Books. Action figures. Weapons of mass destruction. Model cars. Pictures of loved ones. Thumbtacks.* I put it in my pocket.

Mom says, "Kristina's mother says that going to that bar was your idea. We can't figure out where you'd come up with that idea if you haven't been lying to us. I'd like to know when you first went there, and I want to know how you got in and—"

"Wait. What?" I look at her. "What did you just say?" This particular piece of bullshit was fine as a stupid high school rumor, but this is different.

"I talked with Kristina, too. She told me you had to drag her there."

I stare at her. I become Very Serious Astrid. I sit up straight. I take a deep breath. "Kristina said that I dragged her to Atlantis?"

"Yes. She said she'd never thought about it before because she and Justin were meeting their *friends* on those double dates they used to take." She winces a bit with the term *double dates*.

"That's complete bullshit," I say. "I can't believe she said that."

Frank says, "Really? I can."

"I don't have any reason to disbelieve her, do I?" Mom says.

Mom sits there with her eyebrows up in a judgmental arch.

"Like—only her *entire freaking life* was a lie, Mom. And all of you bought it! Only a few weeks ago you were asking me about her and Justin and Homecoming. How about *that* lie?" I yell.

"Well." She stops for a second as if she's about to say something nice. "Until she and her mother come here and tell me they lied, I believe them. They're good people."

"And I'm not?"

"I didn't say that," she says.

"She dragged me there after bugging me for months. She didn't even know about—uh." I stop.

"About what?" Mom asks.

"About any questions I might have about stuff like that." I send love to myself for playing that so vague. *Astrid, man, you're smooth. I love the way you just made that completely obtuse. Nice save.*

"So you're saying the exact opposite? That Kristina dragged *you* there?" Mom says.

"Yes."

Dad sighs. "I don't see why this even matters."

I say, "It matters to me because my best friend just screwed me over when it was all her idea. I'll never trust her again. Maybe the only friend she has in this house is you now, Mom."

Dad looks concerned. Mom looks a mix of confused and smug. Frank S. looks hungry. He gets up and looks in the fridge.

"I checked the story with the few people in town who I trust. They said that's the version they heard, too."

I stare at her. "That's because they're repeating what they heard...from Mrs. Houck, probably."

"Either way, my daughter dragged a fifth of the town's Homecoming Court to a gay bar and got them all arrested."

"That's bullshit and technically, we didn't get arrested."

"Oh, for Christ's sake. I don't know why I bother to try to get an honest answer out of you. You haven't said anything... meaningful to me in years." She goes into the living room and turns on a table lamp and begins to attack the curtains with the hot iron. I sit there and have thoughts about attacking *her* with a hot iron. *Meaningful?* As if she wasn't too busy dressing Ellis up in diamonds and velvet to hear me if I ever did offer anything meaningful. As if she'd ever think anything I said was meaningful. Jesus.

Dad gets up and goes out the back door toward the garage, and I almost want to follow him and ask him if I can have a toke off the pipe just so I can unhear what she just said.

Instead, I go to my picnic table. As I lie here, bundled in my winter coat and scarf, I can smell Dad's wafting pot smoke, and I find three planes all flying in a row in the dusky sky. Once I let go of how mad I am at Mom, I realize that I'm steaming about Kristina. On fire. Smoldering. Exploding.

I think of all the bossy moments and the perfect ponytail moments and the pressuring moments and what she made me do to Jeff Garnet. I'm too angry to lie here. I get up and walk to the edge of our yard and then back to the garage. Then I go past the side door and out onto the street and then over to

Kristina's house, where no lights are on and the minivan is still missing from the driveway. I sit on the back porch and swing on the swing.

I look around for something to vandalize. Something to punch.

I walk over to the back storm door and write *LIAR* on the glass with my finger, but it's so clean, I don't think anyone will see it. I write it again on the siding by the back door and the stone and the pear trees that line the back path. I write it on the garage door. Five times. *LIAR LIAR LIAR LIAR LIAR.*

They say: *Did you see Astrid Jones acting crazy over at the Houck place tonight?*

They say: *I told you they broke up.*

Then, after one last *LIAR* on the black mailbox, I walk across the street to our house and get back on my table.

I find airplanes in the sky. I watch them. I picture the passengers. But I can't find any love at all to send to them. I try my mantra. *I love you. I love you. I love you. I love you.* It's hollow and stupid.

I don't love anyone right now. Not even me.

"This is the longest Wednesday in the history of man," I say to Frank S., who is sitting in his favorite spot on the bench by the back patio door.

"Try being on trial for *impiety* on a Wednesday. It's far worse."

▶ ▶ ▶

When my phone rings, I think it's Kristina feeling all the bad vibes I'm sending out. But it's Dee. The minute her number comes up, I hear it: *Stay away from my daughter.*

"Hey! I was going to call you later." I say.

"I miss you so much!" she says back. It makes me grin a huge grin.

"Me too. It feels like a year went by since—uh—Saturday."

"I am sooooo sorry about that message my mom sent," she says. "It was so uncool. I nearly died when I saw it."

"It's okay." I am so relieved that I forget about Kristina the liar for a minute. And Claire the neglected mother who never gets to hear anything *meaningful*.

"Seriously. I nearly killed her. I'm really sorry."

"Really. It's fine." I say. "I'm sorry I took you out to a bar that got busted. I feel like a tool."

"How would you know that was going to happen? And anyway, you didn't take me. I drove there all on my own."

"Still. I had to say it," I say.

"You okay, Jones? I hear all kinds of shit. Even an entire school district away."

"That's a really long line of whisper down the lane. I can only imagine the discrepancies."

We laugh. It's nice.

"Don't believe what you hear," I say. "Unless you hear that my mother and Ellis have disowned me, and my best friend is a lying bitch," I say. "But I'm not going to jump off any cliffs, if that's what you mean."

"I'm glad," she says. "And, hey, admit it. It feels nice to be out, right? No more hiding. No more secrets?"

"Uh."

"What?" she says.

"Uh. I didn't really tell anyone," I say. "I mean, it's been such a hectic week, and the only person I've really seen is my dad, and he's just—uh—useless," I say. I mean stoned. *Useless and stoned.*

"Hold up. They don't even know about you?"

"Nope."

"But *everyone* knows!"

"Not them. Not yet, at least." I don't mention that they don't know because I haven't told them I know, either.

"What about me?" she asks.

"What?"

"Do they know about me?"

"They don't know about anything."

"Why?" she says. It's slightly whiny.

"I haven't found the right time yet. That's all."

"Dude, this weekend was the right time. Right? That's when I told my mom."

"And she wrote me that text," I say. *Stay away from my daughter.*

"Again—sorry. She doesn't want you to stay away. It was just her reaction. You know. She was being protective. My hockey scholarships. My reputation. I'm *still* freaked out about the hockey scholarships. I even talked to Coach about it, and she's pissed at me." She takes a deep breath. "I asked my mom to call you or text you back to apologize, but she was too embarrassed."

"Yeah," I say. "Tell her not to be embarrassed."

"But you really should just come out, you know? Beats lying. And sneaking around. I'm not sure I can do that anymore."

Oh. She's not sure she can do that anymore. Last week she was fine with it. I reach into my pocket and retrieve my list, and I add things to it.

ME: *Pre-sharpened pencils, halibut fillets, highlighter markers.*

ME: Stop blocking people out, Astrid.

ME: *Used tissues, superhero figurines, jewelry.*

ME: Come on. It's Dee. You have to let your guard down somewhere, right?

Awkward silence for what feels like twenty whole seconds while I talk to myself inside my head.

ME: Why are you doing this to yourself?

ME: It's protection.

ME: It's only going to make you lonely.

ME: And I'm not lonely already?

"Astrid?" Dee asks. "We still good?"

"As far as I know," I say.

35

YOU CAN IRON
THE CURTAINS STRAIGHT.

MOM IS STILL IRONING when I get downstairs at 6:40 AM on Thursday. I can't tell if she's been here all night or if she got up early. I hear Ellis get into the shower and Dad flush the downstairs toilet soon after. This makes Ellis screech and Dad stand outside the main bathroom door and yell, "I'm sorry!"

As I pour a bowl of corn flakes, I count how many times someone in this house apologized to me for flushing while I was in the shower. That would be zero times.

Dad arrives and walks straight for the coffeemaker and makes a cup of very light, very sweet coffee and sits down at the table across from me. Mom continues to iron.

"Any answers today for us, Strid?"

"Huh?"

"About our conversation last night. We just want answers."

"I thought I gave you answers," I say.

"Okay," he says. Then he leans over the table and whispers, so his coffee/morning breath bowls me over. "Can't you just make something up?" He moves his eyes to the sides of their sockets to draw my attention to my ironing mother.

Poor guy. It must suck to get to thirty thousand feet and realize that your pilot is a control freak nutjob.

When I look at her, I see our house as a mini cave, and her fire as a mini fire that casts mini shadows for us mini shackled prisoners. We are a cave within a cave within a cave. Our little house on Main Street (with the immaculately pressed curtains) is part of the Unity Valley cave, which has its Unity Valley fire that casts Unity Valley shadows. And Unity Valley is just a cave inside the big American cave that is a huge fire that casts the biggest shadows of all.

"Strid?" Dad whispers again.

"Stop calling me that," I say. Then I get up and rinse out my bowl and put it into the dishwasher.

When I get to my room and get dressed, I decide that I'm going to skip school for the first time ever.

I walk up the road toward school and then I double back to my car, which has been sitting in the same space since Sunday's trip to the diner. I hop in, start her up and drive to the lake because who'd go to the lake on a cold day like this?

I park in the empty lot and lock my doors. I put my seat back and try to fall asleep, but I can't get past the warning signals in my brain about some ex-convict finding me here and drowning me in the lake after doing unspeakable things. So I sit up and roll down my window.

ME: Maybe you can call that Kim girl from the party that night and go hang out there today.

ME: You're a moron.

ME: No, really. She seemed into you. And you don't have anywhere else to go, right?

I pull out my phone and scroll through the numbers until I get to Kim's number, which I put into my phone under the name *Pizza* in case anyone found it. I look up into the clear sky over the lake, and I start to cry a little.

ME: That's good. Get it off your chest.

ME: *(sobs)*

ME: You'll figure it all out, I promise.

ME: What's there to figure out? My best friend lied about me, and my girlfriend doesn't like me anymore.

ME: Dude, Dee loves you.

ME: Dee has conditions. Kristina has conditions. Mom has conditions.

ME: Everyone has conditions if you look at it that way.

ME: No. Frank Socrates doesn't have conditions, because he's dead. He loves me unconditionally.

ME: Stop being difficult.

I get out of the car and go over to one of the five wooden tables in the grassy picnic area. Inferior-quality tables compared to mine and Dad's. The wood is rotting in spots, not to mention covered in graffiti and gnawed away on the corners by forest animals. The surface needs a good sanding, and I don't move much because I don't feel like getting splinters in my ass. I think today is already sucky enough without splinters in my ass.

This sending-love-to-the-passengers thing is getting old, somehow. I mean, I still have to do it the minute I see a plane—it's a reflex, like covering my mouth when I cough—but I don't want to send my love away forever. I want it to be safe here. I want my life to be easier than this. I mean, I know I'm not some starving kid who has to wash clothes in the Ganges for a nickel, but today just sucks. My guts are all twisted up over Kristina and her stupid lie, and Dee and her pressuring me, and Mom and our lack of *meaningful* conversations.

The sky is amazing at lakeside. It's huge. And it's quiet here. There's no traffic. No bikers because it's ten o'clock on a school day. All I hear are birds.

When I see the first plane, I make a deal with its passengers. I say: *Look, this is a loan. I don't know if love is something I will run out of one day. I don't know if I should be giving it all to you guys or not. Today, I feel like maybe I should have kept some for myself for days when no one else loves me. Not even my best friend.*

My eyes well up with tears again, and I feel stupid and dramatic.

ME: You're not being dramatic. This hurts.

And then I send the love up. It's as easy as it always is, and it's hard, too, because I really don't know the answer to this mystery. Is love something that will always be available? Will it always be confined and untrustworthy like it feels today? Is there enough to go around? Am I wasting mine on strangers?

PASSENGER #980
JAMEY WIEDNER, SEAT 27E
FLIGHT #504
PHILADELPHIA TO CHICAGO

The problem with my job is that I fall in love too quickly. Men come to me for companionship. They pay me to be the good-looking young guy on their arm. They pay me for other stuff, too.

They don't fall in love like I do, though. They have parents and siblings and people who love them already. Some of them have partners. Wives and kids. It's not my business to know, but they tell me anyway. Some guys have a lot of love, and it's still not enough.

But they don't love me. They just use me and then put me on the next flight out.

It's lonely, but I'm okay. I just fall in love a lot, and I shouldn't. And sometimes I end up in the wrong place at the wrong time. And sometimes I don't get paid enough. Sometimes I dream that I'll be rich one day and be able to go to college and get a job. Then I remember that it takes a lot of clients to get rich...unless one of them falls in love like I do.

As we fly over the mountains, I get this feeling I've never felt before. I can't explain why I feel it or how, but it's a big feeling. Bigger than I can put into words. It's all-encompassing, like all the love I've poured into all the someones I've loved is now coming back to me. Like someone *is loving me back* for the first time in my life. And I know that everything's going to work out. Maybe someday, someone will fall in love with me. I'll go to college. I'll be rich. Or at least I can help people like me so they don't have to do what I've done.

I stare out the window and smile because just dreaming it is nice...even if it doesn't happen. Just dreaming it is nice.

▶ ▶ ▶

I don't have a lot of love to send right now. Or maybe I'm being stingy. My heart just isn't in it, so I get up off the table and into my car and start driving toward the college town where Donna lives. I don't remember how we got to the Gamma Alpha Psi house, but I'm sure if I drive around enough, I might find it.

> ME: And what will you do once you get there? Call
> Kim? Run off and get married? What are you
> doing?
> ME: Just driving. Leave me alone.

▶ ▶ ▶

By the time I get on and off the turnpike, I'm starving, so I go to a drive-thru and then cruise the fraternity and sorority houses looking for those familiar Greek letters. It's about noon. The sidewalks are busy with students. I stop to eat my bacon double cheeseburger and watch them. I think: *That will be me at this time next year.*

I've been so caught up in Dee and Kristina and our secrets and now this whole mess that I've forgotten my entire future. No Ellis. No Mom and Dude. No Kristina bossing me around. Not even Dee if I don't want her in my life. I will hear scholarship news in the next few months. My grades rock. I should be concentrating on *me.*

College kids look happy. And free. After I crumple the uneaten part of my burger in its wrapper and stuff it into the bag, I realize my future is only a few months away, and I will be one of the free, happy people. And then I start the car again and head for the turnpike. I turn up the music to block out the sound of my own thoughts. When I get to Unity Valley, I pull over into the Legion Diner parking lot and I text Kristina. *You coming back any time this decade?*

She texts back. *On our way now. Should be back by dinner.*

I park in the fairground parking lot hidden behind Kristina's house and abandoned since the last fair of the season. I walk to Kristina's back porch and sit on the swing, and I start thinking about what Kristina said. And I decide that I'm done being a pushover.

▶ ▶ ▶

"What a surprise!" Mrs. Houck says when she finds me sitting on her back porch. She's got a suitcase in either hand, and after she says this, her face makes a frown. The kind of frown I'd have expected from a mother who thinks I corrupted her daughter. Then Kristina shows up as Mrs. Houck jiggles her key into the back door.

"Dude. You can't live here. I already told you that," Kristina says. She's joking, so I figure this must mean she doesn't know how much I want to kill her right now.

"We need to talk," I say.

She nods and goes back to the car to get more things. "Let me get the rest of my stuff," she says. Her smile has disappeared. She must know why I'm here. I use my finger's imaginary marker on her back as she walks up the path to the driveway. *LIAR LIAR LIAR*, I write down her back. When she gets back with her last bag and a pillow, she says, "I'll be out in a minute."

I get up and pace. I see Mr. Houck is not in the car. Strange. I thought they went as a family. Then I hear Mrs. Houck whisper-yelling through the open door. I don't hear what she says. I don't care what she says. I trace the word *LIARS* onto the side of the house. I face out toward the big barn they have as a garage, and I write it in imaginary letters twenty feet high.

"So?" Kristina says.

"Wanna take a quick ride somewhere?" I ask.

"Where?"

"Anywhere but here, I guess."

"Do we have to?" she asks. "I have to unpack."

I have to pack. I have to unpack. These are things that never mattered to Kristina before Tuesday.

I face her when we reach the driveway. "If you want, we can sit right here," I say.

She sits down on the ground. I sit down next to her.

"So I heard the big lie you told about me, and I can't understand why you'd do it."

She looks a mix of surprised and ashamed. "I—uh—I'm not sure what you mean," she says.

"You know exactly what I mean."

She sits silent for a while then says, "I didn't tell any lie."

"Really?" I'm surprisingly calm. "You didn't tell your mom a lie, which she then told the whole town? About me dragging you to Atlantis...almost against your will? That lie?"

She acts surprised. "What? I never said that!"

"Dude. You told my mom to her face. You said it. And I think you made it up because you can't handle not being the perfect little Unity Valley Homecoming princess anymore."

She smirks at me.

"Well?" I ask.

"Well, what did you lose? Nothing. That's what you lost."

"I lost my sister, my mother—who believes you and your mom and not me—and my father. And my best friend, who would rather lie about me to save her skin."

"You still didn't lose nearly as much as me."

"What the hell are you talking about? What did you lose? You weren't even in school this week to hear anything! And your little lie made you the victim of Astrid Jones's evil gay plot to get you out to a bar, right? Isn't that how you wanted it to play out?" I yell. "And it worked perfectly! Good job,

Kristina Houck. Mission accomplished. You set up your best friend after she kept your secret for over two years, and then you lost her. Nice job." I get up and dust off my butt.

I start walking toward the fairgrounds to my car. "Wait!" she yells. She's following me. "Wait!"

"Did you lie about me or not, Kristina?"

She stands there dumbfounded. I get in my car and drive away.

▶ ▶ ▶

I approach Dad after his evening toke.

"I need a sick note for today," I say. "I totally skipped school."

He looks at me and shakes his head and smiles. "It just keeps getting worse with you."

"Nah. Today was just the day off I should have had on Monday. I want to get back."

"Where'd you go?" he asks.

"Nowhere special."

I hand him the blank absentee card, and he scribbles his signature on it, and I slip it into my backpack before I go to bed.

When I walk through the kitchen to get to the stairs, I look into the living room and see that Mom is still ironing.

36

FRIDAY IS JUST GROSS.

I WAKE UP LATE on Friday and rush to the bathroom to wet my hair and brush my teeth. In the hall, I meet Ellis wrapped in a towel. When she sees me, she grabs the front of the towel and pulls it up to her neck and scurries into her room quickly, as if I'll become aroused at the sight of my own sister in a towel.

I don't have enough gross words in my gross vocabulary to describe how gross that gross thought is. Gross.

While I'm brushing my teeth, I think about how our sisterhood deteriorated. I blame Mom. Of course. But as I look at myself in the mirror, I see some other stuff. My snubbing her when she decided to be a small-town girl. Me deciding she didn't need me anymore when she got old enough to stop watching *The Wizard of Oz*. Me not inviting her when Dad and I would make stuff together. Me deciding that Mom would always like her more...and having it reflect on her instead of just on Mom.

So maybe I helped it happen. Maybe we'd be closer. If I told her the truth, she'd probably accept me eventually, and we could just be sisters again.

None of this changes the fact that what she just did was gross.

▶ ▶ ▶

The janitor took pity on me and cleaned off the wall above my locker, even though I can still see the flecks of red crayon embedded in the crannies of the painted cinder blocks. I know it makes me a horrible person, but after Ellis's grossness this morning, I kinda wish it was still there.

"They closed down your bar," I hear from behind me. It's Jeff Garnet. "Did you see in the paper today?"

I take a deep breath. "It wasn't my bar. And no, I didn't see that."

"Well, they closed it, and they arrested the owner, I think."

"Huh," I say. "I guess that's what you get for serving underage kids." What else am I supposed to say? I turn around so he's not talking to my back anymore.

"I'm really sorry, Jeff. About everything. I shouldn't have lied to you. I was totally wrong, and I—"

"It's cool, Astrid. I mean, I think you're really nice, you know?"

Oh, man. I am so not nice. I am the opposite of nice when it comes to what I did to Jeff Garnet. I want to say *I am scum* because I feel like scum. But before I can, he talks again.

"Your mom called my mom last night," he says.

I just stare at him like I'm totally scared of what he's going to come out with next. Because I am.

"Did you hear me?"

"Yeah. Sorry about her. She's nuts."

"She asked my mom to talk to me about how you just made a mistake and went there so you could drink and dance and stuff. Is that true?"

"Yeah, kinda." *No, not at all.*

"She wanted to know if I'd go out with you again."

"Oh, God," I say. "I'm really sorry. Just ignore her. She hasn't been able to locate her mind-your-own-business medication for years." I think my cheeks are actually purple. They physically hurt.

He's fidgeting as though he's actually about to ask me out again. I can see his leg going all jiggly. "Look, I'm really sorry, but I'm kinda going out with Karen Koch now," he says.

Do I look as relieved as I am?

I say, "I am so happy to hear that! You guys are perfect for each other. God! She's been into you for a long time."

I send my love to Jeff Garnet. *Jeff, I love you. Not in that way, so don't even try it. But I love you since you've been standing here talking to me like a normal person for more than a minute. I hope Karen totally lets you in her pants, okay?*

"Cool. So we're cool?" he says.

"Totally. And thanks for coming to talk to me. You're the first person who's talked to me for more than a few seconds in a whole week."

"Shit—you know it'll blow over. Everything blows over around here." We nod at each other. It makes me feel better. Then he says, "But that Justin and Kristina thing was a bit hard to take, man. I can't believe they lied like that. And I used to change next to him for gym all the time." He makes a cringing, concerned face.

"Don't worry. He's not into you."

"Yeah, but still. It's weird," he says. "I hear he's in jail now."

I shake my head. "Don't believe what you hear."

As he walks away, I think about what he said about Justin in the locker room, and I think about Ellis and her gross towel thing this morning, and I figure out what confuses people so much about other people being gay. They think it's all about sex.

▶ ▶ ▶

Humanities class is abuzz with paradoxes. Most people are still keeping them secret, but one, in particular, is tossed out for Ms. Steck and me to hear.

Penny Uppergrove says, "Love is between a man and a woman."

Ms. Steck continues to work with another student on a computer in the back of the room. Clay turns around and says, "I think that's one of the best ones I've heard."

"Thank you," Penny says.

"So what you're saying is that love *can't possibly* only be between just a man and a woman because that lacks all common sense. For example, a woman can love her child, correct? And a boy can love his dog. And I, personally, love peanut butter and banana sandwiches. Good paradox. Well done."

"But that's not what I meant," she says. Then she gets flustered and starts going through her notes.

"Oh. Then color me confused," Clay says. "What else could you mean?"

"Shit," she says. "So a Socratic paradox is about something that probably *isn't* true, but you make it sound true?" She shuffles through her notebook and finds a part she highlighted in pink. "So I *should* say the opposite."

Clay rolls his eyes. "Whatever you say, you can't really know it's true unless you can truly define it," he says.

She scribbles a little, and I look in my notebook at my paradox that I already sent to Ms. Steck via e-mail. *Equality is obvious.* I think this raises a sufficient amount of questions that I could argue all day about it.

Penny holds up her hands. "I got it! I got it! God! Why does this philosophy stuff have to be so difficult? Give me calculus any day!" She looks at Clay. "How about this?" She's just about to read, and then she stops. "Shit. No. That doesn't work." She goes back to her scribbling.

Ms. Steck stands up and moves to her desk. "Today's the day! I need those paradoxes on my desk before you leave. Don't be worried if you get a better idea over the weekend. Philosophy does stuff to your brain. Makes you change your mind a lot. That's good. I don't care if you come to me Wednesday morning with a completely different paradox from the one you give me today. Just give me *something* today! And don't forget to research what you're going to wear. It all counts toward your grade."

They say: *She gets off on seeing girls in togas.*

Penny hits her desk with her fist. "I got it!" She writes it down and shoves it into her folder.

Ms. Steck sits on the edge of her desk. "Before we go into Plato's cave for the last day, I want to talk a little about next week's Day of Tolerance, because this kind of stuff is what philosophy is all about. I'm sure you all have your own ideas of why the administration is doing it, and I'm sure you all saw the wonderful display I've had on my blackboard for the last few days." She refers to the signs that are still taped on the board. My arrow is still there. UNNECESSARY APOSTROPHE. FAIL.

"Since we all have wildly different ideas about ethics and morality, I was thinking about how to approach this in class, or if we even should. And then"—she snaps—"then! I got a great idea.

"Since you're Unity Valley's best and brightest, I was thinking I could do an experiment." She hands out little pieces of gray quiz paper.

"With all the recent votes and discussions in the news, I think we're all pretty sick of talking about gay marriage. So I don't want to talk about it. Instead, let's vote. I want you to write one thing on the paper I've just handed you. I want a YES or a NO. Yes means you vote YES for gay marriage rights. NO means you would not give gay people the right to get married. Everyone got that?"

We all nod.

"Then toss your votes into the box here." She puts a shoe box on Clay's desk.

Penny Uppergrove raises her hand.

"Yes, Penny?"

"Is this part of our grade?"

"Nope. Just a fun in-class exercise," Ms. Steck says.

I write YES and fold the paper in half and in half again and put it in the box.

After a final discussion about Plato's cave, we are left to our usual ten minutes of free time. Some are still struggling with their paradox, and they summon Ms. Steck to their desks or to the computer lab.

Before the end of class, Ms. Steck takes the shoe box off Clay's desk and tallies the votes. She writes the results on the board.

NO wins, twelve votes to ten. Ms. Steck doesn't say anything. She just leaves the results on the board above the ugly homophobic signs, and all I can think of is what she called us: Unity Valley's best and brightest. And we're three votes short of equality.

I snap a picture of the results and the signs with my phone. Since Justin isn't around, it seems someone should document it.

▶ ▶ ▶

The first and last time I see Kristina today is at lunch. She's sitting at a table with her popular friends. I sit by myself in a booth to the right. When they all look over at me, I can imagine what she's saying. The lie. Maybe even bigger lies. Maybe a skyscraper of lies. I think about what she said to me last night. How I had nothing to lose and how she had everything to lose.

I count eight people at her table. I count zero at mine.

37

I USED TO LOOK FORWARD TO WORKING ON WEEKENDS.

DEVEINING SHRIMP HAS BECOME my Zen thing. I know they're going to ask me to do it, so I look forward to doing it, and I make sure I do it well. Sometimes it means I go a little slower than they'd like, but then they can fire me. I've seen Jorge's cousin devein shrimp. His method is called *mangling the shrimp*.

I have to retrieve a box of shrimp from the walk-in, and I stop for a second once the door closes behind me, and I breathe. In. Out. In. Out. *I'd put my bed there.* In. Out. In. Out. *I'd put my vanity there.* In. Out. In. Out. *And I'd put a desk over there, under the light.* I look at the cage around the lightbulb. I know it's caged for protection—so no truck-driving supplier tosses a box into the corner and shatters the bulb. But I can't help seeing a cage for what it is. Sure, it protects the bulb, but maybe if people weren't so careless, then nothing would need to be caged.

I get my box of shrimp and let the door slam behind me. I'm happy Dee didn't come in after me. I'm glad to see her, but I'm still mad about what she said the other day.

When it's time for Dee to chop veggies, she stops every few minutes and smiles at me. I try not to smile back, but I can't help it. She probably forgot that she even said that thing about how I should come out. She's just in love with me. And then I realize something. Dee doesn't care about all the rumors. She doesn't care about anything except her life, her future, and playing hockey and getting into Bloomsburg and playing more hockey. And being happy. She's like Frank S. but a lot cuter. Except Frank wouldn't require me to place myself in a labeled box in a public place in order to hang out with me. Frank would never want to put me in a cage.

"You okay?" she asks.

I snap out of it and go back to my shrimp. "Yeah. I'm good."

"You ever gonna finish with that shrimp?" Juan asks.

"Metaphysically? No. In reality? Yes. In about four minutes," I answer.

He looks at me quizzically and then goes back to his office.

When I'm done, I rinse the shrimp and then clean up the sinkful of shrimp veins and wash my hands and then get to the dishes. It's a short day again—a dry season until Christmas catering, Jorge says.

▶ ▶ ▶

"I can't believe you haven't told your parents yet," she says. We are in her car with the heater on.

"I don't see what the big deal is," I answer.

"The big deal is that you're still hiding, and it doesn't make any sense because everyone knows!"

"I'm not hiding!"

"You're hiding. And you're ashamed."

"I am totally not ashamed. I just haven't told my parents. Because they know anyway."

"But *you* haven't told them."

"I didn't need to. They had the neighbors to tell them, didn't they?"

I tell her about Kristina and the lie. I tell her about the week at school. Still, she's snarky.

"You should just grow a pair and come out." She tries to say this jokingly.

"I will," I say, feeling like a scolded kid. I get out of the car without a kiss or an *I love you*, and I practice the whole way home in the car.

Okay. I have something to tell you. I love Dee Roberts, and I'd really like it if you could accept her as my girlfriend and we could just put this week behind us.

I'm sorry it took me so long to talk about this, but I was scared. I love Dee Roberts, and I want you to meet her so you can love her, too.

Okay, I can tell you the truth now. I love Dee Roberts, but I'm still a virgin.

Look, I know you need the truth. I'm sorry it took me so long to tell you, but this isn't easy. I have a girlfriend.

When I walk into the house, no one is around. There is no one to say any of my practiced lines to. I use this as a sign from the gods that it's just not time yet. My brain people say: *You will not be pressured.*

After I clean my room, I continue to compile my enormous list of questions for the Socrates Project. It's amazing how many questions can come from *Equality is obvious*. First, to define *equality*. Then to define *obvious*. I mean, I can even try to define *is* if I want, because equality isn't really working in the present tense, is it?

Because equality isn't really obvious to most people.

And I don't mean to say the world is filled with racists or sexists or homophobes. I mean to say: Everybody's always looking for the person they're better than.

In fourth grade, it's the second graders. In ninth grade, it's the eighth graders. Adults look at teenagers like we're the stupidest creatures on the planet, when really we're just lining up to take their jobs in T-minus five years.

I am equal to a baby and to a hundred-year-old lady. I am equal to an airline pilot and a car mechanic. I am equal to you. You are equal to me. It's that universal.

Except that it's not.

▶ ▶ ▶

When Ellis appears at the dinner table, she is in full sulk.

Mom says some stuff to her without looking, and then when Ellis doesn't answer, she turns and says, "That does it! I call an impromptu Mommy and Me night!"

"No," Ellis says.

"I'm not taking no for an answer," Mom says, and she proceeds to drag Ellis from the chair and up the steps.

By the time Dad gets home with the pizza, the two of them are screeching like preteens, and all is back to normal. If you want to call this normal. Mom tells him that she's made reservations at the country club. "Don't wait up!" she says.

He looks at me and tosses the pizza onto the table, and I dish out a little salad and pour iced tea, and we're both on our second piece of pizza when Mom and Ellis leave through the front door without saying good-bye.

I think again about how Dad and I could fix this. I mean, he could be warmer, right? Not so disconnected and stoned? He could at least say "Have a good time!" and demand a kiss or something. And I could giggle with them and show them that it doesn't bug me that I'm not invited. Because I'm over it.

He leans back and reaches into the fridge for a beer.

"Want one?"

I consider it for a second. "No, thanks."

He closes the fridge door, twists the cap off his beer and drinks.

They say: *My God, look at him. He's like a dog in a cage.*

"So, here's to this week being over," he says. He holds up his glass, and I pick up my iced tea and clink with him, and we both drink.

"The curtains look great," I say.

"Shoot me now," he says.

"I'm really sorry I put you through all that."

"You mean the curtains or the other shit?"

"All of it," I say. "I hate lying to you. But I can't tell her anything or else—you know."

"No. Or else what?"

I sigh. "Or else she'll ruin it?"

"Oh, that," he says, and takes another drink. "Yeah."

▶ ▶ ▶

I go to bed after the *SNL* Weekend Update, and I hear him come up at around one. I don't hear Mom and Ellis come in. I remember waking up at around four and fearing that they'd both been in an accident. I remember wondering how it would feel to lose them.

My alarm goes off at five. I take a quick shower and see that Ellis's shoes are on the floor in the bathroom. This makes me happy, because I want to make things okay, because she's my sister and I still want to save her from the flying monkeys.

▶ ▶ ▶

On Sunday morning, I ask Juan, "Why do people love shrimp so damn much?" He shrugs and drops the box on the sink's edge for me, and I start deveining before six. Dee is late and gets in at 6:15.

"Oversleep?"

"Forgot to set my alarm." She turns to Juan. "Sorry."

"Slow day, ladies. You'll be out of here by ten, I bet." He goes to the schedule on the wall. "And no work at all next weekend. Have a happy holiday, yo."

Once I get set up with my knife and my shrimp, Dee asks, "Did you do it?"

"Do what?"

She lets her face fall into a disappointed scowl. "Forget it," she says, and goes back to her brassicas.

"Nobody was home," I say. "What was I going to do? Wake them up at five this morning? I didn't know you were on a strict schedule." I'm aware that came out a little bitchy, but she's being too pushy, so I don't care.

"Sorry," she says.

After some silence, she says, "You ready for your big day this week?"

"Yep," I say. "I still have to make my toga."

Jorge hears this. "You having a toga party?"

"Kinda."

"Jorge, you didn't know that Astrid here is a brain? She's, like, a real live philosopher."

"Seriously?" Jorge asks.

I smile. "I guess."

He nods. "So what's your philosophy on shrimp?"

I stare at the small case of it. "Shrimp is good."

"That's it?"

"Or shrimp is bad," I say.

Jorge looks at me like I must be high. Frank S. gives me a thumbs-up from over by the big industrial mixer. Dee still has a look on her face like she's losing me. Because she might be losing me.

▶ ▶ ▶

At home, we eat DIY dinner because none of us are hungry at the same time. I do leftover pizza. Cold. Ellis eats a can of meatballs. Mom has a salad. Each of us seems to be in our own little world with our own little shadows.

After dinner, I go out to the picnic table and I try to think about the Socrates Project and my toga, but I'm distracted by the realization that I'm completely alone right now. No friends. No family. No Dee. I look at the planes and picture the passengers feeling sorry for me for shutting people out. For having to do what I have to do next, which is figure out all the ways to not be completely alone. I ask them: *Do you think one day they might let me love them again?*

PASSENGER #1008
MIKEY JO MARTINEZ, SEAT 1D
FLIGHT #4430
DALLAS TO JFK

What people don't tell you about this part of breaking up is the embarrassment. I'm Mikey Jo Martinez, man. Always a happy guy. A good father. A good husband. I go to church, and I volunteer at the soup kitchen twice a month, you know? And all I feel is embarrassed right now. I almost didn't make it onto this plane because I thought about taking a bunch of pills last night. That's a first. Mikey Jo Martinez doesn't think about shit like that. Ever.

Donald and Glen told me that divorce was freedom. They said that they have more time and less worries, and no one bitches at them anymore. But they didn't love their wives, either. I do.

More than I ever did before.

You know that saying about how you don't know what you have until it's gone? I already did know what I had, and now that she's gone, I know even more.

Donald and Glen said something about dating honeys. How they go clubbing. Shit, man, I'm thirty-five years old. I don't want to go to a club. I don't want honeys. I want Noelle back. I want my kids back. I want to hit Rewind. So I'm going back to Jersey to see if she'll try one more time.

And I'm landing in an hour, and I don't know what to say. All I know is that nothing I ever said before worked.

She said she loves me. She said she doesn't want to do this to the kids. She said that she really wants it to work out. But she said it's up to me...and I don't know what that means.

I can admit that at first I was a jerk. She gave me some self-help book, and I threw it on the ground, but I was mad. Really mad. And I'm still mad and embarrassed.

What's scary is that I still feel that way on some days. Like I have anger issues. Like I'm some animal. When, really, I know I'm a good guy. I mean, most of the time, you know?

My favorite part of flying is when we break through the clouds. Seeing them from above is magical, but flying through them to see the landscape below is beautiful. As we do it this time, we hit some turbulence, and I focus on some tree-covered mountains in the distance and the dark yellow of the setting sun hitting the edges of the scattered small clouds between me and the mountains. While I do this, I hear Noelle's voice in my head—the last thing she said to me on the phone. She said, "If you're coming back here, then you'd better have something new to say, because I'm not going to sit and listen to the same old excuses, Mikey. You either need to own up to your shit or just stay in Dallas with your mother, because this is your last chance."

She means it, too. Noelle Martinez doesn't say anything she doesn't mean, which is why I love her as much as I do. You can count on people like that.

I look out the window and see the sun getting lower and the mountains in the distance getting yellower, and I feel this sharp pain in my chest like someone just shot me. It hurts, but it's good, too. Like it's letting the pressure out of my chest. It's a relief. Like someone somewhere is releasing the embarrassment and letting me think straight.

Suddenly, I know what I'm going to say.

I'm going to say: *This was all my fault. I'm so sorry. I didn't appreciate you, and I didn't help you.* She will look frightened because Mikey Jo Martinez has never admitted stuff like this before. I will ask her to hug me. When she does, I will ask: *Will you let me love you again?*

38

WHAT WOULD SOCRATES DO?

"HEY," KRISTINA SAYS. It startles me out of my love-sending, and I sit up.

"Ninja," I say. "Didn't even hear you come out the door."

"I snuck around the side," she says. "I don't feel like seeing Claire right now. Or your sister."

"I don't see why not. They still probably like you more than they like me."

"Look," Kristina says. She sits down on the table next to me, our feet on the bench part, and I share my blanket with her. "You have to understand some stuff."

"I understand enough," I say. "You lied about me. I'm not your best friend anymore."

"Please! Just stop!" she says, and she starts crying a little, and I feel like shit—a little like my mother. Twisting the knife once it's in and all that.

She reaches into her coat pocket and gets a tissue, and she blows her nose a few times. Finally she says, "I did make it up. But I had to."

"You *had to*? That's even lamer than denying it."

"Let me finish," she says. "You don't understand what it's like to be from here. You don't understand what it's like to have a family who's *always* been from here."

"And this makes it okay to tell lies about your best friend how?"

"God, you can really be like Claire, you know that?"

"Thanks."

She looks at me and starts to cry again. "I've lost everything! Can't you see that? Everything!"

"No. I can't see that," I say.

"I was Kristina Houck—"

"You're still Kristina Houck!"

"I was Kristina Houck: Homecoming Court, Unity Valley girl. I had a *reputation*. I had status. I had a future. Recommendations to the best colleges. Connections. People," she says.

I interrupt her. "You still have all that stuff. Doesn't explain why you lied about me. Which, if you look at it from my point of view, looks like this: Townie girl with *status* and *connections* makes up lie about her pseudo–best friend who moved here and was never accepted by the townie people, and then denies it and makes a shitload of excuses, as if it's okay for good Unity Valley girls to lie about big nothings from out of state."

She sobs into her hands. I say, "I asked you a while ago to stop being so bossy. It was uncomfortable, but I could kinda take it, because it was the side effect of being friends with Kristina Houck, popular townie girl. I took it with a grain of salt every time you put me down and made me do shit I didn't want to do. And then this week I kinda missed you while all the rumors started and the shit went down with Ellis and everything. I really needed you around, you know?"

"That's kinda sweet," she says. "Thanks."

"But then I heard the stupid lie you told, and I was crushed. Completely crushed. Do you know that my own mom won't believe me unless you tell her yourself that you lied?"

She cries a little more and says, "I should go." And then she gets up and walks around the side of my house toward her house. I watch her walk all slumped over and sad, and I guess she is genuinely sad. Maybe she did have more to lose than I did. I don't know what it's like to be half of the loved Homecoming couple. I don't know what it's like being Kristina Houck, but from where I'm sitting, it doesn't look very easy. So I jog after her and say, "Wait up."

She stops on the sidewalk and takes a deep breath.

I say, "Come back to the table. Before the whole town sees us and says we're breaking up for a second time." I laugh, and it makes her smile. We walk to the side of my house again and around to the table.

"I'm really sorry," she says. "I'll tell Claire I lied. I know that won't stop the bullshit. But at least she'll know I lied."

"That'd be cool, thanks," I say.

"It's fucked up that she doesn't believe you."

I sigh. "You know, she'd take you over me any day."

"Nuh-uh."

"Yuh-huh. I bet you my whole bank account," I say.

"Will you promise you won't get mad if I say something?"

"I can't promise, but I can try."

She lets out a deep breath. "Well, I'm kinda pissed off with you for lying, too."

I wait for her to explain, but she seems to think I know what she's talking about. "I don't follow you," I say. "What did I lie about?"

"Everything. You know. Your big secret."

I look around for Frank S. I sit him on his favorite bench, and he shrugs at me.

"It wasn't a lie," I say. "I just wasn't sure."

"But I was your best friend, Astrid. You should have told me."

I feel myself getting pissed off, so I take a minute to try to figure out how to say what I want to say. Frank S. lights Dad's pipe. I have no idea how he knew where to find it, but I guess if I made him up in my head, he must know everything I know. I feel relaxed by association.

"I see what you're trying to say. But you're wrong. I mean, when did you first know you were gay? And did you tell anyone on that first day? Who is anyone to tell me when to talk about something so personal?"

"But look at me. I'm gay, dude. *And* your best friend. Right?"

"Still, it's none of your business until I'm ready to tell you. Calling it a lie is wrong. And kinda hurtful. I really know what you're trying to say, but try to think about it from my side. It just sucks that you'd hold my own confusion—which tortured me for months—against me. Seriously."

"Huh," she says. "I never thought of it that way."

"I guess I'm just not as confident or sure as a lot of other people. I wasn't really sure about any of it until the night we got busted, actually."

"Really?"

"Yeah. And then all this other shit happened."

She points to the house. "And you still haven't told them?"

I shake my head.

"But you and Dee are okay?"

I shake my head again.

"Shit," she says.

"Yeah."

She says, "Can I be honest?" Like I could stop her from being honest. She smiles uncomfortably. "I don't want to go back to school, and I don't want to live here anymore. I swear to God I'm not trying to be dramatic, but I'd jump off the nearest cliff to save myself from the next seven months of my life."

"I hear you," I say.

"I'm thinking about cyberschooling or something."

"Seriously?"

"Yeah. Seriously," she says.

"Dude, you're not looking at this right at all," I say. "Try to think about it like an ancient philosopher. WWSD, you know?"

"WWSD?" she says. It takes her a few seconds. "What Would Socrates Do?"

Frank S., puffy-eyed and slouching on the bench, gives me two thumbs up.

"Yeah. Seriously. Think about this town. It's a cave where people are chained, right?"

"You need to stop."

"Why? I'm right! All those people who are chained here thinking that their reputations matter and that this little shit matters are so freaking shortsighted. Dude, what matters is if you're happy. What matters is your future. What matters is that we get out of here in one piece. What matters is finding the truth of our own lives, not caring about what other people think is the truth of us!"

"That's refreshing, Asteroid. Really. Thanks."

"Stop being sarcastic. Motion *is possible*. You don't have to be a douche from Unity Valley for all your life. You can stop whenever you want. Up to you."

"I knew there was a reason I should have taken humanities," she says.

"I learned most of this stuff from watching Claire. Look at her. Miserable. So concerned with these people. Your people. You, even. So concerned about having Unity Valley friends that she befriends *you*. *My* best friend. Seriously. If you don't step out of the cave now, that's you in twenty-five years."

She chuckles through her nose.

"You know I'm right."

"Let me go inside and tell her I'm a douche, okay?" she says.

"No freaking way. If you go now, she'll think I bribed you or something."

We walk to the curb.

"I want to fast-forward to next September," she says.

"Or we could just try to have fun while we're here," I answer.

"Ready for the big Day of Tolerance?" she asks.

"Are you kidding?" I ask. "I'd rather poke my eyes out with dull forks. But we have to do what we have to do, right?"

Kristina nods. "I say we tolerate the shit out of it."

39

IN WHICH ASTRID JONES
FINALLY LOSES IT.

ELLIS STAYS IN BED. This was the plan, and I don't care.

If the situation were reversed, however, I'd like to state for the record that I'd go to school and support my assumed-gay sister during the lame-o tolerance rally because sisters do shit like that for each other. Then again, I haven't really told her yet, so I'm pretty much to blame for my own lack of familial support.

The first noticeable sign of Tolerance Day: They moved the NO PLACE FOR HATE sign from in front of the guidance office fourteen feet to a spot in front of the main office. Very exciting stuff.

▶ ▶ ▶

Study hall is out of control. There's a sub, and someone has convinced him that this study hall isn't one of those *real* study halls where people study. I sit by myself until Clay stops by and saves me.

"How you doing?" he asks.

"Good."

"You ready for Wednesday?"

"Yeah. I'm stoked."

"I'm going to kick its ass," he says.

"I have no doubt."

"Have you seen Justin at all?" he asks. "I'm kinda worried about him. And we need him back at the paper soon, you know?"

"I think he'll be back this week. Ask Kristina. He's okay, though. Nothing to be worried about."

He lowers to a whisper. "I heard he went to jail."

I shake my head. "Totally untrue."

He sighs. "Oh, good. So what do you think this whole Tolerance Day will be like? My money is on it yielding a whole bag of nothing."

"Yeah. I've been trying not to think about it, really."

"For what it's worth, I've got your back," he says.

"Thanks."

I spend the rest of the period reading the Socrates Project sheet we were all given at the beginning of the class, which instructs us on the schedule, the requirements and the actual day of debate.

I take a second to think about him—Frank Socrates—

and I decide he's my new hero. Not because he shows up in my life and talks to me when I want him to, but because of who he was and what he stood for.

I just love how he rejected all the boxes.

Then the bell rings, and the tolerance portion of our day begins.

First, to the assembly. I blend into the student body and don't feel the spotlight on me so much as the lights dim and the guy talks. And talks. And talks.

"The world is made of so many types of different people, and we have to learn that though they might be scary at first, they are not inherently bad because they are different." He starts this way and goes on to talk about his days in school as a mixed-race Latino and how hard it was for him growing up. He got beat up a lot. Teased every day.

I start to feel resentful. You mean to tell me that it's 2011 and this guy gets paid to have remedial talks with high school students about how they shouldn't hate other people? Isn't this elementary? Shouldn't it be automatic? What kind of species are we if we have to have people come talk to us about this crap? And how, if we're that stupid, did we get to the moon and help build a space station?

He tells a story about how his mother was from Cuba and how she hated Puerto Ricans. He says, "No matter how many times I tried to explain to her how stupid this was, she never changed. It was just ingrained in her.

"Some of you have it ingrained in you. You weren't born with it. You were taught. No baby has hate for anything." He produces a baby (a real baby) and bounces the kid on his hip. "We were all babies once, right? This little guy doesn't care what country you were born in or what religion you might practice or how much you weigh or who you might love."

At that, I feel the spotlight again. He talks a bit about high school being a time of feeling things out, and after that I kinda block him out for a while because the spotlight is just so hot. And I'm angry. I say to Frank, who is sitting up on the catwalk operating the spotlight, "Frank, that baby is smarter than half of my humanities class. Is this how things have always been?"

Frank nods.

ME: I need to get out of here.

FRANK: Too bad you didn't sit in an aisle seat. You're not going anywhere.

ME: I can pretend I'm going to puke.

FRANK: Do you really think that would be wise?

ME: I just can't believe he gets paid to talk about this stuff.

FRANK: I bet he can't believe it, either.

Then I hear, "I just went to my twenty-fifth class reunion, guys. Let me tell you—people change. The girls who passed around rumors about all the weird kids? Are nice and have their own weird kids. The so-called losers who graduated at the bottom of the class? Are driving luxury cars and running big businesses. The kid who made fun of all the gay kids? Is gay. I'm not saying this will happen to all of you, but what I'm trying to tell you is that high school doesn't end here. You guys will know each other for a long time, and you will get to see how life changes people. I only hope that for right now, you remember that there is no place for hate in a happy life. I don't care who you are, where you come from or what God you believe in. I can guarantee you that if you hate, you will never achieve true happiness."

Someone taps me on the shoulder and a note drops into my lap. It's from Kristina.

Let's skip the 6th-period pep rally thing.

I look around and find her and nod.

After the guy finishes his assembly program, Principal Thomson gets up and talks a bit about why it's important to study diversity in high school, and then two boys walk down the aisles and meet in front of the stage, and they stand there with their arms crossed as if they're bouncers. I think Mr. Thomson mentions something about signs in the hallways and how anyone caught making or hanging hateful signs will be suspended, but I can't be sure. I'm too busy trying to figure out what these two kids are about to do.

One is Ross Bentley, our resident Holocaust denier. The other is some kid who I've seen around, but I don't know. He seems to know Ross, anyway. They're wearing similar T-shirts, but I can't make out what they say in the semidarkness.

Eventually, the lights go on. There is relative calm in the audience, and people start to talk to each other as we are escorted, row by row, toward the gym. Because the lights are on, I can read what Ross Bentley's shirt says. It says DON'T BE GAY, and it's got one of those red circles with the diagonal line through the word *gay*. The kid standing next to him is wearing this one: BE HAPPY, NOT GAY.

Everyone ignores them, and Mr. Thomson and some teachers talk onstage with the presenter, and they smile at the baby, and they're all cooing at it and being normal as if the Day of Tolerance assembly wasn't just infiltrated by negative creeps.

▶ ▶ ▶

We have no chance of slipping out of our organized lines and skipping the pep rally in the gym. Kristina sits four people away from me, and we get seats as near to the doors as we can, but there are teachers everywhere, so we sit and watch.

Turns out the Unity Valley cheerleaders can spell out the word *TOLERANCE* with their skinny bronze bodies. Who knew?

Ross Bentley and his friend refused to sit, and now they stand to the right of Mr. Thomson at center court because "they have rights, too." That's a direct quote from Ross's dad, who has come to stand next to them. His shirt says STRAIGHT PRIDE. He says, "The First Amendment protects our right to free speech as much as it protects yours."

I'm incensed. I never really felt like this before. Maybe because I haven't told anyone yet, and I know that means I can't complain yet, either. I don't know. I just want to freak out on these hater people and tell them that they're bigoted assholes. And then I remember that Ross and his dad don't even believe in the Holocaust. I don't care how many babies we could put on a stage—there is nothing that will change people like this. I'm still incensed, though. Because five hundred people here want to have a tolerance rally. And three people don't.

The cheerleaders do another hate-free cheer while Mr. Thomson asks Mr. Bentley to go to the office and sign in as required by the school rules. We hear this conversation because Mr. Thomson doesn't turn off the mic and because Mr. Bentley is particularly loud. Mr. Bentley doesn't move.

Kristina looks to me, and there's just enough chaos for us to make our way out the side gym door, and we start heading that direction when Mr. Trig, who's standing by the gym doors, says, "Ladies! Where do you think you're going? We're not done yet!"

We don't stop.

I hear one of the teachers say, as we walk out into the hallway, "Some thanks we get for throwing them a pep rally."

That line just eats at me. It makes me sick. I am sick of living around people who want to put me in a box. I am sick of people poking their noses in my business. I am so sick of everything to do with Unity Valley that when we get into the main hallway and Kristina turns around and says, "So, did you tell Claire and Gerry last night?" I just explode.

The explosion is internal at first. And then it forms this sentence, which blurts out of my mouth about three times too loudly and right into Kristina's face.

"Will you PLEASE just let me do this my own way?"

"Dude," she says. "I was just asking. I thought we were cool."

"Nothing is cool! Everything is fucked now! EVERY-THING!" I say.

"Uh, wow."

"I don't give a FUCK about anything anyone in this town thinks anymore! I'm fucking so sick of the gossip and the bullshit and the stupid secret code of Unity Valley, where no one ever wins unless they're the same five people who always win because they lie to the most people! I'm done! Okay? I don't care who knows I'm gay!" I say. "I'M GAY! Okay? I'm fucking GAY!"

I stand there in the long hall and hear it echo back at me. *She's fucking gay. Okay?*

Frank Socrates, who is stationed at the water fountain, echoes, too. "She's fucking gay, okay?"

I smile at him. He smiles at me.

"Miss Jones, would you like to take a walk with me?" The voice comes at the same time the vice principal grabs my elbow. I walk with him and leave Kristina standing there looking angry and completely confused. Frank S. takes a drink from the water fountain, readjusts his toga, and walks out the front doors.

▶ ▶ ▶

I'm suspended. Just the rest of today and then all of tomorrow. Unity Valley High School doesn't tolerate lesbian freak-outs that include the *F*-word.

Oops.

I guess when I finally lose it, I lose it.

Dad has to pick me up.

It's like a tradition.

40

I CAN'T DECIDE
IF I WANT HIM TO DRIVE
SLOWER OR FASTER.

I SIT IN THE FRONT SEAT.

He says, "I have to go across town for something Mom needs."

"Okay."

For the first ten minutes of the drive, I take to ripping my suspension notice into pieces. When I get each tidbit so small I can't rip it in half again, I add it to the pile in my lap. My goal: confetti. Celebration. A bon voyage.

He doesn't say anything until we get on the big road. Then he does an awkward half cough to clear his pot-smoky throat and says, "I assume that sucked?"

"It sucked the suck off of suck."

I look at him as he drives on the big highway, keeping his half-cocked eyes on the road. He glances over at me and smiles a little.

I am not in the mood to smile. "Does Mom know you're stoned all the time? Because it's really obvious. I think if you're going to do it, you should be more discreet," I say. "You need to either stop smoking pot or buy some cologne or something. And breath mints. The fact that Claire doesn't know yet is insane. She must be in some sort of denial."

He makes a face like he never thought of this before. Make no mistake—weed kills vital brain cells, dulls critical-thinking skills and reaction time. "Wow. What brought this on?"

"You asked me to stop lying, so I've stopped lying. Watch and be amazed," I say.

He glances at me again, no smile this time. He almost looks scared, except he's too stoned to be scared.

"Furthermore, Mom dislikes me. Don't argue or talk me out of it. And don't make excuses for her. She's never liked me, and that's *her* problem. Eventually, she'll be sorry she was such a bitch."

He doesn't answer for a minute, then says, "So far, I get that you think I smoke too much weed and that Mom is a bitch who doesn't love you. Is that right?"

"I don't *think* you smoke too much weed and Mom doesn't love me. I *know* it," I correct. "If you guys are so cool about diversity, then why don't you act it?"

He nods and says, "I know it's hard to believe, but your mother is a really hip lady. Or—she was. Once."

I go back to ripping the suspension notice into tinier and tinier pieces. "I remember when she was still nice to me, you know. I remember those walks we used to take around the block when I was little."

"I bet you do."

"I never understood why we moved here. I mean, I understood you guys wanted us to have a different childhood, and she wanted to buy her grandmother's house, but I don't get it. You said fresh air and grass and space and country fairs and stuff, but I guess I could never figure out why you thought that was better. Different, yeah. But better? I don't know."

He nods.

"It wasn't any better for you guys, was it?" I ask.

"Definitely not for me."

I stare out my window again for a minute. I remember the move. I remember Ellis and me crying in the backseat of the car. We held hands the whole drive to Pennsylvania. We were so close. When we got to the house, which we'd already seen a few times, we sat on the love seat in the quiet room because it was closest to the door.

"We really thought you'd move us back," I say.

"Yeah."

"Like if we'd have stayed on that green love seat for long enough, you guys would just change your minds."

"Ellis took it hard," he says.

"We all took it hard."

"Not like she did, though. You don't remember the whole doctor thing?" he asks.

"No," I say.

He sighs. "You don't remember the problems she had in school and how we had to send her to the psychologist?"

"I don't remember any of that," I say. *Why don't I remember any of that?*

We park outside an office store. "You coming in with me?" he asks.

I go with him. We buy an extra-long USB cable and something that has to do with the word *Ethernet*. I make him go to the car first, and then I buy him an ergonomic stapler because I think he should have one.

When we start driving toward home, I take a deep breath and say it.

"So I've had a girlfriend since July, and I love her."

"Okay," he says.

"I don't know why this is so important for me to tell you, but I'm a virgin. Seriously weird for me to be telling you that, I know, but this whole thing, it's not about sex. I just fell in love, and it happened to be with a girl."

"O-*kay*," he says.

"When I told you I didn't know if I was gay, I was telling you the truth. I just know I'm in love—with a girl. I had no idea of anything past that. It's very Socrates, you know? I'm not questioning *my* sexuality as much as I'm questioning the strict definitions and boxes of all *sexualities* and why we care so much about other people's intimate business."

He nods.

"But there's a problem with that."

He nods again.

"If I do all this Socratic shit the way I've been doing, I end up living in this weird limbo that's no good for anyone. The world is made up of clear definitions, which is exactly why Socrates was put to death. People didn't like him messing with their clear definitions, you know?"

"Okay," he says. I'm so glad he's stoned right now.

"So, I'm gay. Until further notice. That way, I don't have to think about it, my girlfriend doesn't have to wonder about it and I can actually enjoy being in love with her because she's awesome." I have just ripped the last of the suspension notice into its tiniest parts, and I stuff the confetti into my sweatshirt pockets. "You and Mom don't have to think about it, either. You can just be the couple in town who has a gay kid right alongside Kristina's parents and whoever else. And Ellis can just figure out a way to grow up and be my sister again.

"And if any of you has a problem with any of it, then it's *your* problem. Being gay is hard enough without having to worry about your family being weird about it."

"Gotcha."

We look out the windows for a while.

"For what it's worth, we're not like that. We have gay friends, and we're fine with it."

"Yeah, but gay friends isn't the same as a gay daughter," I say. "Plus, you haven't been fine with it, really, have you?"

"That's different. You got busted for underage drinking."

"At a gay bar," I add. "And you told me I was ruining Ellis's reputation."

"We worry about her. Because of—you know—the whole doctor thing when we moved, I guess."

"Did you stop to think about what school was like for me last week?"

"We worried about you. But we knew you'd get through it, too. You kinda had to, right?"

I shrug.

He says, "Either way, you have to tell Mom now. I'll help you, but you have to give her a little time to catch up. She's not like me, you know?"

"By *like you*, do you mean stoned all the time?"

He opens the glove compartment and pulls out a pack of peppermint Life Savers and pops one. "See? I'm not completely stupid."

We pull up to the curb. I give him the stapler. "Thank you for being so cool about this," I say.

He's too stoned to know what to say, so he just looks at the stapler and then back at me, then at the stapler again.

"What the hell happened to us, Dad? One minute we were hammering shit together in the garage, and then we just stopped."

He lets a minute pass. "I dunno. I guess stuff happened," he says.

"I miss making birdhouses. How are we going to keep our freak reputation if we don't make them anymore?"

He takes his hand off the wheel and raises it in an oath. "I promise we will make more birdhouses."

"Good."

"Maybe this weekend?" I ask.

"You bet."

As I walk onto the porch, where Mom is standing with her arms and lips folded, I say, "Yay! Astrid is home!" and toss my suspension-notice confetti as high as it will go, and because I ripped it up so small, it seems to stay in the air forever, like light snowflakes.

41

CAN YOU SAY *AWKWARD?*

"YOU'RE GAY NOW?" she says. Dad and I recoil a little. "You're sure? You're gay?" Her frown wrinkles two deep vertical lines between her eyebrows. "Because last time we talked you weren't gay, remember? And you didn't know if you were gay. Remember that?"

I nod. "Yeah. I remember that."

"So couldn't we get here without all the lies?"

"They weren't lies."

She gives me a judgmental look. "Astrid, I know what a lie is. I've been around for forty-seven years."

"You don't understand."

She sighs as if I am the biggest pain in her ass ever and then says, "Exactly how don't I understand?"

"I needed time to figure it out. It takes a while, you know? You don't just wake up one day and *know*," I say. "Or at least I didn't. I wasn't lying. I was just figuring it out."

"And I'm guessing we're the last to know?" she says.

"Depends on who you include." I so want to tell her that no one in Russia knows, but her sense of humor hasn't shown up for this conversation (or any conversation in the last decade), so I keep it to myself. Also, probably no one in Africa knows, and that's *a lot* of people.

"We shouldn't be the last to know," she says. "It makes us look like we don't know our own children."

And there it is. The Claire moment. I cock my head. "So you're angry because this makes you look bad? Because I didn't tell you first? Am I getting this right?"

"No. I'm not angry at all. I'm just—uh—dis—"

"Disappointed?" I say. "Not the best word choice."

She looks genuinely frazzled. "I didn't mean it *that* way. I mean that I just wish I knew before now."

"Well, you know now. Believe me. I told you as soon as I could." I lean into the table toward her. "It's just not easy to tell you stuff."

She waits a second, and I think she's going to be totally cool, and then she says, "How is this my fault?"

"Who said this had anything to do with fault?"

"You just did."

Dad puts his hands up. "Astrid was saying that it's hard to talk to you. That's why she found it hard to tell us the truth."

"*Hard to talk to me?* Are you saying that, too, Gerry?"

"Mom, you're doing it now," I say. "Anyway, it doesn't matter. I just told you."

"Yes. You did."

Silence.

Awkward.

"Well, I guess that's that, then," she says.

"Yep."

Dad says, "Thanks for telling us, Astrid." He walks over and squeezes my shoulders from behind and gives me a hug from back there while I'm still sitting down. "Doesn't change a thing about how we feel about you."

"That's right." Mom leans over and holds my hand. "You're our daughter no matter what."

Not *we love you no matter what* but *you're our daughter no matter what.* Not all that warm, but it'll do.

At least it's over.

▶ ▶ ▶

Things do not miraculously become normal, either.

First, we go out for lunch to the Legion Diner. I order a grease-dipped grilled cheese sandwich. Mom orders a waffle and link sausage, and Dad orders the breakfast-all-day special.

While we wait for the food, Mom says, "I talked to Kristina this morning."

I raise my eyebrows.

"She told me that she lied," she says.

"And?"

She seems stuck. "And that's it. Thought you'd want to know."

"Well, yeah," I say. "Thanks for letting me know." I look at her and wait for the apology, but it doesn't come. This time, though, instead of flaming up inside, I send love to her. *Mom, I love you even though you can't say you're sorry or admit you were wrong. If only you'd stop thinking there's such a thing as perfect, then you'd feel a lot better about yourself. And me.*

While I eat my sandwich, I tell them that I'm not going to hide who I am in school. "I mean, I pretty much came out already. With *F*-words, apparently." I laugh. "I hope that's okay. It's easier to just be real at this point."

"But it's still going to be hard, you know?" Mom says.

"Yeah," I say.

"For all of us," she adds.

We eat in relative silence until I say, "Do you think Ellis will ever stop being so freaked out about it?"

"Well, I certainly didn't raise her that way," Mom says.

Dad chews.

Mom chews.

I chew.

"I think you're the only one who can help her with this, Claire," Dad says. "She only listens to you."

Mom chews.

I chew.

Dad chews.

"What do you mean, she only listens to me?"

No one answers her question.

"You did it?" Dee yells into the phone.

"I didn't just do it," I say. "I did it and got suspended for doing it so loudly."

"Holy shit, Jones."

"And you're right. It does feel better. So far, anyway," I say. "Meet me at the lake?"

It's warmer today, and I'm too hot in my scarf and gloves, so I leave them in the car before we climb up the hill.

The ground is wet, so we lie on a picnic table.

"They took it pretty well," I say when she asks me how it went. "My dad was stoned, so he didn't care. Mom was... Mom."

"Your dad was stoned?"

"Yeah. You're in the inner circle now. I can tell you shit like that, right?"

"Inner circle, huh? How'd I get there?"

"You wanted me to come out. I came out. Now we're bound for life or something. Isn't that how it goes?"

"I didn't want to force you out. I just thought—it's just easier," she says.

I point to the sky. "Look at that. Three in a row—all 747s, I bet."

"You can tell that from here?"

"Sometimes. Those are pretty high up," I say.

"Sweet." She points. "What's that one? It seems smaller."

"It's a little jet. Probably an ER4."

We watch it zoom across the sky. "I like this," she says. "I'd have never known that you knew anything about airplanes if we didn't just hang out sometimes."

"And I wouldn't know that your favorite food is roast beef."

She laughs and turns toward me and looks at me with that smile. The smile that brought me here—to this. To her. To the truth about why I didn't really want to kiss Tim Huber while we were dating last year. To the truth about why I buried my head in all those books for my whole life.

When I kiss her, I place us in the future, where ~~we are just like Mom and Dad~~. No. Scratch that. I place us where we are a happy couple who are madly in love, and we are kissing the way people kiss on their wedding day. With joy and relief and love. Without guilt. Without shame.

I say, "Abracadabra."

Dee kisses me and then says, "You know what? I don't want to rush. I want to have fun and fall in love and actually— I don't know," she says. "It's like you're teaching me to slow down or something."

I don't say anything, but I'm somehow not embarrassed that I just finally said *abracadabra* and she's all *no, thank you.*

She continues. "Must be all that Socrates shit rubbing off on me, but I got to thinking about how since I came out, all I've done is work on being sexual, and while that's fun and all, I never took a minute to really just relax and feel loved, and I like it."

"It's nice," I say. "No doubt."

"My first few times were kinda awkward and fast."

"Oh," I say.

"Actually, that thing you said a few weeks ago? About how I was a fiend and all that? Reminded me of my first girlfriend and how—uh—I guess—pushy—she was. It was fun, and I liked her a lot, but she didn't love me," she says. "I think she just wanted to pop my cherry, you know?"

"Yuck. I hate that expression."

"Me too."

I think about all those guys in school.

They say: *I popped her cherry last night!*

They say: *She bled all over my varsity jacket!*

"So okay," I say. "*Abracadabra* whenever it comes naturally. How's that?"

She nods and kisses me again. "I never asked you what your favorite food is," she says. "And I really want to know."

I turn to look at the sky and rest my head on her shoulder. "Well, I know it's sure as hell not shrimp."

We laugh, and then she gets serious. "You sure everything's going to be okay? At home? School? Do you feel like you did the right thing?"

"I have no idea. I'm sure people will still be weird about it. Ellis will probably come around. My mom might manage to say she loves me before I graduate college. My dad probably forgot it already."

She laughs. "Some people will always be a pain, but all in all, it's easier to be yourself, I think. I mean, now that the pressure's off to be perfect."

I stay quiet for a minute and let that go through my head a few times. *The pressure's off to be perfect.*

"Jones?"

"Yeah. Sorry. I think I just got a message from Socrates. I have to go."

She laughs. We get up and walk down the hill to our cars, and when she takes off, I open a notebook and grab a pen from my glove compartment.

My paradox is all wrong. I write out a whole list of other paradoxes until I come to the one I most want to argue. I want to argue it with everyone in this town. Everyone on TV. I want to argue it with Claire and Kristina and even with Dee, who puts too much pressure on herself to play well and run enough. Or Juan, who swears at himself every time he makes a tiny mistake in the kitchen. Or Ellis, who is still a scared little girl trying to fit in.

I want to tell them: *Nobody's perfect.*

42

THE SOCRATES PROJECT.

LET'S START HERE: Wearing a toga to school is totally boss. Given free roam of the school in order to pick fights with anyone who looks willing is also totally boss. I mean, I'm usually Astrid Jones, pacifist poet type who doesn't usually pick fights outside of correcting your grammar. But now I'm Astrid Jones, recently out lesbian who just got back from being suspended for saying the *F*-word several times right in front of the vice principal. This is a little different than I'd imagined it all quarter.

I have a small sign with my paradox on it. Nobody's perfect. I find most people won't argue with this, so I have to ask them related questions. I start with teachers. Mr. Trig walks by me after first period. "What is perfect, Mr. Trig?" I ask. "And can you say that anyone's achieved it?"

"We're all born perfect," he says.

Good answer.

"My right foot is a half size smaller than my left foot," I say. "Is that perfect?"

He waves me off and winks because he has to get back to class.

Mr. Williams walks by me, and I ask him, "Is perfection possible?"

"No."

"How are you so sure?"

He says, "Everything is a matter of perception."

"So does that mean nobody is perfect or everybody is?" I ask. "Because if it's a matter of perception, then either could be true."

"Up to you," he says as he walks away toward his room. I could have kept that going for a while, though. This whole notion of perfection intrigues me. *How can we say nobody's perfect if there is no perfect to compare to? Perfection implies that there really is a right and wrong way to be. And what type of perfection is the best type? Moral perfection? Aesthetic? Physiological? Mental?* I write this down in my project journal.

During the five minutes between second and third periods, I start to rant on my crowded pseudo-street corner (which is the hallway next to the gym).

"If perfection were possible, which type would reign? Moral perfection? Mental perfection? Would the smarter man win, or the stronger? The dark-skinned or light-skinned? Would the winner be the most beautiful?"

"Perfection is equal," someone says. "Beauty is in the eye of the beholder."

This draws a laugh from someone in the crowd.

"There is such a thing as a perfect race," he says.

"A whole race of perfect people?" I say. "Really? How do you know this?"

"God said so. It's in the Bible," he says.

"The Bible?" I ask. "What's that? And which god are you talking about? Zeus? Hermes? Poseidon?"

He flips me the bird while he's walking to the library wing steps.

Someone yells, "Perfection is stupid!"

"I like that!" I say. She can't hear me, but I riff on it. "Perfection is stupid! So, what is stupid, then?"

"That toga," Kristina answers as she slips by me and into the classroom to my right.

"I believe that's a matter of perception, Ms. Houck. My toga is not stupid. If the rest of Unity Valley wore togas, then I would be at the height of fashion."

During third and fourth periods, we have the group debate in the gym, and Ms. Steck invites some of the school administrators to watch and argue with us. We each sit with our signs pointing out, waiting to be picked on by audience members. Camus-loving Clay gets the superintendent all wound up about the true meaning of education by saying that in recent years, our highly paid administrators are simply puppets for yahoo school boards who don't know anything about the tenets of a good education.

"That's ridiculous!" the superintendent says.

"What's ridiculous is the cutting of the art program in the elementary schools this year, sir. And the simultaneous building of a soccer field when we already have one soccer field." Score for Clay.

An African-American board member—Jimmy Kyle's mom—asks me why I chose *nobody's perfect*. "Isn't this whole town built on the idea of perfection and standing in the community? I've never lived here, but I hear things. And I mean no offense by this," she adds, nodding to the other administrators in the room.

"I've heard it said, too," another person says.

"I don't think it's Unity Valley. I don't think it ever ends— this feeling of having to be perfect. Look at our culture. Look at the computer-enhanced people we compare ourselves to. Look at the expensive cars and trinkets we're all supposed to have. Look at how many people are wrapped up in that! Imagine how much money and worry we'd save ourselves if we stopped caring what kind of car we drove! And why do we care? *Perfection*. But there is no such thing, is there? And if there is, then everyone is perfect in their own way, right?"

"I agree," she says. "Not a popular view, but logical."

"My toga is also not a popular garment," I say, "but it's very comfortable."

I consider this statement a big score for my humanities grade. I see Ms. Steck scribble something in her notes.

We eat lunch at a special table in the cafeteria, and when we're done eating, we are allowed to roam the caf and talk about our paradoxes.

I go straight to Ellis's table and say, "Hello, fine people of Unity Valley. I'm taking the day to talk about perfection. Do you have an opinion one way or another?"

Aimee Hall says, "Some people are better than others." She looks at Ellis and then at me. Something isn't right here. Ellis looks more than her usual color of emo blue. It's like she swallowed a wheelbarrow of drowned adorable kittens.

"Is there a way you can tell who those better people are?" I ask.

"Yeah," Aimee says. "First place you look is their wallet."

This makes a few others at the table laugh.

"You know I'm Socrates, and I'm a poor man, yes? So by your definition, I am less perfect than you because of how much our wallets hold?"

"And other things. And news flash, you're not Socrates."

"How interesting. So would all of you be willing to show me your wallets?"

They stare at me. Aimee Hall digs into her purse and then realizes she's the only one doing it once she opens it and dumps a bunch of cash onto the table.

"How much is that?" I ask.

"I don't know. Probably about eighty bucks," Aimee says. "And don't forget these." She tosses out two credit cards.

"So this eighty dollars makes you more perfect than everyone else at the table, then?"

"Yeah. In some ways," she says. "Can you just go away now?"

Her friends look at her like they feel sorry for her. Ellis gets up to put her trash in the trash can.

"Hold on," one of the other girls says. I stop walking away as she pulls her own wallet from her purse. She pulls out two hundred-dollar bills. "I think this makes me more perfect. Right?"

As I walk away, I hear Aimee Hall ask the other girl how much her credit limit is, and I look around for Frank so he can see how proud I am that I may have just poked a hole in Unity Valley's perfection myth, but he's nowhere.

By the end of the day, I'm exhausted. Frank S. must have been one hearty guy to argue on the streets of Athens all day the way he did. Our humanities class enjoys a bunch of snacks and a Socrates Project party in the humanities room, where we all debate one another's paradoxes and are reminded by Ms. Steck to question everything and continue to challenge others with our open minds long after we remove our togas.

▶ ▶ ▶

The stack of lit mag submissions is huge since the first-quarter poetry and short-story classes have finished. Ms. Steck is still cleaning up from the Socrates Project party, and I refuse to take off my toga.

"It makes me feel smart," I say.

Justin laughs. "It makes you look dumb, though." He

snaps a few pictures, and for fun I pose for him in the hall with my sign, pretending to argue with invisible passersby.

"Also, it doesn't flatter your ass. Just sayin'," Kristina adds.

"Don't care. I like it," I say.

I pick up the stack of submissions and put it into my bag, and I say good-bye to Ms. Steck.

"Good job today, Astrid. Socrates would have been proud."

I nod. It's true. I think Frank would have loved to see that he is legend and that he didn't drink hemlock for nothing. I try to make him show up again, but he won't. So I'm guessing he thinks I don't need him anymore. He's probably right.

Before we leave, Justin's phone buzzes, and he gets that look again—that Chad look—and he shoves his reading pile into his bag and moves to the hall. Kristina and I walk home with him and make sure he doesn't trip over stuff while he texts without looking up once.

Three people beep because of my toga. I show them my sign, which I still have tucked under my arm. NOBODY'S PERFECT.

43

THANKSGIVING IS NOT
A DIRTY WORD.

THE TURKEY GOES IN at ten thirty—covered in butter and salt and pepper and celery and carrots and onions. Mom is in penny loafers, not high heels. They're new.

We have omelets for brunch and a bowl of fresh fruit. Ellis doesn't say much except, "Skip the cheese for me, please," and "Orange juice, thanks." Still no eye contact. I guess that's her problem for now. I can't try with her until she's ready to try.

Mom insists that we all have a piece of her freshly baked courgette bread, which makes me want to scream, *They're called zucchinis, okay? Zucchinis!* I don't scream anything, though. If she wants to use obscure European words for everything to feel better about living here, then she can. We all have our own ways of coping.

I go out the back door toward my table, and then I walk around the side of the house and stand on the sidewalk. I put my hands in my pockets and look down Main Street. I see a few people out walking their dogs or talking to neighbors, and even one guy starting to put up his Christmas decorations. I listen to the air. I don't hear a thing. Not one thing.

They say:

They say:

▶ ▶ ▶

Ellis still won't talk to me, and I'm really not sure why.

She walks past the living room while I sit here writing in my Socrates Project journal. She doesn't stop and say hi, even though she slowed a bit as if she was going to come in and watch TV. Makes me feel like I should go to the quiet room instead because this is the only TV room we have, but then I figure if she wants to watch TV, she can come in and watch it. I forget about it and go back to writing.

"Where's your father?" Mom asks.

She starts to move toward the back door, and I say, "I think he's clearing off the bench so we can make a new birdhouse."

"That one in the maple is about to turn to dust. It could use a replacement." She stands and drums her fingers on her thigh and then walks away.

I watch her walk away, and I realize that maybe I have more in common with Claire than I think. Maybe deep down, she doesn't want to be here, either. Deep down, I do think I'm smarter than those twelve NO votes in humanities class last week. I did use Jeff Garnet as a disposable person—and while it was Kristina's idea, I still went along with it, using his annoying leg-jiggling as an excuse. And really, who cares if the kid jiggles his leg?

▶ ▶ ▶

Dinner is at three, and as tradition dictates, we all go upstairs and dress up a little. Dad puts on his cubicle blazer and a dress shirt with his jeans. Very Dude. I'm pretty sure he's not stoned, too, which is great.

Mom puts on a work suit. With heels. Of course.

I wear a cool miniskirt I got last Christmas and my favorite turtleneck and a pair of black dress boots I never wear because they're a little too small for me and they hurt my feet if I have to walk in them. I'm pretty sure the last time I wore them was last Thanksgiving.

While Mom carves the turkey, Dad dishes the carrots and corn and mashed potatoes and gravy into their respective bowls, and I fill the water glasses with ice cubes and water.

Then Ellis arrives at the table in sweats. I'm pretty sure they're dirty sweats. She smells a bit like a hamper. She doesn't offer to help, and just sits in her seat while the rest of us do stuff.

When the turkey is on the hot plate and covered in sufficient gravy, we sit in our chairs, and Mom starts the toast with her wineglass raised.

"To family," she says. She tears up on the second syllable of *family*. Sniff. "To all the things we have to be thankful for."

Dad clears his throat and raises his glass. "To a new start." He nods to me.

I raise my water glass. "To love," I say.

We all look to Ellis. Her hand isn't anywhere near her glass. She's just staring into space until it's time to eat.

Mom says, "Ellis."

She acts deaf.

Dad says, "Ellis."

She sighs and raises her glass. "Here's to bullshit," she says.

And I can't help it—I laugh so hard that I make her laugh, too. And that makes Dad and Mom laugh, too—in that order.

"To bullshit!" I repeat, and take a gulp of water.

"To bullshit!"

"To bullshit!"

▶ ▶ ▶

"You smell," I tell Ellis while we're doing dishes.

"I tried," she says.

"Dude, we have a lot of Thanksgivings in front of us. Why don't we agree to make them atypical and cool instead of bullshit?"

"Are you going to wear those boots every year?"

"Probably. Why? Do they bug you?"

"You bug me."

"Damn. You're pissy."

"I was kidding."

"You need to warn a girl before you turn on her like that," I say.

"I was kidding," she says again while I'm passing her a really hot rinsed dish so she can dry it.

"No, you weren't," I say. She fumbles the dish and blows on her fingers.

We wash and dry in relative quiet for a while. I finally get to the soakers—the rack from the turkey and the bottom of the roaster—and I fill them with scalding-hot water and leave them to sit in the sink while I wipe down the kitchen table and the countertops.

"I'm gonna go get dressed," Ellis says.

"Good."

She starts toward the stairs.

"You know, you bug me, too. I'm just nice enough not to mention it," I say.

"You just mentioned it."

"So we're even, then."

I wipe down the stove top and replace the covers on the rings and then rinse my dishcloth and drape it over the drying rack.

Mom and Dad are bloating on the couch. I choose not to interrupt, and go to the quiet room and close the door. I dial Dee's number.

She answers and says, "Hey! Happy Thanksgiving! Tell me everything!"

"How about I miss you? Like crazy?"

"That's a good start. How are your mom and dad dealing?"

"It's been okay, I guess," I say.

"They didn't beat you with canes or anything, did they?"

"Sorta."

"What?"

"No, Dee. They didn't beat me with any canes. Seriously."

"You still love me?"

"More than a pilot loves air traffic control, baby. You still love me?"

"More than I love to nap after eating too much turkey."

▶ ▶ ▶

After a twenty-minute conversation, I check on my soaking dishes and find Mom attacking the roaster pan with a scrub pad.

"I was going to do that," I say. "After they soaked."

"It's fine. You did all the rest. Go and relax."

Dad is in the living room with his eyes closed, his pants unbuttoned, and the TV on. Ellis is sitting next to him, watching whatever is on TV. I decide I need to have a chat with my passengers because everything is different now, so I put on my coat and scarf and hat and grab the wool blanket off the back of the couch.

I hoist myself onto the picnic table and lie down, and as

my eyes adjust to the bright four o'clock sky, I squint a little and look for planes.

They're flying low, heading for the small regional airport. I'm pretty sure one of them is a twin-engine commuter. The other is a military plane. I concentrate on the commuter and send my love.

Everything ended up working out okay so far. Even with my parents. And maybe even with Ellis.

The nice thing about the passengers is they can't say anything back. I can't see any faces full of disappointment. I can't hear them saying bad things about me. I can't hear them call me the politically correct term for Indian giver...on Thanksgiving Day. Anyway, it's not like I want my love back. I'm just slowing down business. They can have a little. I can say, "I love you!" when I see a plane. I probably always will. But they can't have all my love.

I have too many uses for it now.

Are we okay? I ask them. *Will you be okay without me?*

▶ ▶ ▶

The back door slams. The blanket is warm, and when Ellis lifts it up and pushes me over with her hip, I open my eyes and say, "Dude. You're killing my perfect nap."

"I want to know what you do out here," she says.

"Uh—obviously, I lay here."

"Yeah, but why? What for?" She snuggles close to me and sucks the warmth out from the whole blanket. "You know, most people don't lie around looking at the sky for hours on end."

"I'm not looking at the sky," I say. "I'm watching the airplanes."

"Oh. I didn't know you were so into that shit."

I gesture to our yard full of birdhouses. "I think it's the freedom they represent," I say.

Ellis pauses. "It's not like you're in a burka and living in North Africa or, you know, severely oppressed."

"Depends how you look at it, I guess. Anything can be true or false if you turn it upside down."

"That philosophy stuff is making you weird."

"Maybe."

"So then, what freedom do you see in the birds and the planes and the table here? Freedom from us? Freedom from high school?"

I don't say anything. She'll laugh. And I can't trust her not to repeat it to Claire. But then I realize this is an opportunity. Ellis wants to talk. And if I don't open up now, I might not get another chance with her.

"You promise not to tell anyone *ever*?"

She pulls her hand out from under the blanket and points her pinkie at me. I link mine into it. "Sister swear."

"Okay. I sent them my love because I didn't need it here," I say. "Mom never loved me, and Dad was too busy doing other stuff, and you didn't love me because Mom had turned you against me, and then when Dee came along, I knew I couldn't love her even though I love her more than anything. But I knew I wouldn't be allowed. Not by Mom, not by Unity Valley. Not by you. Not by anyone."

"You didn't think you needed love here?"

"Right."

"And by Dee, do you mean Dee Roberts? Because that is total news to me."

I realize that I didn't really tell Ellis anything yet. "Yes."

"Wow. I had no idea," she says.

"Glad to hear Unity Valley gossip lines are still overlooking the obvious stuff. God, you'd think Aimee Hall would have been all over that."

She snaps her hand up. "Never say that name to me again." Then she starts sobbing, which is out of place.

"El?"

I give her a minute to get her head together. "There's something I'm not telling you."

"So tell me," I say.

She breathes a few times and gets a grip. "I caught Aimee Hall talking about you on Monday at lunch. I walked in late, and she was saying the usual stuff, to the usual audience, you know?" she starts.

"But then she said that you'd once tried to kiss me and that I'd told her that, and I was sitting right there and I said that I didn't say it and that it never happened and that it was wrong to make up and say shit like that."

"Oh," I say. Tame. Seriously. *Morons exist*. There's a paradox for you.

"And rather than say she was kidding or whatever, she exploded in front of everyone in the caf and said I *did* say that and that I was lying about never saying it."

"Shit," I say. "That's harsh."

"Just wait," she says. "So I say, no way, I would *know* if I ever said that because it was about my own fucking sister and that it was wrong to say that you'd tried to do *anything* to me and that you aren't some sort of weirdo lesbian rapist or anything."

"Ew."

"Then she said that yeah, I told her you tried to kiss me, but the truth must be that you did kiss me and I liked it. She said—and I mean, still in front of everyone, including the usual tennis people and whoever was earwigging from the tables next to us—she said that it must run in the family and that we were probably sleeping together and with a mother like ours, it was easy to see why we chose to become lesbians."

I try not to laugh at the last part, but I can't not laugh. "Sorry," I say. "I'm not laughing at you."

"I'm glad you can laugh. I can't."

"Dude, in a week it will blow over, and Aimee Hall will make up a new story about someone else. You know it."

"But this shit lives on! Like—Tim Huber will probably always believe that you only dated him because you felt sorry for him. Doesn't that hurt?"

"Something tells me that Tim will be quicker to remember that after he broke up with me, I started dating girls, you know?" I say. "Eventually, I think most people will notice, you know, when you find some cute guy and marry him and have a bunch of kids, that you might not be gay and sleeping with your lesbian sister. If they believe lies, then that's their problem, not yours."

I see her watching a plane. I think she's sending love to it.

"You know, in ancient Greece, Aristophanes would write plays about how much of a dipshit Socrates was and perform them right there in Athens. Talk about cutthroat, right?"

"Maybe we can do that with Aimee Hall."

I laugh. "That would be hilarious," I say.

"We could make the backyard into an outdoor playhouse on the weekends in summer and run a play a night."

"We can call it *Believe Nothing*," I say.

"You're reading too much Plato, Astrid. I think we should call it *Aimee Hall Is a Secret Lesbian Who Has Slept With All of Your Mothers*. Bet you it will draw bigger crowds."

"True," I say. I'm watching the same airplane as she is now.

"Are you going to keep sending your love to them?" she asks.

"Probably a little."

"I just did it, and it feels nice." She's lying there, staring up, and I'm looking at the side of her face. We used to lie like this as kids, when Mom and Dad would let us have pretend sleepovers in the living room.

She sighs. "I'm officially freezing." She sits up and stretches her back. "I'm outta here. Want to watch a movie together? *Wizard of Oz*?"

"Definitely," I say with a smile. This is serious progress.

▶ ▶ ▶

When the flying monkeys appear, Ellis still curls her feet under herself and grabs my arm for safety. It's more comforting than a lot of things I can think of right now. In fact, as I watch the

Wicked Witch of the West peer into her crystal ball, I realize it's probably the most comforting thing I've ever known.

I see us old and wrinkled and visiting each other a few times a year and watching *The Wizard of Oz* and Ellis grabbing my arm when those monkeys appear. I will always make her feel safe.

"They're just actors in flying-monkey suits," I'll say.

44

MOTION *IS* POSSIBLE.

BEFORE MOM, Dad and Ellis get up the next morning, I'm in the garage rolling out self-drying clay with a coffee can and cutting it into rounded tiles. There's this design for a dovecote that Dad and I have been looking at in our design book for years, but we never had the guts to try it before. It's not a huge dovecote for actual doves, but it's big and it has four floors for four different families and this cool conical roof covered in little handmade roof tiles. So I figured I'd start there.

It's a crisp, sunny day, and I figure the clay will dry faster in the sun, so when I'm done, I take the two trays of tiles to my table and put them there.

Mom is in the kitchen making coffee when I walk in the back door. She jumps.

"Oh, my God, I didn't know you were up," she says.

"Sorry."

"You want coffee?"

She's never asked me this before. I tilt my head and ask myself the question. Do I want coffee? "Yes, please."

"Great. I'll make a big pot."

She shuffles back upstairs as the coffeemaker starts to gurgle. I take a shower.

I check my phone, and I see I missed a call from Dee. No voice mail. I flop onto my bed in my shirt and underwear and call her back.

"You rang?"

"You doing anything tonight?"

"Grounded."

"Oh. Does that mean people can still come to you?"

I say, "I don't know. Why? You planning a long walk?"

"How about three o'clock?" she says.

"Let me ask and I'll call you back?"

"Sounds good."

▶ ▶ ▶

There's coffee waiting for me on the counter—extra sweet and light. Mom is in the living room in her robe. This is new. A day off? Relaxation?

"Your father is out there waiting for you," she says.

"Cool. And, uh, I know I'm grounded, but can I have friends come over here?"

"Sure. I guess. How many?"

I don't understand her question at first.

"You said *friends*. Just curious."

"No," I say. "I just meant one friend."

"That's fine with us," she says.

▶ ▶ ▶

Dad works on the door detail and the internal floors, which make him swear a lot but he finally figures it out. I spray-paint the roof tiles and then coat them with a few layers of weather-proof lacquer. When we break for lunch, I call Dee back, and she says she'll be here at three.

I can't figure out whether to tell Mom and Dad over lunch about Dee's visit. I mean, I *should* tell them who's coming, shouldn't I? But do I have to tell them that she's my girlfriend?

▶ ▶ ▶

We finish the birdhouse before three. I have red paint on my fingers, and I'm wiping it off with turpentine and a cloth when I hear Dee park. I'd know the rattling sound of the Buick's engine anywhere. I walk up the side driveway to meet her before she gets to the front door.

"Come with me," I say. "I'm just finishing up."

She stops and looks around the backyard. "Daaaamn. That's awesome."

I cross my arms and nod.

"I mean, I'd heard about the birdhouses, you know?" she says. "But I didn't understand it was like *this*."

"Yes. We're freaks. We know."

I walk into the garage and get back to my can of turpentine, and I load the rag up again and wipe off any leftover paint. Dee looks around and spots the nearly finished dovecote on the bench.

"Did you just make that?"

"It's nice, isn't it?"

"I had no idea you could do shit like that, Jones. *And* you're a poet and a great kisser," she says, moving in and putting her hand on my hip.

I take her hand and lead her in the back door and to the kitchen table, where Mom is sitting reading the weekend section of the paper. Dad appears from the powder room, still drying his hands on a paper towel.

Dad points and says, "I know you! Dee Roberts! Mount Pitts! Number thirty-four!"

Dee smiles. "Hi, Mr. Jones."

I smile shyly and put my arm around Dee's shoulder, take a deep breath and say, "Guys, I want you to meet my girlfriend, Dee."

▶ ▶ ▶

Mom could have been nicer. Dad could have been less goofy. Ellis could have pulled out her hockey stick and invited Dee into the backyard to hit the ball around a little. Instead, they left us alone. So now we're here.

"What's that one?" she asks, pointing.

"That's a Cessna. Single engine. Probably a 172. Nice day to take the family up for a ride."

She laughs. "I think that's what you just did."

"I hope they learn to be less awkward."

"They will. Don't worry," she says. She grabs my hand and holds it in hers.

I spot a reflection in the sky—a high-flying 747. I send it a little love to let it know I'm here.

PASSENGER #587
JESSICA KIMBALL, SEAT 2A
FLIGHT #78
MINNEAPOLIS TO PHILADELPHIA

She put me in a window seat because that way she can control when I go to the toilet and who I talk to. Never. And nobody.

I am her prisoner.

My own mother.

I'm her prisoner until she delivers me to the camp. Gay camp. Conversion camp. Whatever you want to call it…it's where I'm going.

I look out the rounded airplane window and marvel at the clouds. They are miracles from every direction. The blue of the sky is so deep, I wish I had a parachute and could jump into it. Or maybe…we could skip the parachute.

Below the clouds I see vague ridges of mountains and dark

forests. I see a lake. I see a large building—some sort of enormous warehouse that is visible from this high up.

I ask it: *What do they store in you, warehouse? And can I jump out of this plane right now and work in you? Anonymous. Unpaid. I'd do anything to get out of this plane before I am handed over.*

An even bigger lake appears. I had no idea Pennsylvania had lakes. All I knew about it before now was that it had my father, who is worse than my mother.

Lake, can I jump into you, and will you keep me safe underwater until I can escape? There are no other options. My mother has said it.

"There's nothing I can do about it," she said. "You'll stay at that camp until they make you right again."

My father said, "Your mother didn't discipline you right. These people will."

I wrap my love for Marie into a tight ball of mental swaddling. I wrap it in a soft flannel blanket, four, ten, a hundred times. I wrap it so well that nothing can hurt it. And then I look out the window and down at the green-and-brown landscape, and I toss my love to whoever might be there to keep it safe.

Maybe if you catch this love, you can keep it safe? I ask them. *Maybe someone down there knows what to do with it while I go and get brainwashed by people who hate me?*

▶ ▶ ▶

Dee says, "What?"

I try to think of what just happened, but I can't explain it. All I know is that a huge, overwhelming feeling of love has just landed in my heart, and I have to keep it safe for a while.

"Nothing," I say. "Don't worry about it."

I'm left with this feeling, though. A lucky feeling. I squeeze Dee's hand and kiss her on the cheek. I can do that now. I can do whatever I want.

I look at the plane, and I send my love. *Don't worry. I'll keep it safe. Stay strong.*

ACKNOWLEDGMENTS

Thank you to my family and friends—you know who you are, and you rock.

Topher, you get an extra line because you're Topher. Big love.

Thanks to my awesome editor Andrea Spooner and to Deirdre Jones, who held this book's hand until it found its way. Thanks to the entire team at Little, Brown for making me feel so welcome and for everything they do.

Thank you to my agent Michael Bourret, who knows my Vulcan secrets.

A huge thank-you to Rosemary Hauseman and Bob Fleck—my humanities teachers from high school. That class was where I (unintentionally) wrote my first piece of fiction and where I met Socrates, who has traveled with me through life. Thank you also to an unnamed fellow student from that humanities classroom who reminded me what a refuge it was.

Thank you to Detective Courtney Garipoli, an old friend and invaluable resource for all things police-related.

And an awesomechutney thank-you to every fan who has ever written to me or come to see me at events, and to every librarian, teacher, bookseller and blogger who has supported my work. Your support means the world to me, and I will be forever grateful.

AN INTERVIEW WITH A.S. KING

Several of your novels contain elements of magical realism, such as Lucky's dreams about his grandfather in Everybody Sees the Ants *and the pagoda in* Please Ignore Vera Dietz. *Where did your inspiration for Astrid's connections with the passengers come from? Is there a passenger in this book whose story you particularly connect with or are most moved by?*

I write by the seat of my pants, so when the passengers showed up, I gave them space to tell me their stories. What I learned was that Astrid's love was positively affecting those whom she sent love to even though she didn't know them personally. I feel strongly about this idea, as I've been sending love to random passengers in airplanes since I was a child and always hoped it did someone some good.

I am moved by all the passenger stories in the book because of the effect that love can have on a human. There's a fearlessness to following one's heart, and I think no matter the conclusion (to leave one's partner, to propose marriage, to return to try to fix a broken relationship), the catalyst is pure. For me, there is nothing more moving than a determined human being who takes a risk to improve his or her life.

Many readers and reviewers of Ask the Passengers *have commented that this book is perfect for anyone who is struggling with labels, not just those dealing with coming out. What kinds of choices did you make while writing the book that allowed the story to speak to such a wide audience?*

When I was first writing the book, by the end it had converged into something far narrower and more specific than what's there now. I am so grateful for the patience of my editor...especially on the day that I called and asked her if I could replace the final 25,000 words of the book. Thankfully, she allowed this, and the result was a wider book about accepting *everyone* instead of about sexuality. I have always been of the mind that people's sexuality is their own business, really.

I also enjoyed the challenge of tying that first scene — the one where Astrid is sending her love — in to the rest of the book. This isn't romantic or sexual love. This is human love. This is universal. We all need it, whether we get it or not. It is a form of respect for other humans. It is a form of positive energy that we can choose to share and that will return to us if we just put it out there. Wouldn't it be a far more fabulous world if people loved random other people? If we sent love to random strangers instead of judging, gossiping, or trying to find fault or a reason to be better all the time?

▶ ▶ ▶

Were there experiences in your own teen years that inspired elements of this book?

Many. From sending love to passengers in airplanes, which I've done since I can remember, to questioning everything…including my sexuality. Yes, I'm straight, but I questioned it then, and I'm not ashamed to say I did. I was lucky to know that questioning was perfectly normal, no matter what those awful gossips and bullies said to me in high school. I was lucky to have an openly gay sister who gave me unconditional love and showed me that life would be just fine no matter what the answer to my question was.

▶ ▶ ▶

As you were writing Astrid's story, did you consider having her explore the possibility that she might be bisexual? Or was Astrid forced to use the labels that her community uses, as she states on page 257: "'The world is made up of clear definitions.... So, I'm gay. Until further notice. That way, I don't have to think about it, my girlfriend doesn't have to wonder about it and I can actually enjoy being in love with her because she's awesome.'"

Your assumption is correct; society uses the labels they best understand, and in turn, in many people's minds, those labels seem to be the ones available for making choices. They certainly were in my case at that age. More important, though, is that Astrid never really likes a boy in this book. Even her feelings toward her (only) boyfriend the year before this story takes place weren't the same sort of attraction as she has toward Dee. Since Astrid is not actively attracted to boys, and is only actively attracted to Dee, in my mind her logical questioning wouldn't include that of being bisexual, because she isn't attracted to boys at all.

▶ ▶ ▶

When did you first read Plato's Allegory of the Cave, which is sometimes required reading for high schoolers, and what made you decide to use Socrates and the Socratic method as a major theme in this book? Were you particularly inspired by these philosophical ideas in your teens, or did their importance and applicability to your life become more apparent as you got older?

I was introduced to Plato's Allegory of the Cave in my senior humanities class, thanks to two of the best teachers I have ever met. It was one of the only times in my very sketchy high school academic experience that I remember being completely engaged by an idea. The cave stuck with me for many years and became the lens through which I viewed the world. It even led to my eventually giving up watching television, because I refuse to go into the "cave" of TV and believe the shadows of the "real" world it shows me. I'm pretty sure the Allegory of the Cave and my subsequent lack of TV have a lot to do with how I view consumerism and how I ended up as a self-sufficient hippie freak in Ireland for a decade. That time taught me that all the information I'd been fed until that point was bunk. We don't need any of the things they're selling us; we could totally live like *Little House on the Prairie* and do just fine.

In the case of Socrates, back in college when I first studied him, I used to think he was just some devil's advocate who liked to wind people up with his explorative reasoning. But then I learned more about him and I really respected his lack of ego, his lack of possessions, and his seemingly pure need to make people think. I bonded with him, in a way. I recently had a reader tell me that she wasn't sure if she liked the book or not, so I asked her if it made her think. She said she hadn't stopped thinking about it for over a week. I told her that I didn't really mind how she felt about the book, so long as she kept thinking. I like to think Socrates would dig that, too.

▶ ▶ ▶

As with Everybody Sees the Ants *and* Please Ignore Vera Dietz, *this book is set in Pennsylvania, which is also where you live. Do you find inspiration for your books in your immediate surroundings, or do you set them in this area simply because it's most familiar to you?*

I never thought I'd move back to the United States from Ireland, let alone move back to Pennsylvania, where I was born. But I definitely find inspiration here because I lived away from home for so long. It's a funny thing, nostalgia. You think it's rooted in a time period, and it is, but it's also rooted in a landscape. So when I drive through places in my hometown now, I get feelings from the memories that I once experienced here. They are really powerful, because I said what I thought was a permanent good-bye to this place and my memories of it so long ago. But now I get to see it all again—like a landscape that rose from the dead. It's very strong and very visual, and I take my inspiration from that. For example, I can show you the house of every character I write, so now driving around Berks County is extra fun for me.

▶ ▶ ▶

For many teens, Unity Valley is very similar to the place they call home. What do you hope these readers will take away from Ask the Passengers?

Honestly, I can't believe how many people write to me to tell me that Unity Valley is just like their town. It makes me sad, really. I wish things were getting better faster, but with the rise of technology and social networking, we are seeing a rise in deplorable behavior and rumors that spread far faster than they once did.

I hope readers will think about the book and the idea that they can only control their own behavior and that they will be happiest if they act kindly toward others and gossip and judge less. I really hope readers take Frank Socrates from this book and allow him into their lives to help them question those things they have made definite decisions about. Frank Socrates was invented to help break boxes open; he was invented to help break us free from the cave.

▶ ▶ ▶

Do you have any more books coming out soon? What are you currently working on?

Reality Boy will be coming to fine booksellers near you in October 2013. After that, in fall 2014, *Glory O'Brien's History of the Future* will appear. I am also presently working on several adult novels, as well as an idea for a top secret young adult book for 2015 or thereabouts. My lips are sealed on that one.

DISCUSSION GUIDE

1. How would you describe Astrid's relationships with each of her family members? In what ways are these relationships dysfunctional, and in what ways are they healthy? Even though Astrid gets along best with her father, would you say that her relationship with him is any less dysfunctional than her relationships with her mother and sister?

2. Throughout the book, Astrid makes references to what "they say" and what "they think." Who do you think "they" are? What do you think "they" would say after reading this book?

3. Why does Astrid send her love to the airplane passengers flying above her? Do you think the passengers are truly affected by Astrid's love? Is Astrid somehow impacted by the passengers, other than her finding solace in talking to people who can't talk back to her and judge her?

4. Sometimes people's external perceptions of others don't match those individuals' internal truths. Which characters in the book does this concept describe?

5. How do Astrid's secrets change over time, and what impact do they ultimately have on how she handles speaking about her sexuality?

6. How do people define Astrid, and how do those definitions change over time? How does Astrid define herself, if at all? Do you think definitions are a useful or detrimental tool?

7.   Do you think the ultimatum that Dee presents to Astrid about coming out is more helpful or harmful to Astrid? What does it tell her about Dee?

8.   How does *Ask the Passengers* use the Allegory of the Cave as a metaphor for Astrid's journey toward publicly acknowledging her sexuality?

9.   A key theme in this book is the power of loving oneself. How does Astrid's journey toward this goal provide perspective on who you are and the relationships that you have with others?

HE'S NOT THE BOY YOU SAW ON TV.
AND HE'S ANGRY THAT YOU STILL THINK HE IS.

A fearless portrayal of a boy on the edge
who finally breaks free of his anger by creating
possibilities he never knew he deserved

COMING OCTOBER 2013

Turn the page for an excerpt.

I AM
REALITY BOY

I'M THE KID you saw on TV.

Remember the little freak who took a crap on his parents' oak-stained kitchen table when they confiscated his Game Boy? Remember how the camera cleverly hid his most private parts with the glittery fake daisy and sunflower centerpiece?

That was me. Gerald. Youngest of three. Only boy. Out of control.

One time, I did it in the dressing room at the mall. Sears, I think. My mom was trying to get me to try on some pants and she got the wrong size.

"Now you stay right there," she said. "I'll be back with the right size."

And to protest having to wait, or having to try on pants, or having to have a mother like her, I dropped one right there between the wicker chair and the stool where Mom's purse was.

And no. It wasn't excusable. I wasn't a baby. I wasn't even a toddler. I was five. I was sending a message.

You all watched and gasped and put your hands over your eyes as three different cameramen caught three different angles of me squeezing one out on the living room coffee table, next to the cranberry-scented holiday candle ensemble. Two guys held boom mikes. They tried to keep straight faces, but they couldn't. One of them said, "Push it out, kid!" He just couldn't help himself. I was so entertaining.

Right?

Wasn't I?

Gerald the spoiled little brat. Gerald the kid who threw violent tantrums that left holes in the drywall and who screamed so loud it made the neighbors call the police. Gerald the messed-up little freak who needed Network Nanny's wagging finger and three steps to success.

Now I'm a junior in high school. And every kid in my class has seen forty different angles of me crapping in various places when I was little. They call me the Crapper. When I complained to the adults in my life back in middle school, they said, "Fame has its downside."

Fame? I was *five*.

At five years old, did I have the capacity to write the producers a letter begging Network Nanny to come and help me stop punching the walls of my parents' swanky McMansion? No. I did not have that capacity. I did not write that letter. I did not want her to come.

But she came anyway.

So I got madder.

1

IT'S WWE NIGHT. That's World Wrestling Entertainment, or *Smackdown Live!* for any of you non-redneck-y people who've never watched the spectacle of heavyweight wrestling before. I've always hated it, but it brings in good money at the PEC Center.

The PEC Center is the Penn Entertainment and Convention Center. That's where I work.

I'm that apathetic kid in the greasy shirt at the concession stand who asks you if you want salsa, cheese, chili, or jalapeños with your nachos. I'm the kid who refills the ice because none of the other lazy cashiers will do it. I'm the kid who has to say *Sorry. We're all out of pretzels.*

I hear parents complain about how much everything costs. I hear them say *You shouldn't be eating that fattening stuff* right before they order their kid some chicken fingers and fries. I hear them wince when their kid orders a large sugary Pepsi in a WWE commemorative cup to wash it down. At WWE, it's the fried stuff, cups with wrestlers on them, or beer.

I'm technically not allowed to work this stand until I turn eighteen and take a class on how to serve alcohol responsibly. There's a test and everything—and a little certificate to put in your wallet. I'm almost seventeen now, and Beth, my manager, lets me work here because she likes me and we made a deal. I card people. I check for signs of intoxication—loud talking, lower inhibitions, glassy eyes, slurred speech; then, if everything checks out okay, I call Beth over so she can tap them the beers. Unless it's superbusy. Then she tells me to tap them myself.

"Hey, Crapper!" someone yells from the back of the line. "I'll give you twenty bucks to squeeze one out for the crowd!"

It's Nichols. He only comes to this stand because he knows I can get him beer. He comes with Todd Kemp, who doesn't say much and seems embarrassed to be around Nichols most of the time because Nichols is such a dick.

I wait on the three families in front of Nichols and Todd, and when they get here, they barely whisper what they want and Todd hands over ten bucks. Two Molsons. While I'm covertly tapping the beer, Nichols is saying all sorts of nervous, babbly stuff, and I do what my anger management coach taught me to do. I hear nothing. I breathe and count to ten. I concentrate on the sound of the WWE crowd cheering on whatever big phony is in the ring. I concentrate on the foam at the top of the cup. I concentrate on how I'm supposed to love myself now. *Only you can allow yourself to be angry.*

But no matter how much anger management coaching I've had, I know that if I had a gun, I'd shoot Nichols in the back as he walks away with his beer. I know that's murder and I know what that means. It means I'd go to jail. And the older I get, the more I think maybe I belong in jail. There are plenty of angry guys like me in jail. It's, like, anger central. If we put together all the jails in this country and made a state out of them, we could call that state Furious.

We could give it a postal abbreviation like other states have. FS. I think the zip code would be 00000.

I wipe down the counter while there's a short break in the hungry, thirsty WWE crowd. I restack the cup lids. I count how many hot dogs are left in my hot drawer. I report to Beth that I am completely out of pretzels.

When I get up from counting hot dogs in the next drawer over, I see her walking through the crowd. Tasha. My oldest sister. She's with her boyfriend, Danny, who is about two staircases more than a step down from us. We live in a gated community of minimansions. Danny lives in a rented community of 1970s single-wide trailers. They don't even have paved roads. I'm not exaggerating. The place is like the hillbilly ghetto.

Not like I care. Tasha is an asshole and I hate her. I hope he knocks her up and she marries him and they have a hundred little WWE-loving pale redneck babies. I wouldn't shoot her, though. I enjoy watching her fail too much. Watching Mom swallow her Tasha-dropped-out-of-college-and-is-dating-a-Neanderthal soup every day is probably the best thing I have going for me.

It's probably the only thing keeping me out of jail.

2

I LIVE ABOUT ten miles away from the PEC Center, in a town called Blue Marsh, which is not blue, not a marsh, and not a real town. It's just a bunch of developments linked together with shopping malls.

I get home at ten and the house is dark. Mom is already sleeping because she gets up so early to power walk and invent exciting new breakfast smoothies. Dad is probably still out with his real estate friends smoking cigars and drinking whatever equity-rich assholes drink, talking about this economy and how much it sucks to be them.

As I near the kitchen hallway, I hear the familiar sound of Tasha getting nailed by Danny the hillbilly.

If I brought a girl home and did that to her that loud, my parents would kick me out. But if Tasha does it? We all have to pretend that it's not actually happening. One time she was whinnying away down in the basement with Danny while Mom, Lisi, and I ate dinner. This was last year when Lisi still lived at home. Mom talked nonstop to block it out, as if the three of us would magically unhear what was going on. *And did you see that Boscov's is having a white sale this weekend? We could use new sheets and towels and I think I'll go over on Saturday morning because the selection is always better early in the day and I really would love some that are blue to match the upstairs bathroom and last time I ended up with those red sheets and as much as I like them, they still seem too rough and they usually have nice flannel this time of year and I think it's important to have flannel sheets in winter, you know? Blah blah blah blah blah.*

I got about seven mouthfuls into a nice plate of roast beef and mashed potatoes and I finally couldn't take it anymore. I went to the basement door, opened it, and screamed, "If you don't stop planking my sister while I eat dinner, I'm going to come down there and kick your ass. Have some fucking respect!" and I slammed the door.

My mother stopped talking about towels and sheets and gave me that look she'd been giving everyone for as long as I could remember. It said *Tasha can't help it.* It said *We just can't control what Tasha does.*

Or, in Lisi's words, "Tasha is out of control and for some reason our mother is totally fine with it. Don't know why, don't care, either. I'm getting as far from here as I can the minute I can."

And she did. Lisi went all the way to Glasgow, Scotland, where she's studying literature, psychology, and environmental science all at the same time while balancing a waitressing job and her years-long pot habit. She hasn't called since she left. Not even once. She e-mailed Mom to let us know she got there okay, but she never calls. It's been three months.

Anyway, Mom should have named Tasha "Trigger." Not just because of the horse sounds she makes when she's getting planked by the redneck, either.

She is my number one trigger.

That's the term the anger management coach uses to describe why I get angry. It's the self-controlled, acceptable word we use for *shit that pisses me off.* That's called a trigger. I have spent the last four years identifying mine. And it's Tasha.

At least on that night—the time we had the roast beef and Lisi was still home—Tasha and Danny shut up. Which was good, because I was completely serious. As I ate, I had my eye on the fireplace set in the living room, and I was wondering what kind of damage the iron fire poker could do to a human head. I pictured an exploding watermelon.

My anger coach would say *Stay in the present, Gerald.* But it's hard when nothing ever changes. For sixteen years, eleven months, and two weeks, I've been drowning.

I I ■ I I

Dad arrives home. He'll hear it, too, the minute he gets out of the car.

Basement sounds—especially Tasha's whinnying—go to the garage first.

Giddyup.

I hear his dress shoes *tip-tap* on the cement floor and the door open...and he finds me standing in the dark like some freak. He gasps.

"Jesus, Ger!" he says. "Way to give your old man a stroke."

I walk over to the living room doorway and switch on the main hall light. "Sorry. I just got in, too. Got distracted by the, uh—you know. Noise."

He sighs.

"I wish she'd move out again," I say.

"She doesn't have anywhere to live."

"So? Maybe she'll learn how to get a job and not sponge off you guys if you kick.her ass out." I don't know why I'm doing this. It's just raising my blood pressure. "She's twenty-one."

"You know how your mother is," he says. *You know how your mother is.* This has been his party line since Lisi moved out.

We move into the living room, where it's quieter. He mixes himself a drink and asks me if I want one. I usually say no. But tonight I say yes.

"I could use it. Busy night."

"Hockey game?"

"Wrestling. Those people never stop eating," I say.

"Heh," he says.

"Is Lisi coming home for Christmas?" I ask. He shakes his head, so I add, "There's no chance she'll come back with Tasha in the house."

He hands me a White Russian and flops himself on the couch. He's still in the suit he wore to work this morning. It's Saturday, and he worked at least twelve hours before he went out with his real estate group. He takes a sip from his drink.

"Those two never got along," he says. Which is bullshit. Tasha never got along. With anyone. And it's partially his fault, so he has these excuses. *You know how your mother is. Those two never got along.*

"Thinking about what you want for your birthday?" he asks.

"Not really." This isn't a lie. I haven't been thinking about my birthday at all, even though it's just over two weeks from now.

"I guess you have some time," he says.

"Yeah."

We look at each other for a moment, and he manages a little smile. "So what are your plans after next year? You gonna leave me here like Lisi did?"

I say, "My options are limited."

He nods.

"There's always jail." I let a few seconds pass before I say, "But I think Roger has reasoned all of that out of me." Roger is my anger management coach.

At first he looks shocked, and then he laughs. "Phew. I thought you were serious there for a sec."

"About that? Who'd want to go to jail?"

Right then, Danny the hillbilly opens the basement door and tiptoes into the dark kitchen and grabs a bag of tortilla chips from the cupboard. He goes to the fridge and grabs the whole carton of iced tea. Dad and I notice that he is completely naked only when the light from the fridge shines on his pecker.

"Maybe next time you steal from me, you could put on some clothes, son," Dad says.

Danny runs back down the steps like a rat.

That's what we have. We have rats in our basement. Sponger rats who steal our food and don't offer us shit for it.

I'm still thinking about my last rhetorical question to Dad. *Who'd want to go to jail?* I thought about going nuts once and hitting the mental institution. We have one of those here, only a few miles down the road, too. But Roger said mental institutions aren't really the way they used to be. No more playing basketball with the Chief like in *One Flew Over the Cuckoo's Nest*.

"So where to, then, Ger?" Dad asks, swirling his drink with his index finger.

I don't know what to say. I don't want to do anything, really. I just want a chance to start over and have a real life. One that wasn't fucked up from the beginning and broadcast on international TV like a freak show.

3

EPISODE 1, SCENE 1, TAKE 3

YES, EPISODE ONE. As in, they did more than one show of the Crapper. I was such a big hit with all those troubled parents around the country, so they wanted more chances to watch poor little Gerald squat and deposit turds in the most peculiar places.

I could almost hear the relieved parents of normal tantrum-throwing children saying *At least our kid doesn't crap on the dining room table!*

So true. So true.

What they didn't know was this: I didn't become the Crapper until those cameras were mounted on our walls. Until the strangers with the microphones did sound tests to make sure they could pick up every little thing that was going on. Until I became entertainment. Before then, I was just a frustrated, confused kid who could get violent—mostly toward drywall…and Tasha.

If I was to give a postal abbreviation to my house while I was growing up, it would be UF. I was furious, yes. Livid. Enraged. Incensed. But only because everything was Unfair. Postal abbreviation UF. Zip code: ?????. (The zip code for UF probably changes every five seconds, so there's no point trying to give it one.)

I can't remember a time when I didn't want to punch everything around me, out of confused, unacknowledged frustration. I never punched Lisi or my parents. But then, Lisi and my parents never begged me to punch them. Walls did. Furniture did. Doors did. Tasha did.

From the moment I saw Network Nanny, I didn't really believe she was a nanny. She didn't look like a nanny or act like a nanny. She had starlet hair—something you'd see at a red-carpet movie premiere. She was skinny. Bony, even. She dressed up, as if she was attending a wedding. She didn't smile or possess any warmth. As if she was…acting.

They'd sent us a fake nanny.

I didn't know this for sure until I was older, but it was true. Nanny was really Lainie Church, who was really Elizabeth Harriet Smallpiece from a small town in the south of England, who'd wanted to make it in Hollywood since she was five. Her first acting jobs were in commercials, and then she got a stint for a while in Iowa as one of those fake meteorologists who don't know anything about weather but act like they do. She had a very convincing Iowan accent, too. But Network Nanny was her breakthrough role.

Alongside our fake nanny was a less camera-ready *real* nanny. She wasn't allowed to interact with us, but she winked at me sometimes. She told Fake Nanny what to do to play a good nanny. This arrangement made me mad. I remember sitting there watching them set up and wondering what I could do to really show the world how wrong things were in my life.

After meeting with her makeup artist for a half hour, Fake Nanny got into costume and character and came into the living room, where my family sat waiting. She clapped her hands and looked at the three kids. I was five, Lisi was seven, and Tasha was nearly eleven.

Then she looked exclusively at me while she talked. "Your parents have called me in because your family needs my help." She stopped and checked her reflection in the TV screen. "Your mother says you fight all the time and that's not acceptable behavior."

To imagine Nanny properly, you have to give her an English accent. She dropped her *r*'s. *Behavior* was *behay-vyah*.

"Sounds to me like you need the three steps to success in this house. And we'll start with some old-fashioned discipline. Gerald, do you know what that means?"

The director told me to shake my head no, so I did. I tried not to look into the cameras, which was why it took three takes to film scene one. How can a five-year-old not look into a camera that's right in front of his face?

"It means we're about to start a whole new life," she said. "And this will be a whole new family, easy as one, two, three."

|I ▓ II|

Nanny only came around for a day and then she left her crew of cameras and cameramen there to film us being violent little bitches to one another. Then, two weeks later, she came back and decided, based on that footage, who was right, who was wrong, who needed *prop-ah punishment*, and who needed to learn more about *responsibility*. She taught Mom and Dad about the naughty chair and how to take away screen time. They made homemade charts with rows, columns, and stickers. (The girls got cat stickers. I got dog stickers.)

Nanny didn't actually help make the charts, because her fingernails were too delicate and chart-making wasn't in her contract. "Anyway, it's not my job to parent these children," she said to Mom and Dad. "It's yours."

What the cameras didn't see was: Everything that made us violent little bitches happened behind closed doors or just under the radar of those microphones. And so Nanny (well, really, the *nannies*) only saw part of the picture. Which was usually me or Lisi running after Tasha, trying to hurt her.

Or me squatting on the kitchen table that day—the most-watched YouTube clip from our time on the show—after Nanny took my Game Boy away for throwing a tantrum. That was my first crap—first of many. After I spent the rest of the day in my room, she asked, "You know pooping anywhere but the toilet is dirty, don't you?"

I nodded, but the word *dirty* just kept echoing in my head. It was what Mom had said to me when I accidentally pooped in the bathtub when I was three. "Why did you do this?" Mom asked. "Why would you be so dirty?" I was so little I didn't remember much else, but I remembered that five minutes before, Tasha had told me she was going to help me wash my hair. Which is not what she did.

Nanny said, "Every time you poop and it's not in the toilet, you clean it up yourself and then you go to your room for the whole day. Does that sound fair?"

I shrugged.

She repeated, "Does that sound fair?"

I ask you: Imagine any five-year-old who's surrounded by cameras. Imagine he lives in the postal area UF. Consider that he has so little giveashit that he has started crapping on the kitchen table in front of video cameras. Then ask him this question. He will not know how to answer.

So I freaked out.

I screamed so long and loud, I thought my throat was bleeding when I was done. Then Nanny came over to me and sat down and ruffled my hair. It was the nanniest I'd ever seen her act in the two weeks I'd known her. She asked me why I was so upset, but she laughed when I told her.

"Your *sist-ah* isn't trying to kill you, Gerald. Don't exaggerate."

BOOKS ON THE SQUARE

Where lively minds meet.
401-331-9097

358640 Reg 2 ID 144 12:16 pm 12/27/13

```
S ASK THE PASSENGER   1 @  10.00    10.00
S 9780316194679
SUBTOTAL                            10.00
SALES TAX - 7%                        .70
TOTAL                               10.70
VISA PAYMENT                        10.70
Account# XXXXXXXXXXXX6767
Authorization# 000508        Clerk 144
```

I agree to pay the above total amount
according to the card issuer agreement.

BOOKS ON THE SQUARE

Where lively minds meet.
S 9780316194679
SUBTOTAL   10.00
Account# XXXXXXXXXXXX6757
Authorization# 000508   Clerk 144

I agree to pay the above total amount
according to the card issuer agreement.

Ask about our Frequent Buyer Plan. No
cash refunds. All exchanges/returns must
be within 30 days of purchase.

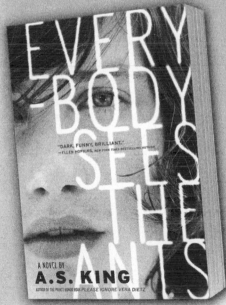

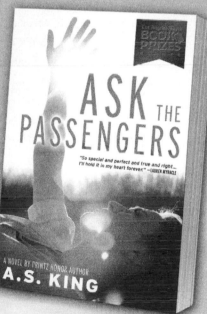

"A.S. King gets better with each book."

–stackedbooks.org

Three powerful stories that will keep you thinking long after the last page, from Michael L. Printz Honor author A.S. King

A.S. KING is the author of the highly acclaimed *Ask the Passengers*, which was a Los Angeles Times Book Prize winner, received six starred reviews, appeared on ten end-of-year "best" lists (including *Publishers Weekly*, *SLJ*, *Kirkus Reviews*, and *Library Journal*), and was a Lambda Literary Award finalist. Her previous book, *Everybody Sees the Ants*, also received six starred reviews, was an Andre Norton Award finalist, and was a 2012 YALSA Top Ten Best Fiction for Young Adults book. She is also the author of the Edgar Award–nominated, Michael L. Printz Honor Book *Please Ignore Vera Dietz* and *The Dust of 100 Dogs*, an ALA Best Book for Young Adults. When asked about her writing, King says, "Some people don't know if my characters are crazy or if they are experiencing something magical. I think that's an accurate description of how I feel every day." She lives in rural Pennsylvania with her husband and children, and her website is www.as-king.com.